THE NEST KEEPER

THE
NEST
KEEPER

Beth Krewson Carter

Palmetto Publishing Group
Charleston, SC

The Nest Keeper
Copyright © 2019 by Beth Krewson Carter
All rights reserved

First Edition

Printed in the United States

Paperback ISBN-13: 978-1-64111-208-6
eBook ISBN-13: 978-1-64111-361-8

To my own bloodline,
Rick, Laura Brooke and Will
With love

CHAPTER 1

I t was late in the evening when the final decision was made. She knew she had to do the right thing.

After talking to both of her parents, Susan was sure that the time had come for her to get involved. It was actually past time. The whole thing had become just a tough situation. And now there would be a long drive to help them.

Somehow in the middle of the night, her eyes opened for an hour. She could not stop herself from making a mental to-do list for the morning.

By the time Susan had fallen back asleep, the first gray streaks of dawn were falling across her bedroom floor. Her arms were now stretched into the empty space beside her. Right before she drifted off again, she realized that the bottom sheet on the bed was cold. Instead of feeling good to her, the cool cotton linens had been almost too chilly to be relaxing. Rolling on her side and sliding into her dreams, she sensed that her hand was reaching for something warm. Someone was not beside her.

The ringing startled her and made her jump. A loud sound filled the entire bedroom. Reverberating down the hall, she wondered for an instant if the noise was inside or outside the walls of her house.

Susan propped up on her elbow and reached for the telephone. Her landline blared out a staccato rhythm. The caller ID flashed the name David Upton. It was her parents.

"Hello," she said slowly. There was something instinctive about an early morning call that made her fear the worst.

"Hello, dear." Her mother was on the line. Her voice sounded happy and awake, with just a hint of fatigue in her voice.

Susan relaxed. She stretched back out and rubbed her eyes.

"Is everything okay?" Her words were focused as she pulled herself into wakefulness.

"Oh, it's fine," answered her mother. "I just wanted to see what time you were leaving today."

Susan could picture her mother, Sylvia, wrapped in her heaviest bathrobe, probably sitting in the kitchen, talking on her telephone. It would be the old yellow one on the wall. Her parents still had a home phone that allowed anyone to travel at least fifteen yards while they were tethered by the long curly cord.

In her hand, Susan held onto her own hard plastic handset as she shifted under her beige comforter. Everything made her wonder why she still had a landline. The telephone was one of the few vestiges of the last decade that she still owned. She told herself that she kept it because a client might call on her house number, and wisdom mandated having as many ways to communicate as possible. But the truth was that all her business these days was done on her cell phone and by email.

"I'm leaving as soon as I can make a few calls and get organized," Susan said calmly. Her voice was low and husky in the morning. She said it like she was talking to a friend.

Years ago she would have been less patient with her mother's questions, but cancer had changed that between them.

"All right," said her mother back with equal patience. "Well, I'll have some dinner for you for when you arrive."

"Don't go to any trouble," Susan told her. "Remember, I'm coming to help you."

"Call me when you're on the road, but don't call when you're driving on the highway. That's not safe." She said the words as if her daughter needed reminding of the basic facts of life.

Susan smiled as she cradled the phone against her shoulder. When her mother worried about the family, she could hear the love in her voice. It was protective, like the hard coating layer on a chocolate candy.

"Don't worry," Susan assured her. "I'll call you later."

As Susan put the phone back on her nightstand, she realized that Harvey was now on the end of the bed. There was always something comforting about the weight and warmth of his body against her legs.

A swinging foot went over the edge of the bed. That was when she heard them.

"Don't forget your science project!" The voice belonged to Cynthia, from next door, calling to her children. She was obviously in the driveway. Jack's truck could be heard idling. Heavy doors were slamming shut.

Susan stood now, trying to find her slippers and bathrobe. Stopping to listen, she realized that this was the least favorite part of her house.

Suburban Memphis was wonderful, she had often told herself. Her cul-de-sac overflowed with classic southern charm. Except that her bedroom just happened to be a bit too close to the fence. And that made it all a bit too close to the neighbor's driveway.

"I'll pick you up at three! Kisses!" Cynthia called again.

"Bye, Mom." Claire answered.

"Bye, hon. Get some rest. I love you," she heard Jack say.

He was obviously taking the kids to school, Susan surmised.

Ever since the neighborhood Christmas party, when Cynthia told the whole cove that she was expecting her third child, Susan had noticed that Jack had clearly been helping out more with the kids. It was sweet, really, it was. But all the goodness and consideration that Susan had to witness from her neighbors had begun to make her feel like she was living next door to the sunshine family. They were always bright and warm and cheery. And that had somehow left Susan feeling a bit like an old shadow this winter.

As she pulled on her bathrobe, Susan could hear the noise of her too-close neighbors and their too-big pickup truck begin to fade. She sighed as her toes pushed into her other slipper. Looping her bathrobe sash into a sloppy bow, Susan knew that she really did like the family next door. Even though she hadn't sold them the house two years ago, they were great neighbors. They never had loud parties and their two kids were cute, especially at Halloween.

She was still thinking about Jack and Cynthia as she headed into her bathroom. Susan Abbot had sold real estate long enough to know that there really were no perfect families. Just like there really were no perfect houses, people could be deceiving. Even in the tidy bubble of Germantown, nothing was ever as good as it looked. No one could possibly know what went on behind the manicured front lawns and neat brick facades of any of the houses. It was just that Jack and Cynthia really were good people, living in a nice house. They clearly loved each other and their kids. They weren't perfect, but they were kind of perfect.

As Susan emerged back into her bedroom, she pulled her hair into a ponytail with an elastic. Even though she was forty-three, she was growing her hair out in the new year. A *Style Watch* magazine that Susan had seen had claimed that longer hair made everyone look younger.

Quickly she surveyed the open suitcase on the chair in the corner. Her packing needed to get finished. In the early winter light, she saw a sweater that she probably should add. It rested right next to the scattered framed photos on her dresser. Susan glanced at old family snapshots and sighed. With a long day ahead of her, she needed to get going.

Padding down the hall, she tightened her long bathrobe. Her cotton camisole and flannel sleep pants now disappeared under the heavy white knit fabric as she rubbed her smooth face.

Harvey circled at her feet, and his black and white colored fur looked fluffy. Susan knew that he would wait expectantly to be fed. In his world, his needs were always first on the list.

But the weather was colder this morning. A winter chill had filled the kitchen and seemed to settle across the tile floor. Susan moved slower than usual. Early January, even in southern Tennessee, held a raw cold. Susan had noticed the year-round humidity when she'd moved to Germantown. The dampness gave birth to a kind of temperature drop that felt like it settled into her bones in the winter.

Harvey's food dish sat in the corner on a mat that said I AM PURR-FECT in big block letters. From the floor, his eyes appraised her. He was waiting.

Dry food and water were put in the dishes in the morning. Susan could handle that much first thing. There was something about opening those little cans of wet food that had to come later in the day.

Susan scoped his crunchy brown food into his dish from the cat food bag in the pantry and filled his water bowl with frigid tap water. Harvey opened his eyes wide with excitement. He could hardly wait to hunch over the two saucers and begin his breakfast.

As Susan started her coffee, she thought about the list of things ahead of her. She checked the clock. The microwave numbers announced that it was early, just before seven. That left her plenty of time to start her plan.

Her first thought centered around Ryan. She would call him, but not until later. Susan had learned her lesson about morning phone calls. Ryan would only grunt at her if it was much before nine in the morning. Even last semester when he had a co-op job at the Nissan plant, he rarely wanted to talk to her in the morning. He was always busy, always working. Her call would often roll to voicemail and only later in the day would she hear from him.

Sons at age twenty did not want long conversations with their mothers, she had learned. Her friends all said the same things happened with their male children. The lack of talking was like a slow dance of moving away from each other and there seemed to be nothing that she could do about the process.

A whiff of steam arose from the coffee maker. The aroma of warm roasted beans filled the kitchen. Susan poured the black liquid into her department store mug from the shelf.

Just last night, she had been reading a book in bed to unwind after she'd talked to her parents. The bestseller had been all about the bad whites of life. Almost surprisingly, nothing in the chapters had been about race relations. Rather, the entire volume centered around white sugar, white flour, white rice, and all of the other white foods of the world. The book had outlined the benefits of meals without anything processed. They called it a clean diet. Susan had read late into the night and thought about the things the author suggested. Everything made sense. She could do that kind of thing. Giving up all that junk would be a good idea. Maybe she would even run a 5K this year.

Now Susan moved over to the refrigerator. Of course, this was January. The new year was always a good time to make changes. But that being said, if she started this, then it would mean saying no to a lot of things. The usual culprits, like desserts, would have to go. Okay. That much was to be expected. But then the whole thing would have to go a bit farther. There would be no pasta, no pizza, no bread. Now that would get hard. Eating out would be limited to a salad with no real dressing to mention. And of course, then there would be no appetizers, because the book had said that you couldn't trust them either. Susan grimaced. Then she remembered one more forbidden thing. It would be inevitable.

"Dear God," she muttered under her breath, "There would be no wine."

With that, Susan opened up the refrigerator and reached onto the top shelf. Her hand pulled out the shapely container of French vanilla coffee cream. She poured the thick liquid into her cup until her coffee matched the color of dirty blond hair. It was settled. If she was going to start some sort of dietary hell, today would not be the day.

Holding her mug, Susan began to plan the other things that she would do. After eight, she would call the office. Thank goodness for the month of January. The market was so slow these days. Nobody was looking at houses right now, certainly not mid-week. Her absence should not be any big deal. And she would come back on the weekend if she got a call.

Then, of course, there was the vet. She would have to make a call there, as well. Harvey would have to load into his teal carrier in the garage. She could almost hear him start to whine. All that fuss he made, just to go to the "luxury kitty condo."

Susan walked over to the bay window in the breakfast area as she took her first sips of coffee. When she opened the blinds, there was frost on the lawn.

The phone call from last night was on her mind. Actually, she had been thinking about the conversation for most of the night, until she made herself drowsy with a book that banned most of the real food in her life.

"With Aunt Julia's estate not settled, your father is so agitated," reported her mother at the beginning of the phone call. "He told Peter that he needed a full accounting of the estate, but then he received only the last quarterly statement of the remaining investments."

"Peter is being very difficult," her father had said hotly, when he got on the line. "He won't even return my phone calls."

And it was true. Everything seemed to be stuck in neutral.

So, in the end, she had decided to go. Doing the right thing meant that she needed to put her eyes on everything. It was time for a visit, anyway. After all, wasn't that what a good daughter was supposed to do?

Susan caught a glimpse of her reflection in the window pane. A scowl spread across her face.

There was always uncertainty about helping them. Settling the entire estate would still take time. Everyone would probably be headed for more delays. The most likely outcome would be that be that Susan would just end up feeling underappreciated, unvalued and a host of other things.

Harvey jumped onto the tweed chair in the living room. From her spot in the kitchen, Susan could just see him. He gazed over his shoulder at her as if he were royalty. His eyes narrowed, and his stare was piercing. Susan thought about her parents and Dory as she studied the cat.

Susan could handle heading home and helping. She could get to the bottom of some of the details, she felt sure. But talking to her father about anything always required effort.

"I'll look at all the documents with you when I get there," Susan told her father when he got back on the line at the end of the call.

"I don't know," replied David Upton. There was a slur to his words, followed by hesitation. "I've been working on this for Dory. You can come and help your mother, if your work schedule is flexible. I just don't need to pull through everything. I don't have the time for that right now."

His response was typical. After all, Susan had grown up accustomed to his abrupt comments.

Except the words and the tone her father had used had rolled around in her head all night. Something was different. It felt off somehow. Susan looked into her almost-empty coffee cup and wondered. What was he not telling her?

CHAPTER 2

Harvey started with a low growl. After that, he extended his large splayed paws, claws first, to resist his fate.

He does this same thing every single time, thought Susan as she gave him a gentle shove. His black and white fur stood at attention as he plummeted into the cat carrier.

"For goodness sake," Susan said out loud. "All this fuss for a stay away from home." She had wanted to say "stay at the vet," but changed the words. She was being was silly. It wasn't like the cat could understand English.

Susan layered a gray long-sleeve tunic on top of her oversized pink T-shirt. With black leggings and flats, she would be ready for the drive. With two hands, she pulled her dark wavy curls into a clip that made the bottom strands of her hair cascade down towards her neck. She guessed that she might look rounded and mature in her outfit. Hopefully, people would just think of her as curvy.

The cat carrier was loaded into her blue crossover. All the pet supplies went on the passenger seat. Her suitcase rested in the back.

The drive to pet boarding at the animal hospital was less than nine blocks from her home. Susan just had to exit her subdivision onto a major road and turn left in four miles.

Harvey was now making loud, whining cries. Occasionally, he would hiss. It was the longest five-minute drive of the day.

"You know," Susan said softly to the cat, "you might try to like your vacation. You'll stay in a carpeted cat condo. They feed you and clean up after you. Every bit of your day sounds pretty good to me." Harvey was wriggling inside the carrier. Susan looked at him. He had turned his back to her.

"Well, that figures," she said, more to herself than to the cat.

She parked the car in the almost-empty lot. A quick glance around the pavement revealed the reason: The time read 8:22 a.m. Of course, she realized, not a soul had arrived except the staff.

Most people who were boarding pets, the ones who were going somewhere wonderful, would still be at home. Susan could just imagine their day. They would be packing up and excitedly ready to take on a new adventure.

She shook her head. Her trip would be nothing like that kind of thing. Leaving town for Susan involved helping her aging parents and her unconventional cousin. She just hoped that she could do it quickly. Getting home and back to work remained important. Being present, even in a slow market, was essential. Any buyer that she might get during the winter would be a boost in an almost-stagnant off-season market.

Out of the car, she struggled to gather up everything that she needed for the cat. With Harvey's carrier, her black purse and the plastic bag containing cat food, Susan pulled open the glass door of the boarding facility. Entering the warm pet hospital with her awkward armload, she felt weighed down and struggling, like a homeless woman carrying all her belongings at one time.

"Hi, Harvey," said the petite receptionist behind the granite counter. She wore pink scrubs, and she had a small face and a blond bob cut that tapered at her chin. The cut made the most of her fine, thin hair.

Susan looked around at the redone office space. It had rustic country décor, with lots of exposed beams and tile. At her last visit, Susan had decided that her ongoing vet bills had most likely paid for the fancy stone counters and updated atmosphere. She had consoled herself with the knowledge that at least they knew Harvey there, and they seemed to care about him.

"He's just here for a short stay this time," Susan said breezily as she forced herself to smile. She placed the pet carrier on the floor as the disgruntled cat started to claw at the door.

What she really wanted to say, but hadn't, of course, was that maybe this would be a short stay and a small bill. She looked around the room again. There was no need to pay for any more granite than she'd already paid.

"Do you have his food, Mrs. Abbot? What day will you come and get him?"

Susan hoisted Harvey and her almost-designer purse from Target on the black-flecked counter. The bag of cat food plopped next to the carrier. From deep within her handbag, she pulled out her wallet. She was evidently going to need her money.

"I'll pick him up in four days, so that's the twenty-second, I think," answered Susan.

"Okay. I just need a credit card to hold his spot," said the receptionist. Her nametag said Megan. Susan looked at the youthful employee and noticed that her eyebrows were too dark for her light hair. As she handed over her credit card, she could not stop staring at Megan's face. Multiple silver studs protruded from the sides of the young woman's dark set eyes. Susan tried to smile pleasantly.

Megan was about her son's age. Susan still paid attention to things like the age of young people. She wondered if the girl had gone to high school with Ryan.

As the receptionist inserted the credit card into the chip reader, Susan noticed a tattoo of Mickey Mouse on her right inner wrist. The bracelet on her left arm that looked like a spikey dog collar. Susan said a silent prayer for Ryan not to bring a girl home like Megan. She almost immediately felt guilty about thinking like that, let alone praying about it. That sort of thing just wasn't very Christian. But she couldn't stop herself. Ryan was her only one. He needed to find a nice girl, one without a tattoo and extra piercings.

"Bye, guy," Susan said to Harvey. He now sat in silent anger. His flicking tail was all that she could see. She handed that carrier over the ledge to Megan.

Susan gathered her handbag and went out the door. There was really no need to elongate the moment or dwell on the cat's bad attitude. After all, she told herself, the animal hospital advertisements always promised that luxury awaited all the felines.

Back in her car, she started the motor, fastened her seat belt, and headed out of the parking lot. Black, cold asphalt spread in every direction. She pulled out of the parking lot and into the steady Monday traffic of her cozy bedroom community.

As Susan's car accelerated up the ramp that lead to the highway, she went over the mental checklist of her day. She looked down at her gas gauge. It was at a good level. No need to stop for fuel until almost Knoxville.

She noticed that I-40 heading east had traffic moving at a good clip. Predictably, a long line of trucks had already packed the right lane of the concrete highway. One of the true drawbacks to heading home to the mountains of North Carolina was the constant pulse of nonstop vehicles on the only real main artery across the state of Tennessee.

Susan felt fine at the moment, but she knew that a stop would have to occur in Jackson. Nature would call, especially after two large cups of coffee. But with a drive so long, she had learned the value of stopping often. It was one of the many life lessons that came from living by herself.

As she drove along, listening to music, she had plenty of time to think. These long drives provided lots of mental space for planning. Nine full hours of car time stretched out for the day.

Susan would definitely stop for barbeque in Crab Orchard. Years ago, she and Neil had stumbled upon a little shack restaurant right off the highway. The eatery marked the exact halfway point to her parents' home. With its dilapidated wooden exterior, crowned by a single smoke stack, the place had beckoned them to take a chance. And that's what they'd done back then: take chances and try adventures. Both of them had decided that it would either be the best pulled pork outside of Memphis, or it would be the worst. And after they had stopped, Susan had spent the rest of the car trip stealing pieces of tangy meat out of the extra takeout box they had intended to take to North Carolina.

"What you want, doll?" the ancient man behind the sticky wooden bar had asked Susan that first time they visited.

"What do you have?" Susan asked, regretting the question as soon as it had left her mouth.

"Barbeque. Just barbeque," the man replied almost wearily. He had a face that was the color of a wrinkled old prune with a cigarette that dangled from the side of his mouth, bobbing up and down with each word.

"You two together?" He nodded toward Neil. She could see the old man squint at her husband. Neil had on his usual crisp cotton shirt and pressed pants. Susan affirmed with a nod of her big fluffy hairdo.

"I give you two pounds then. Comes with bread, beans and slaw and tea."

Susan once again let her bouncing neck do the talking.

"Pardon me," asked Neil, over Susan's shoulder. "But do you have unsweet tea?"

The old man behind the counter put his hands on his hips. He narrowed his eyes again at the man before him. There was silence for at least thirty seconds.

"Nay," he finally said. "The tea is sweet. Made right." He paused again and looked at both of them. "You's gonna like it."

And everything had been wonderful. It turned out to be the really good kind of barbeque, the kind that made both of them lick their fingers.

That day was one of those times that they had eaten and laughed and always remembered how good taking chances felt.

In all the years that the three of them had lived in Germantown, Susan could always remember the times that they had made this drive.

When Ryan was young, the trips had been challenging. Just to arrive without feeling frazzled seemed like a miracle. Susan became convinced that it would be easier when he was out of a car seat. By then, Susan had been hoping for another child. She had told herself that even if car trips would be tough, they would find a way to travel. But then Neil was never excited about the thought of more children, so things had just kind of stalled. And then everyone got older, life had changed, people had shifted.

Susan could hear his words in her head above the car stereo as she drove along the crowded highway: "I did the best I could. It hasn't always been easy for me. This wasn't how I wanted it all to turn out in life." They had been a good family, a happy one, for most of the time.

Thinking and chatting had always been Susan's role on all the driving trips they had taken. She recalled with a half-smile all the traveling the she had done with Neil. Although they had flown on most of their trips, her husband had loved to rent a car and just go once they arrived at their destination. Susan always thought that it was the pilot in him. The need for control, being behind the wheel, and picking the course demanded his attention. All of that was so Neil.

She found herself wondering now what her ex-husband would say about her father and her Aunt Julia's estate. Her mind would sometimes ask those sorts of questions. She would find herself wondering what Neil would do. He had always known the wise thing to do; that is, until he did the unwise thing.

Even now, Susan could hear the words. "But I love you. I haven't stopped loving you, but there is someone else." How could he?

She'd asked herself that a million times. Everything had all torn apart. They had been good—not perfect—but good up to that point. Their marriage had certainly been worth fighting for, at least for Ryan's sake.

And the last four years had been hard. At first it was the anger. But after almost a year, Susan had realized that feeling that way just took so much energy. She had become tired, too tired to keep being so mad all the time. Initially, Susan had tried to walk out her resentment during that first year, then to jog out her feelings, until finally she woke up to sore knees and the dull realization that she needed to feel more than bitter indignation.

These days, her life just felt like something else. Now it was called loneliness. Most of the time the feeling was like a dull ache. Susan had somehow learned to live beside the feeling of emptiness the past few years. Thank goodness, she still had Ryan. He was the child that she had longed to have. She had wanted him so much, and he made moving forward worth it. Besides, she owed him one decent parent.

Susan reached for her phone. She needed to hear Ryan's voice. Looking at the time on the screen, she hung up after realizing that he would not be awake yet. He loved to stay in bed if his classes were later in the day.

"You sleep until the crack of noon," she would always say to tease him.

But Susan couldn't blame him for being tired. He had surprised her by having a paid internship last semester. Every week, he spent his time working as well as taking online classes. His mechanical engineering degree program was already opening doors for him. Just like Neil, Ryan had always loved cars. Engineering was the perfect fit for him. And Ryan had been so mature about it all. He even found his own place to rent this year, moved himself in, and started back to school without her help.

She checked the road signs and saw that the Jackson exits were only a few miles in the distance. A Starbucks on the edge of town created a quick stop. Susan exited the store with an extra-hot latte in her hand, eager to get back on the road.

As she resumed her speed on the highway, the terrain began to change. Driving east, the land was always more rolling in the middle of the state. Susan had been born in Appalachia, and the hills of this part of the trip always seemed to pull her forward.

By late morning, she saw her first mountains. Growing up in western North Carolina had taught her that the seasons changed first on the sloping hillsides. Now, in the bright cold light of January, Susan could see the bare tress. Their trucks and open, naked limbs looked like kitchen brooms standing on end as they marched up the mountains.

After getting a quick pulled-pork sandwich to go, Susan was back in her car. She ate and drove, determined to make good time before she lost daylight.

As she crossed into Eastern Time, Tennessee was falling behind her car in the late afternoon winter light. Mount Robert waited in front of her. Maybe it was her increasing fatigue, but she felt a push, like a second wind, to speed up and arrive before dark.

The Christmas holidays had only given her a quick few days with her family. Her father had sounded hopeful during her last visit that the New Year would bring closure to Aunt Julia's estate. But now Peter was not communicating, and no one seemed to know where the sale of the property stood.

It was time for a fresh set of eyes on the paperwork, and certainly a conversation with Peter. After all, he had been her first boss. Surely, he would meet with her. They could talk about the estate. There had to be a way to get the house sold and the fossils and artifacts moved appropriately. Dory had been living with her parents for so many months that the arrangement had turned into years. The whole thing needed to be finished.

Susan had her cruise control on as she zoomed over the North Carolina state line. The road was a winding black snake clinging to the mountain side. Snow dusted the elevated terrain. She told herself that the next few days would be busy but doable. But if all that was true, she wondered why the sensation in the pit of her stomach would not end. Something made her feel only one thing: a lingering sense of dread.

CHAPTER 3

fter seeing the first signs for Asheville, Susan headed north, exiting the highway, and pulled onto a familiar secondary road. Slowly, the two-lane stretch of asphalt began to narrow and curve. Mount Robert came into view.

"What a beautiful place," she murmured to herself. The words were involuntary, but the thought was always the same.

On every return trip, the sights of her hometown would once again charm Susan as she approached. There was a freshness to the mountain city. The heart of the town never seemed to change. Somehow the hamlet was more than just a quaint college town. The picturesque community was far enough from the urban areas of the state to retain the feeling of being unique while still somehow managing to remain vibrant.

She slowed her car down and turned into the well-known neighborhood just as the streetlights started to flicker to life. Easing up the driveway, her mother's small car sat empty before her. When she turned off the engine, Susan became aware of the quiet. The intense silence enveloped her as she approached the house.

A quick double knock came before she tried the old, brass handle. Turning the unlocked knob opened the door.

The house was warm, almost too warm for January.

"Hello!" she called. "Mom?"

"I'm in here," returned her mother.

The house was old. It had been painted white for as long as anyone could remember. Growing up, Susan had always known that the historic registry in Robertson County listed their Victorian residence as architecturally significant for the town.

"Okay!" Susan called.

She made her way through the darkened house. With the living and dining areas to the left of the front door, and the three small bedrooms lined up on the right, the location of anyone at home became almost predictable.

The only light that Susan could see came from the far back of the house. Years ago, a previous owner added a small den. The tiny sitting room and kitchen had enjoyed a "modern" update in the 1960s.

Susan came to the doorway. The area remained a family room of sorts. Lined in old auburn paneling, with sturdy, slightly sagging furniture, it was the only room that ever had a television.

"Mom," Susan said as she moved to embrace her mother.

Her mother reached out to hug her. Toby, the family dog, thumped his tail from his spot on his brown fleece bed.

"How was the drive?" Sylvia asked. There was fatigue in her voice.

Susan noticed that her mother sat dressed in a plain navy pair of knit pants and a matching top. She recognized the clothes as ones that she had purchased from Old Navy over the holidays. Her mother's head was wrapped in a colorful scarf, hiding the ravages of chemotherapy. An old quilt covered her lap.

"Uneventful," answered Susan. "Which I suppose is good. Where's Dad?"

Almost before the words left her mouth, she regretted asking the question. Obviously, he wasn't there. That had been the story of most of their lives. She glanced at the window. The sky was dark gray and the nightly temperature already felt lower.

"He's here," her mother answered. "He went outside to feed the birds."

Of course, Susan would have guessed his location, had the hour not been so late. If there was one interest for her father, one love, it was the birds. Susan had grown up always watching her father obsessed with his winged muses.

"I'll go find him," Susan told her mother. She headed for the kitchen, the only other dimly lit room in the house. Her father would be in the backyard with the bird feeders.

She walked towards the kitchen table. Only a small electric light glowed above the aluminum kitchen sink. Susan peered out into the deepening twilight. Frigid evening air filled the kitchen where the door had been left ajar.

Out in the yard of now barren fruit trees and dormant waist-high azaleas, stood her father. In his old canvas coat, his back faced the house. Disassembled bird feeders rested in his gloved hands. At his feet, Susan saw a bucket of seeds. She could just make out the old coffee can on the top, the one that her father used for a scoop.

Even in January, the birds were flocking to her father. They seemed to know he was their champion, their kindred spirit in the world.

David Upton finished most of his days in his backyard. Darting feathers often danced around his head. He had lived his passion constantly for decades. If he wasn't teaching at Mount Robert, then he was instructing or writing about ornithology.

Her father turned slightly when he heard the screen door close with a soft whack. Birds started to scatter, aware that an intruder entered their midst.

"Hi, Dad," Susan said as she came out into the yard.

"Hi, there," returned her father. "I was just finishing this with the last of the light."

He turned, pushed a stock of unruly gray, wavy hair from his forehead, and gave a slight smile. Susan knew instinctively that she had interrupted him from some deep thought or observation. His expression made her feel like an uncomfortable intrusion, even now.

Her father attached the base of the feeder and gently hung the top back on a branch. As he headed towards the house, his arm opened for a light hug. It was the kind of embrace he always gave; all chest, his head held high with a quick pat on the back. The hurried touch felt reminiscent to Susan of her childhood, and always managed to appear slightly awkward.

Back in the kitchen, he set his bucket down by the washing machine and took off his worn green coat. He put his gloves on a small shelf above the dryer. In the sink, David Upton began to wash his hands.

"How was the drive?" he asked.

"Okay, I guess," answered Susan. "It was kind of long, so I'm tired.

"I have food in the refrigerator if you're hungry," began her father.

"I'm fine," Susan said. "Now about talking to Peter, I think we should—"

The ringing cut her words to a halt.

"I need to take that in the den. There's a file on the kitchen table," her father shot back as he went to pick up the telephone in the other room. "Take a look, and we can talk later."

For the first time, Susan noticed a thick cream-colored folder resting on the round table. She moved over and opened the top flap. Newspaper and magazine articles were stacked in neat piles.

Susan sifted through the sheets of paper. Everything centered around Peter Elliott. He had been featured in countless interviews. Susan was amazed. She never knew that so much had been written about him in the last few years.

A large article in the file celebrated Peter Elliott as a new benefactor to the Children's Home Society of Greater Western North Carolina. Susan studied the pages. Under the current news stories were old headlines about Aunt Julia and, of course, Uncle Hal. Flipping to the very back of the folder, something caught her eye. There was a story from the Asheville paper. The small column appeared to be several years old, but the sides had been neatly clipped, Susan presumed by her father. Peter had been named as a leader of the forty most influential people under forty years old.

Every tribute was written in a glowing tone. When she'd worked for him, Peter had only handled small cases and the occasional business disputes of Mount Robert. Her Uncle Hal was the most prestigious client he'd ever represented. Years ago, the Upton family had merely retained the legal services of the Elliott firm because there were so few attorneys in town. Susan shook her head in disbelief. Peter now had quite a reputation.

Well, some things in Mount Robert do change, thought Susan, as she looked at the file. She just couldn't help wondering why if Peter was in fact so truly well connected, he had not been able to simply settle her aunt's estate?

CHAPTER 4

The front door to the Mount Robert Animal Shelter opened as late afternoon sunlight slanted through the lobby windows. It was the last thirty minutes of the day. Next to the reception desk, Dory rose from her knees next to the kennel she had been checking. Two women stood blinking and whispering to each other in the lobby.

"We want, like, a labradoodle. You know, one of those dogs that doesn't shed and is hypoallergenic," said the taller blond.

"Yes, and it needs to be cute and quiet. Oh, and house trained, too," added the other almost identical girl in her matching pink sorority sweatshirt.

Dory looked at both of them from under her heavy eyelashes and thick black eyeliner. *My god,* she thought to herself. *I have died and gone to hell.*

"Well, we have lots of great dogs here at the shelter," answered Dory in a measured tone. "Most of them are already house trained, and many of them are short haired, so they don't shed much."

"Yeah," said the taller one. She leaned closer, intent on revealing her big idea. "But, like, are they designer dogs? We really want a designer one. You know, like, everyone will know that it's a designer dog."

Dory could feel the throat tightness begin. The first indication of a problem was always in the back of the windpipe, followed by nostril flaring. Four-letter words caught under her breath. Shifting weight from one red high top sneaker to the next, she locked eyes with the sorority girls, fingernails extended. Suddenly, she made the choice to scratch her own head. Up and down, bobbed her dyed black ponytail. She took a deep inhale. The stress of the moment made her nose ring quiver.

"I don't know if we really have designer dogs," Dory said slowly. She tried to remember that they had lots of pets that needed a home. Proceeding with careful words remained important. It was not a good idea to piss off prospective adoptive families.

"Oh," both the sorority sisters said in an identical pout.

"Let me see if I can bring out a few of our friends to meet you," answered Dory. She forced a smile. Turning to the far end of the lobby, she caught the eye of her boss at the front counter. Bess rolled her eyes and smiled.

The steel door closed and Dory let out a single scream. The syllables left her lips as she pressed her back against the heavy side wall. With all the dogs now barking, nobody could hear a thing. Dory had learned long ago how private the back of the shelter could be. She said a lot of things in front of the kennels that she didn't want anyone to hear.

"What a bunch of spoiled brats! Girls like that . . . no wonder I hated school."

Charlie, in the back right cage, danced with excitement as she opened up the metal latch. He looked at Dory and wagged his tail. Like every dog in the shelter, Charlie was a mutt. Dory had picked out his name when he first arrived. There was something about the furry face that reminded her of Charlie Chaplain. He had also been at their facility now for a good two months. Even though the Robertson Country Animal Shelter proudly claimed to be a no-kill safe haven, the goal of moving dogs out to potential families remained. There were always more animals arriving that would need the space.

"Come on, fella," Dory said as she held the leash. Charlie jumped at her black leggings. He knew that this was a chance for an extra walk.

Dory plastered a fake smile on her face and opened the steel door. The dog lurched forward, yanking his lead.

"Here's Charlie," Dory introduced the friendly mixed breed to the blond pair. "I'll let you get acquainted."

As she watched the co-eds petting the dog, Dory went into the small office at the front of the building to the answering machine. She needed to get away from the Greek sisterhood, and she always checked the telephone before she left for the night.

As she walked into the tiny space that the staff called the office, the late afternoon shadows fell across the desk and illuminated the dust and short hairs that were floating through the air. That was where Dory heard the noise. She knew the sound; a chain rattled with a thump, followed by a small whine.

Dory was moving out of the office now, her sneakers quickly thudding past the front door of the building. The man had his back towards her, and got into a white pickup truck. He wore a baseball cap and a denim jacket. A cab door slammed shut.

"Hey!" shouted Dory. "Hold on, wait a second!"

The truck kicked up gravel and sped down the winding driveway. Dory couldn't see the license plate with all the dust from the tires. She took a few fast steps to follow, but running was futile.

Dory looked down to the ground behind her and found the discarded family. A mother dog, her tits elongated, stood shivering with a heavy chain around her neck. The face was scarred, revealing a crusty left eye. Her ribs were showing. One moving box, ever so slightly swaying, sat next to the mother dog. Dory peered over the rim. There were four puppies; one was not moving.

"Son of a bitch," Dory said. She put her hands on her petite hips. Her oversized fleece shirt was synched in like a dress over her thin legs.

"How could you?" she sputtered. Gently, Bess put her hand on Dory's shoulder. She had followed the noise and stood outside to survey the commotion.

"Come on," Bess said softly. "Let's get them inside."

Dory wanted to say something, but what? She knew that Bess had often witnessed the worst of human behavior as the manager of the shelter. The air felt cold outside. As always, her boss was right.

In her cargo pants and old blue sweater, the arthritic back of the older woman bent over and picked up the box.

"It looks like one little fella didn't make it. Let's see what Doc Simpson says about them when he comes in tomorrow."

Dory went to the mother dog. She whimpered and shivered. The sight of a human hand made her draw back.

"Nobody's going to hurt you, girl," Dory said softly to the dog. She released a long lead of chain and started a soft nudging pull towards the building. Bess was holding the glass door open with her back. The mother dog recoiled. Fear filled her eyes.

"Go on in!" Dory called. "Just bring me some of those jerky treats. I'll try to get her in with those."

Light was fading from the mountain sky. In the steel-blue twilight, Dory could see her breath. She needed to get this girl into the shelter. The weather was downright frigid and it would definitely freeze before dawn. Hopefully, they had an extra pen inside for the family.

Bess appeared with a handful of square treats. They were the good ones. Dory knew the ploy would work. As the smell of ever so slightly fake bacon filled Dory's hand, the mother dog started to wag her tail instinctively. Dory dropped a greasy goody. Bingo.

After ten minutes of careful maneuvering, the mother and puppies rested in the main reception area. Dogs barked loudly from unseen cages, somehow aware that new canines were in their midst.

The sorority girls had forgotten about Charlie, and they were crowded around the box of the puppies.

"Oh, these are so cute," said the shorter one. "I could put it in my purse and just take this one with me to class."

Bess now intervened. "They are cute, and they'll be up for adoption in a few weeks. But they're too young right now to be separated from their mother."

The two blond heads whipped around to see the mother dog. She was eating the snacks from Dory's hand. Scabs covered her face and neck, and protruding angles on her large frame revealed a hard life.

"Ugh," said the taller girl to her companion. She pointed in Dory's direction. "Hallie, we don't want a dog that grows up to look like that. We'll come back later. It's getting late."

The young women were out the door without any further comment. Bess and Dory just looked at each other. They shook their heads.

The rule at the shelter was to tell possible adoptees to come back in a few weeks. There would always be new dogs to see. Dory and Bess knew that they could have paraded more pets out of the back kennels, but neither of them had said a word to the departing Barbie twins.

Dory found bolt cutters to take off the chain. The dog began to squirm violently, sure that she would be hit with the tool. Instinctively, Bess placed her hands on the back of the mother. Dory moved quickly and the chain came off in her hand. A collar and a leash went over her head.

"Put the mom and pups in the cage in my office. Make sure you feed her well. I'll put up Charlie. We're starting to overflow in the back. They'll be fine in the office until the Doc comes in the morning," Bess said.

When Dory had returned to the lobby, she grabbed the broom. Bess was seated behind the reception desk sorting papers.

"Go on, Dory," said Bess. "I'm going to finish up a few things. You go on and go. The sweeping can wait."

"No, that's okay," she answered. "I want to stay." There was an honesty in her words. It wasn't like there was anywhere else to go. She could head home to her aunt and uncle. But another evening with Sylvia and

David Upton felt mind-numbing. They were always bringing up going back to school and her future.

Bess gave a silent nod. She had come to a slow understanding of Dory in the last two years. Some days, Bess felt less like a boss and more like a mother to her young employee. She had also become an expert at reading Dory's moods.

Looking up from the floor, Dory saw the sky beyond the glass doors was the color of India ink. She caught a glimpse of her own reflection in the lobby mirror. With her multiple earrings and oversized Mickey Mouse sweatshirt, she looked like groupie going to a Disney concert. But when she really looked at herself, her eyes told another story.

First, her father, and then her mother, had gone. Being alone in life had forged her love of the shelter. The animals and Dory shared a common past. Nobody knew how it felt to be lost quite like she did. Caring for the rescued pets had become her calling.

Wind blew against the building and rattled the front doors. Bess started to turn out the lights. The barking began to lessen as slowly the dogs were settling down for the night.

"Let's walk out together," Bess offered.

With her boyfriend working late, Dory had already decided to head back to her uncle and aunt's house. She had learned long ago that she never fit into the preppy bar scene in town. Mount Robert was a small place, and there wasn't always a lot to do if you weren't attending the local college.

As she pulled her old leather bomber jacket around her thin shoulders, Dory headed out of the lobby. Bess held open the outside door while she fumbled with the keys and lock. Dory looked at the darkened building and hoped that eventually she would have more in her life than just her relatives' house at the end of a day. Someday, she wanted a living arrangement beyond her temporary situation.

Bess stopped for a hug, and Dory embraced her boss.

"I'll see you tomorrow," Bess said softly.

"I'll be here," assured Dory.

As she headed to her car, the word played in her head. Dory thought about tomorrow. Maybe that would be the day that Peter Elliott would call about settling the estate. She just needed to be patient a little while longer, to get things settled. Her eyes looked back at the darkened shelter as her driver's side door shut. Maybe if she hung on a little bit more, then she would finally have her own real home.

CHAPTER 5

———

"Well, look what the cat dragged in!" Susan announced as the back door opened.

"Hey, yourself," a winter-bundled Dory answered as she stepped inside the house. The response was the same one that she had given to Susan ever since they could both remember.

Silently, Susan marveled as her cousin entered the warm kitchen. Over the holidays, the entire family celebrated together, yet Dory seemed different tonight. She had an adult look about her, Susan realized. Although still petite, Dory was growing more angular, now in her twenties. Named for a shared paternal grandmother, Doris, the clear resemblance to the Upton side of the family rested all over the young woman's face.

Perhaps, Susan thought as she studied her cousin, *Christmas went by in a hectic whirl. Maybe Dory matured without anyone noticing.*

Susan quickly calculated the numbers in her head. The math never changed. Based on Ryan's age, she knew that Dory could almost be a senior in college; that is, if she had decided to stay and not drop out of school.

As Dory's jacket enveloped her in a bear hug, Susan noticed something. The smell of dog shampoo rose faintly from the leather. But there was something more than that on the coat. Dory's hair brushed her cheek and Susan caught another reminiscent aroma. It was weed. She made a mental note to talk to Dory before heading back to Tennessee.

Pulling back from the embrace, Susan forced her face to look happy and relaxed. She felt a twinge of awkwardness with her young cousin these days. While Dory had grown up declaring that Susan was her favorite relative, their closeness in recent years had been marred by their opposite views on practically everything. Susan had to force herself not to be judgmental. She needed to remember that Dory had suffered too many losses for someone her age.

There has just been too much togetherness the last two years, Susan decided as she smiled at the young woman. Living all together under one roof had created an undercurrent of tension for everyone. Dory was someone that Susan loved, but the challenge came in liking her moment by moment.

"What are you doing?" Dory asked her uncle and Susan as she took her small backpack off her shoulder.

"Well, we're looking over this file so I can talk to Peter," answered Susan. She was trying to sound upbeat. Susan gave a quick glance to her father. It was unclear to her if David Upton was sharing details about the estate with his niece.

"The douchebag is dragging his feet," Dory retorted as she pulled off her gloves and unzipped her coat. "Do you know that every quarter he takes a fee from the estate? All the cash is gone, and now the extra fees will have to come out of the sale of the property."

"Yes," Susan answered calmly as she joined her father at the table. "That's why I came back."

"Oh, not just to see me?" Dory teasingly shot back at Susan as she placed her backpack on a hook by the door.

"Of course to see you, but I also need to have a meeting with Peter— that is, if he's in town. I never knew that he was all over the western part of the state these days," Susan replied as she looked at her father again.

They had just been discussing Peter's newfound success. Now Susan wasn't so sure that it would be easy to reach out to him.

"Oh, he's here in town, all right," replied Dory. "Only the Great Peter Elliott drives a black BMW. I saw it on the square today." She rolled her eyes. "He could feed a small nation with the cost of that car."

"Okay. Well, that's good. I'll just call his office in the morning and I'll see what I can arrange." Susan tried to sound confident, but she could see her father shift uncomfortably in his kitchen chair.

"I, um, have not had much success with Peter," he said quietly. Resentment colored his tone.

"Dad," Susan put her hand over his fist that rested on the table, "that's why I'm here. Let me take a crack at Peter. He was my first boss. I can probably get fifteen minutes with him."

Susan knew that she was trying desperately to give off an air of certainty. The only problem was that she felt anything but certain when it came to Peter. And after looking at all his accolades in the file that her father kept, she suspected that maybe he wouldn't even talk to her.

Dory hung her coat on an adjacent hook next to the back door and studied both her uncle and cousin gathered around the kitchen table.

"Well, good luck with that," she said with more than a hint of sarcasm. "I just want the day to come when I'm done with him. I want everything from my mom settled."

She moved across the room.

"Where are you off to tonight?" Susan's father asked as he watched Dory stroll to the doorway. She was in perpetual motion, the way only a young person could move.

Susan watched her head out of the kitchen.

Somehow she understood Dory so perfectly at certain moments. The impatience with life, and a need to keep going, were feelings that she shared with her cousin. It was a desire to move forward that came from losing relationships.

Both of us can speak the same language. The thought ran across Susan's mind as she watched Dory.

"I'm going out," Dory answered.

"Out where?" her uncle asked, studying her back while she swayed out of the room.

"Out with a friend. Out to the Tiki Room!" Dory called from the main hallway.

"You mean that place is still around?" Susan said as she looked her father and smiled. "That was going strong when I lived here."

Her father gave her a tired smile. "It's alive and well."

Susan gave him a questioning glance.

He started to chuckle. "What? Mount Robert is a small college town. My students still go there. I know where they go."

Susan had not seen him amused in a long time. She felt herself starting to enjoy their conversation. Just being home and thinking about the past made her miss all the times they hadn't talked this way. Susan wondered if maybe these small connections were the pieces of her family that had slipped pass them. Maybe life—even family life—had just become too hard over the last few years. There were too many changes and not enough joy. They'd just forgotten how to laugh.

Dory reappeared in the kitchen and grabbed her backpack. She pulled out her phone and scrolled across her screen.

"Who's the friend?" Susan knew that her father wanted to ask, but she also knew that he would be relieved if she took the lead.

"Oh, just someone I know. He's a friend." Dory was on the move again, disappearing down the hall in quick strides.

"She's been seeing Dan, the cook at the inn," her father said softly. "She thinks that I don't know who she goes out with, but I do."

"The inn? The one on South Main? You mean the old Magnolia Hotel?" Susan asked.

"Yes. A young couple bought it a year or two ago. They made it into an inn. The food is good, and I've taken your mother there a few times. They brought a chef from Asheville to run the kitchen."

"Hey," Dory appeared again at the entrance of the kitchen. She wore a vivid yellow miniskirt over her black leggings, topped by a black silk shirt covered in tiny white stripes. Her dark eyeliner had been reapplied, giving her eyes a pointed look, next to two elevated pigtails. "I can hear you. The walls are paper-thin in this old house," Dory continued as she put back on her coat.

Susan had to bite her lower lip to stifle her own laughter. Dory looked like a cross between a bumble bee and a pasty goth as she moved towards the door.

"Yes, I'm going to meet Dan. He's getting off from work soon. Yes, we're going to the Tiki Room. No, I don't want to answer any more questions."

The kitchen door slammed shut before anyone could say another word. David Upton looked at his daughter and they both shook their heads.

"Well, that's life with the twenty-year-old crowd," said Susan.

"Yes," said her father. "She's just like you were at that age."

"I was not like that," replied Susan in surprise. "I wasn't so quick to come in, go out, and announce my intentions."

"Oh yes you were," nodded her father. "Just like that, and then some."

Susan found herself smiling at the memories. She rose from her chair and reached out for the file that she wanted to study in bed.

Her father grabbed her hand. His large fingers went over her wrist. Worry filled his eyes.

"Be careful," he said. "Peter's not the same small-time attorney that he used to be. He's become powerful. He's quite well connected these days. This relatively small piece of business with your aunt's estate doesn't worry him."

"But Dad," Susan answered, "he's the executor. He has a legal duty here. Whether he likes it or not, this business must get finished."

David Upton still looked anxious. "Peter is one of the biggest attorneys in this area now. He seems to win at everything. Now he's even on the board of the college. If you make him angry . . ."

"Let me help you. At least let me try," pleaded Susan.

"Just be careful. He won't be pushed. I've seen what happens to people who try to force their agendas with him. It's not pretty."

"Okay," said Susan. She was touched by her father's protectiveness, but it also made her wonder. She needed to know what she was up against with Peter.

"What does Peter do to those that push him?"

Her father looked up with concern. His own brown eyes darkened.

"He breaks them."

CHAPTER 6

S usan pulled her crossover close to the curb. In the late January
morning light, the town square of Mount Robert looked slow and
sleepy, enveloped in the cloudiness of damp mountain fog. The college semester was three weeks old. Students were settled into a routine of
classes, which finally created ample parking on the historic main street.

Turning off the engine, Susan glanced at her cell phone. The clock
showed fifteen minutes until her appointment. She felt good about the
time, but nervous about everything else. What would she say to Peter? "Hi,
how are you? Yes, it's been a long time since we last saw each other. What
will it take to get my aunt's estate settled?"

In her head, all the words sounded whiney and naïve. She checked her
makeup in the rearview mirror. There was relief that she avoided putting
lipstick on her teeth. Taking a deep breath, she opened the car door.

Walking across the quiet street in her career pants and sensible heels,
Susan realized that just getting an appointment with Peter was a feat. It
almost hadn't happened.

The woman who answered the office phone kept Susan waiting for
a good ten minutes. Sitting on hold felt like some sort of preparation for

rejection. Susan started thinking about a back-up plan. The problem was that she felt completely out of ideas and lost in thought when the receptionist finally came back on the line.

"Mr. Elliott can see you at eleven o'clock today," she announced.

"Oh, thank you," gushed Susan into the telephone with a sense of relief. "Tell him I'll be there."

She had probably sounded far too eager, but didn't care. Getting a meeting with Peter was the first step to solving all the estate business and getting back to Germantown.

As Susan stepped onto the sidewalk, she noticed that the oak door to Peter's law practice looked exactly as it had years ago. Only when she got close to the entrance did the realization hit her. Something had changed. From a distance, the entryway looked like all the other brown wooden business fronts. But Peter's door appeared different in the morning light. The brass fixtures were handsome, thick and solid. But there was no mistake. The door was made of steel.

Pushing open the heavy metal, she stepped into an instantly recognizable lobby. Memories of her first college job flooded Susan's mind. The furniture was new, an upgrade from the past. Everything was elegant, even slightly modern. Years ago, this choice surprised her. Susan thought all law offices were wood-paneled rooms that were decorated to look like old libraries. But she recalled that Peter's taste ran a bit more contemporary. He had loved glass tables and sleek chairs. His office interior always departed from the other businesses in Mount Robert.

A young woman with flawless makeup and long, wavy blond hair sat in the reception area. Susan noted that she was young, maybe a college student. Walking across the thick white carpet, she approached the desk.

"Hello, I'm Susan Abbot. I have an eleven o'clock appointment with Peter Elliott."

The young woman looked up as if she had just noticed her. Susan felt sure that the receptionist had been watching her approach the front door.

A large window facing the town square sat directly across from the lobby desk. If Susan remembered correctly, it was the perfect view to the street.

"Just a minute," she said softly. "I'll tell Mr. Elliott that you're here."

She stood silently, and disappeared into a door at the end of the hall. Susan caught a glimpse of the young woman's shoes. They were definitely designer heels. Susan wondered what Peter was paying her. No one in Mount Robert wore shoes like that. Well, she decided, Peter was certainly compensating this young woman better than he had with employees in the past.

Susan sat down on the sleek gray sofa in the lobby to wait. Geometric-patterned pillows, plumped carefully along the tall, steel backs of the furniture, added a pop of color to the neutral room. But the thin, modern cushions on the bench sat a bit too low. Susan decided to stand. She didn't want to rise awkwardly when the beautiful, well-paid receptionist returned.

The artwork in the room added the only other hues to the office. Large oil canvases without frames covered two pale-beige walls. One painting had blue on the top half and the bottom colored red. Somewhere Susan remembered reading that pictures like that symbolized duality. They always left Susan with the feeling that she should hang up her real estate license and start picking up a paint brush. The other piece was definitely better, in her opinion. On the adjacent wall rested a hazy impressionistic view of a sunset. Susan was immediately drawn to it. Staring at the thick brush strokes, she could feel the heat from the moment just before the sun set over the Smokey Mountains.

She checked her watch. A full twenty minutes had elapsed. The office was incredibly quiet. She began to pace the reception area. What would she do if the girl didn't return? Should she leave at some point? She wondered if this was like a college class and you were supposed to know to wait fifteen minutes and then depart.

The door opened quietly and Susan turned from the window. The young woman brushed the hair off her shoulder and spoke softly. "Mr. Elliott will see you now."

Walking past the receptionist, Susan noticed the fragrance that filled the doorway. As the office door shut behind Susan, the scent of male cologne, clung ever so slightly to the disappearing young woman.

"Susan," boomed the tall man behind a gleaming black desk. He seemed to unfold from the chair. Before she could speak, he extended his hand.

"Peter," Susan said. She had already thought about this. "Mr. Elliott" sounded too formal, even though that was how she had addressed him for years. Better to be on equal, friendly terms, Susan decided.

"It is so good to see you," said Peter pleasantly as he continued to hold her hand. "What has it been? Maybe fifteen years?"

"Actually, I think it's more like twenty," said Susan with a small laugh. She noticed how large and strong his hand felt on her fingers as she spoke.

"Twenty? Really?" asked Peter. "It can't be that long. If that's true, then I'm just old, and you're still young and lovely."

Susan laughed again and felt herself relax ever so slightly. Peter was charming. She remembered that his allure had always been a trademark of his appeal.

"What brings you to Mount Robert?" he asked as he stepped back and took a seat behind his desk. There were two chairs grouped in the middle of the room. Peter motioned, and Susan took one. She noticed that Peter was back behind his polished, massive desk, five feet in front of her.

"Well, I'm here to try to help my father," Susan began. Peter raised his eyebrows in question.

"My Aunt Julia's estate is moving slowly—too slowly," Susan began. She had rehearsed the words in the mirror that morning. "Dory is living with my parents, and there's the house to sell and all the artifacts that need placement."

Peter nodded with a noncommittal expression on his face.

"We also need the full accounting details of the estate," Susan continued. "We need to look at the fees and the remaining money and—"

Peter held up his hand to her as if he were stopping traffic. "I thought that might be why you called to stop by today," he said smoothly. "I realize there's some anxiety over this estate. But you must realize that it's not that simple. Your Uncle Hal had extensive fossil and specimen collections. They're part of your aunt's estate, since she was the surviving spouse. We have to dispose of these items with care."

"Yes, but that's part of the concern. For me, for us . . ." Susan's voice trailed off as she tried to choose her words carefully. "Have the artifacts even been inventoried? They're valuable if they can be organized for sale."

Peter smiled at Susan as she spoke. His expression was pleasant, but his dark eyes, the exact shade of his perfectly slicked-back hair, stared intently.

"The artifacts that your Aunt Julia had in her estate from your uncle were quite unique. I've been in touch with several parties to see if there might be interest in obtaining them," Peter answered knowingly. "As you can imagine, there's not a huge retail market for archeological specimens."

"Well," Susan began. She had been prepared to hear this, and decided to press for action. "Could they not be donated? Say, to the college? It might negate some taxation. And we also need to sell the house. The grounds of the property are adjacent to the school and are technically part of the college. Dory can't really stay there by herself; the house is too large and the upkeep is too expensive. The money from selling the house would let her finish her education."

Even as Susan said it, she knew that the last sentence was a lie. Dory never wanted to go back to school. Anyone who knew anything about the young Miss Upton had probably heard that school was not a happy fit for her. Even though Mount Robert was a small town, Susan hoped that Peter was too busy to know anything about Dory and her future plans.

"Well, believe me when I say that I'm working on it," Peter came back.

"My father is, um, distraught." Susan hated to use that word, but what else could she say? "Is there something that I could do to move the process along?"

"Susan," Peter dropped his voice now. "I completely understand. Believe me when I tell you that I'm trying to contact the right people and organizations that might be interested in your uncle's private fossil collection. I'm also looking at what it will take to get the house on the market."

"Yes, but surely there must be something that we could do," Susan replied. "I'm sure that if we—"

Peter held up his hand again. He seemed to be intent on stopping the flow of Susan's words as if they were cars at an intersection. "Don't worry your pretty little head about all of it. I'll talk with your father. We're going to settle this; it's just a matter of time."

Susan was ready to press further, when Peter changed the subject.

"So, how is Nashville, isn't it? I remember your father said you were in Tennessee."

"Yes, I'm in the Memphis area," Susan replied, making a quick decision. Maybe if they continued to talk, she could find out where the estate really stood.

"And you're doing what in Memphis?" Peter flashed her one of his winning smiles. He was smooth.

Susan shifted in her seat, trying to figure out how to come back to her aunt's legal issues. "I sell real estate," she answered confidently.

There, Susan had said it. Maybe now Peter would know that she really could handle the details of her aunt's possessions and home sale. She assumed that the statement made her sound very professional, but as she stared back at Peter, she also silently hoped that he didn't ask her about her husband. The divorce, even now, was something that Susan hated to bring into discussions. The whole thing still made her feel vulnerable and exposed whenever conversations shifted to the topic of marriage. She felt as if she were saying that yes, she had been married, but no, he really hadn't liked her enough to stay. It was like admitting that Susan could find a partner, just not keep him.

"Well, that's great to hear," he responded. Peter didn't seem to miss a beat, or to appear the least bit impressed with Susan's home-selling career. "And you have children?" he asked cordially.

"A son," Susan smiled, still aware that Peter was being charming. "He's already twenty, and working on an engineering degree."

"Well, that's wonderful. Now, if you'll excuse me, I have another appointment." With that, he stood and extended his hand. "Tell your father that I'll be in touch," Peter said as he held out his large arm.

Susan caught a glimpse of an expensive watch under his cuff.

"I, um, we do need this matter to be settled." Susan was determined to make a parting speech, to implore Peter to act. She took his outstretched hand as he came around the desk and moved her to the door.

"I understand," Peter soothed. His hand went on her shoulder. "I'll be working on it."

Peter opened the door and leaned forward into the outer office. He spoke to his receptionist. "Tiffany, could you please come in here? I need you." He turned to Susan. "Thanks for stopping by. It was good to see you again. Give your family my best."

His receptionist was in the doorway before Susan could say another word. As the young woman moved towards Peter, Susan found herself nudged into the hallway. The blue eyes of the receptionist were locked in Peter's gaze. His hand on the opened door had gently fallen to the small of her back.

Susan knew that the appointment had ended. She'd wanted to have a productive discussion with Peter, but she'd accomplished nothing. What would she tell her father? The meeting had been polite but also incredibly patronizing. They were in such a humiliating position. What was her family going to do about the house, the fossils, and the money for Dory?

Susan stepped back into the lobby and tried to decide what to do next. The office was silent. As she headed toward the exit, she stopped and turned back to stare at Peter's closed office door. She was sure that she heard little Miss Prada giggling.

CHAPTER 7

Back on the street, the traffic increased as the lunch hour approached. Cars went by in steady succession as students, bundled against the cold, walked with their heads bowed to their destinations on the square. Susan pulled her wool cape around her frame and started walking down the street.

She wasn't sure exactly where to go. Most of the business fronts along Main Street had changed over the years. If she could find a quiet spot to check her work messages, maybe she could come up with a game plan. She just needed to go somewhere to think. Susan already dreaded telling her parents about the meeting.

On the corner, she spotted a place. Where the one-hour dry cleaners once stood, a coffee shop now flourished. Students and town locals were coming and going from the entrance at a brisk pace. Called the Mojo Café, the little restaurant advertised trendy beverages on a chalkboard by the door.

Susan suddenly realized that she felt resoundingly tired. Only the air of defeat clung to her morning. A cup of coffee was exactly the medicine she needed. There had to be a way to salvage some plan of action to help her parents and Dory.

Entering the small shop, Susan marveled at the décor. It was very chic, and yet incredibly cozy. Bistro tables filled the middle of the room, while a long glass counter lined the back wall. Heavenly roasted smells made her wonder why a café like this had only appeared in town after she had long since moved away and started another life.

"What's up?" the young man with blond dreadlocks asked from behind the counter.

Susan smiled. The chalkboard that hung on the back wall listed a variety of special blends.

"I'll have a cup of your daily grind," Susan answered.

The young man nodded his head in a slow movement. Susan nodded her head, too, acknowledging the order with the millennial waiter in front of her.

"Size?" the young man finally asked Susan. He looked tired, as if he was oblivious to the caffeine jolts around him.

"A medium with warmed cream," Susan answered.

Paying for the coffee made her wonder about the waiter behind the counter. He looked so incredibly young. Taking note of people who were about Ryan's age had become a habit. It was just one of the casualties of motherhood, Susan told herself.

Holding the warm cup, she thought about life. Maybe she was just at an odd place, and getting older. While she did have a college-age son of her own, Susan felt neither old enough to be truly wise, or young enough to be very hip.

Spotting an empty table in the middle of the room, she made her way to the tiny bistro set. A large bulletin board covered the side wall.

Intrigued, she slowed down and stopped to look at the display. Years ago, the only community notices ever posted were thumbtacked on a dilapidated wall in the old feed-and-seed store. Those messages had mostly been about livestock and farm goods. In the age of social media, Susan wondered what would be posted in a college town like Mount Robert.

Advertisements for textbooks and places to rent filled the board. Random businesses in the community, including medical and legal services, were listed. Everything was about what Susan had expected to find in a small town centered on higher education.

As she settled into her table, her mind started racing. What was she going to do? Her father and Dory needed closure on the estate. The house and its contents were worth enough to give them all a nest egg, so to speak, if properly invested. Her mother was in remission, at least for the moment, thanks to a new experimental drug. But what if the cancer came back? How long could her father cope with a twenty-year old, a sick wife, a teaching load, and a perpetually unsettled estate? Susan wondered, now more than ever, what would become of her family.

She reached into her oversized bag and pulled out her smartphone. A quick email check for work revealed nothing. Given the slow month of January, it was hardly surprising. She consoled herself with the fact that at least she wasn't missing out on potential clients while she was visiting her parents.

Susan decided to call her office.

"Hello," she said.

"Hi, Susan. How are the mountains?" Marcie, the receptionist at the real estate office sounded genuinely pleased to hear from her.

"Oh, it's fine," lied Susan. "How is business?"

"So slow," responded Marcie. As she spoke, Susan could almost picture the secretary filing her nails as she answered the phones. "Are you heading back soon?"

"Oh, yes, um, soon," Susan promised. "I'll call you when I'm driving back."

"Well, don't rush back here. Nothing is happening as far as showings. They're almost nonexistent. Hopefully, the spring will bring in more business."

"Okay," Susan responded, somehow feeling better about her absence.

Ending the call, Susan stared at the screen in front of her. She would have to find professional help for her family. After all, what choice did she really have at this point?

A quick search under the phrase "estate help" yielded names of every lawyer in Robertson County. Susan was surprised there were so many attorneys in the area. Growing up, there had only been one or two legal professionals that she could remember. Now the names before her covered not only Mount Robert, but all the counties surrounding Asheville, as well.

Scrolling down the list, she knitted her brow in concentration.

"Um," she muttered to herself. "Lots of ads for drunk-driving offenses, or getting out of jail on bond."

Disregarding most of them at a glance, her eyes fell to the bottom of the page. She saw something familiar in a name.

A tab on the screen stated legal help with family matters, security concerns, and estate services. She clinked on the link and saw that the attorney was named Craig Cartwright. His page seemed simple, almost a bit stark, just a picture of justice scales in front of the courthouse. Claiming fifteen years of experience, his specialty listed was family law.

She looked up from her table. Of course, she had just seen the same logo on the community board. She rose quickly, grabbed her bag, and almost spilled her remaining coffee. She moved over to the wall. There it was. The same logo. The same name. A simple white sheet with a phone number repeated on slips that could be pulled off the bottom of the paper. Susan took one.

Heading for the door, she needed to make a phone call in her car. Privacy would be important.

Hiring an attorney could be expensive, but what was the alternative? Peter was doing nothing—that was evident—and her family was in limbo. In another day or two, she would need to head back to work. Even if Mr. Cartwright could not help her, maybe he could point her in the right direction.

As Susan pulled her gray wool cape close to her, the winter wind blew dry leaves down the street. Maybe she'd just found a solution to her problems—or at least a place to start.

CHAPTER 8

Craig Cartwright leaned forward in his beat-up hatchback and adjusted his camera. He was near the railroad tracks, on the back street of some condominiums that had seen better days. His small digital camera sat perched on his dashboard, aimed at the front door of a unit that was halfway down the block. The parking spot for his car hugged the corner. Hopefully, the setting sun would not interfere with the pictures he needed to get.

He reached down and took a small sip of water from a bottle on the floor of the passenger seat. His strong jaw muscles moved carefully while holding the liquid in his mouth. One lesson that he'd learned the hard way was never to drink too much while gathering evidence. The evening would only be uncomfortable if nature called when it remained unclear how much time a stake-out would require.

Checking his watch made him realize that at least two hours had passed. How long would this observation drag on before Mr. Benson emerged, hopefully with his new honey in tow?

Craig had been hired by Mrs. Benson. She was a fading southern beauty, her patience worn thin by her husband's perpetual affairs.

"He hit me," she'd said to Craig. Her left eye was swollen and purple on that day in his office. "I ain't never going to put up with that."

Craig nodded. "What can I do for you?"

"I want a divorce," she answered flatly.

"Are you sure you're ready—really ready—for that?"

It was a standard question Craig always asked each client who came to him seeking an end to their marriage.

"Yeah," she responded. "'Cause he's having an affair, too."

Craig nodded sympathetically. He did a lot of head movements with people that were hurting when they first came to see him.

"The woman that he's with is married, too, so I guess that makes it twice as bad." There was disgust in his new client's voice.

Craig continued to affirm understanding with his bobbing chin as he started to write down details.

"It's like my mama always said," she continued through clenched teeth, "'Hurt me once, shame on you, but hurt me twice, then shame on me.'"

And without children, the case looked like an easy one. The only problem was that Craig soon learned that all the assets were listed in the husband's name. The wife would get her share only after a lot of legal stalling. That meant that an attorney's fee would only be forthcoming after a lot of stalling as well. So, being the proactive and resourceful lawyer that he claimed to be, Craig decided to help the entire situation move to an inevitable conclusion.

He rubbed his neck, his fingers combing the curly blond hair at the base of his collar. At this point, all he needed were a few photos of lover boy and his very married companion.

In Craig's experience, many cheating spouses quickly came to the table to negotiate if there was a belief that a jilted husband might take matters into his own hands. More than one of his female clients had benefitted from a decent divorce settlement only after an angry visit was paid to their roaming spouse. Ultimately, it would all come out in the end. So what if a cheating liar ended up with a mouthful of fist or his own black eye? Craig held an unwavering conviction that the law should always be on the side of those who needed help the most. That was how the Cartwright Firm viewed justice.

Shifting his broad shoulders around in the old vinyl seat of his Ford, he tried to stretch. Stiffness spread across his back. Adjusting his legs reminded him to sit still.

These type of surveillance evenings came with the territory these days. When Craig began his family law practice, he'd hired a young man to do most of his intelligence for him. Roger had been the most average-looking guy in the world. And that, Craig learned, was what made him so extraordinary. That, and the fact that he came to Mount Robert College in the ROTC program with a plan to study computer reconnaissance for the army. Roger taught Craig the fine points of getting information on people.

"Always use a camera with a good long shot so you can stay back," he told Craig. "Be patient. And know that people will have vices that never change."

It was excellent advice. Craig proved to be a quick study, and tried to follow the lessons that he learned from his military employee.

When Roger finally graduated and took his commission, he left Craig with a final tidbit of useful information. "Always drive an old car, something that people will never notice."

The instructions had been an invaluable crash course in reality. Because of his superior talent for surveillance, Roger remained one of the few people who Craig never resented paying. Today, his advice still aided many cases involving infidelity that found their way to the law firm.

On his last night in town, Craig took his employee out for a beer and confided in him. "If you ever get tired of military life, you can make a fortune as a spy or a hacker."

Out of sheer boredom, Craig picked up his cell phone. One hard and fast rule was to never do more than check his last few calls when he worked on a case. The phone could be distracting, and he recognized it. One time, an elusive, estranged spouse almost escaped his camera because of voicemail.

An unknown number flashed across his screen. Craig played back the message and started to smile. The voice belonged to some woman. She sounded nice enough, and wanted to meet with him about a family estate.

He shifted again in his seat. Dusk started to settle over the mountains. Craig felt tired. If the right shot happened, then he could call it a day. There was always time at home to return calls.

Ultimately, Craig would take any job, but he was relieved and delighted that it wasn't another sobbing, wronged spouse with a marriage in shreds. Settling an estate might prove great for his bottom line. Constantly worrying about his payroll in a small town, with its thin profit margin, was wearing on him.

Craig suddenly sat upright and put his hands on the steering wheel. He could feel what would happen in the next few minutes. His heart started to race. Now, the work began.

The foyer ceiling of the condominium illuminated and light spilled out from a window above the door. Craig guessed that the glow came from a fairly dim overhead fixture, probably with a light bulb or two missing. As he sat there, a side room went dark. Most likely a bedroom lamp had been turned off, one that had been hard to see in the daylight. He knew that lover boy and his squeeze were most probably done with their romp in the hay.

With his experiences at these types of stakeouts, Craig could almost sense what would come next. Unless he was mistaken, the cheating husband intended to take his play toy out for a big steak. Their choice for a destination might involve either Asheville or Boone so they could avoid meeting any of the locals.

This is where Craig's need for accuracy played the greatest part. It was always risky to follow a car for long distances. Too many things might happen, including tipping off the happy couple. But there would be no need to go that far if he could get the right pictures.

The front door opened. Craig had his hands on the dash, reaching for the camera. A slab of dull light fell onto the front walkway as two people emerged into the twilight. They seemed to be noticing several squirrels chasing each other through the yard. The man and woman pointed and laughed.

Craig started snapping images. The best part of digital photography was the sharpness and the speed. The soon-to-be ex-husband started running his hands through his greasy hair. At the truck, he stopped to tuck in his shirt. The woman appeared to be a blond thirty-something with big hair and a peasant blouse. It was a safe bet that under the ruffles that covered her chest, she had decided to forgo a bra.

"Got it," he whispered to himself.

A smile of satisfaction spread across his face. The camera clicked away, and his video recorder was streaming. They were almost to the vehicle in the driveway. The stupid husband had even driven his own HVAC truck with his name on it. Craig shook his head and let out a low chuckle. He learned long ago that people like the Romeo in front of his camera always thought they would never get caught. They were the same people who routinely believed that the rules did not apply to them. There would be no doubt about anything in his photos.

As the woman got into the passenger seat, his client's spouse let his hand linger on her backside. He gave her a squeeze, and she laughingly turned to her lover. With a nod, Craig was finished. He had everything his case would need.

CHAPTER 9

S usan rolled around and punched her pillow, hoping to magically plump the filling into a vertical cloud of neck support. She felt restless and fretful in her old childhood room. It wasn't just the single iron bed with the less-than-new mattress that seemed to be the problem, nor was it the old white dresser against the opposite wall, covered with a row of staring dolls that bothered her. Closing both eyes again brought everything back. The whole argument replayed in her mind.

"You can't tell me what to do, Sylvia!" Dory shouted at Susan's mother.

Ever since Dory started living with her aunt and uncle, she insisted on calling them by their first names only.

"Dory," Susan mother said. Her voice sounded weary, but the words held an edge of sharpness. "Think about what your mother would have wanted. She wanted—she expected—you to go back to college."

Dory glared at her aunt. "I'm not going back. I hated sitting in class with all those preppy bitches. They all think they are so special. And don't even get me started with the teachers. They all think they're God, or something."

Susan's father took another turn. He tried to use logic. "Dory, think about the expanded good that you could do, in any field, if you got your diploma. It could open doors for you."

"You, of all people, should respect my 'no'!" Dory shouted back at her uncle as she grabbed her purse and headed for the front door.

"Now where are you going at this hour?" The voice of David Upton rose into a booming crescendo to match Dory's outbursts.

"I'm going out!" Dory yelled as she opened the door.

"Hang on!" Susan's father shouted in anger.

Dory turned in the foyer, staring at her uncle. "David, go fuck your-self," she spat out of her mouth.

With that, Dory was gone. The front door slammed behind her. Susan just stood there, a witness to all the turmoil. She had not been able to get a word in edgewise.

The dog followed the family to the front of the house as they watched Dory storm out into the night. A small mirror in the front hall vibrated with the banging of the old entryway. The three of them were left in the sudden quiet of the still rooms. It reminded Susan of the void right after a clap of thunder, when her muscles were still tight, waiting for the next rain cloud to break. Only Toby, the senior dog that Dory rescued from the shelter, gave a whine at all the noise, and headed for the den to curl up on his bed.

Susan opened her eyes again and looked at the old doll collection. Her vision adjusted in the darkness. She had a sudden idea. Over the holidays, Susan causally threw a scarf over the empty, expectant faces on the dresser when they seemed too unsettling. Maybe that was the thing to do that now, she thought. But somehow there was certainty that nothing would help her sleep.

No, it wasn't the old room, left practically as a time capsule to her youth that had Susan tossing restlessly in bed, nor was it all the nighttime sounds of the old house keeping her awake. She felt exhausted, but images filled her mind. No one knew that the meeting that morning had been a disaster. Trying to have a meaningful conversation with Peter only resulted in total failure. And then there had been the fight with Dory.

She closed her eyes and threw her arm over her head. At the moment, the only need was to breathe; think, and breathe. Maybe it would all fall into place if she could just relax and go through things from beginning to end.

Everyone needed the estate to close. Dory had been living with her aunt and uncle now for almost twenty months. And while Susan's parents were all the family that her cousin had left, the situation was obviously taking a toll on each one of them. Her mother's breast cancer managed to return last year. More chemotherapy and a new drug for her tumor meant the need for more peace and quiet.

Dory was just so head strong, Susan thought as she stretched out in bed. As a young woman, she came and went as she pleased, rarely coming home before midnight. And then there was the constant "dating" of young men most people classified as losers.

Susan sighed. But the big problem was school. When Dory had refused to go back to college, constant tension filled the house. Earlier in the evening, the family "discussion" about the possibility of enrolling in some summer classes only created a front-row seat to chaos for Susan and her mother. Dory left the house in a tirade of door-slamming and name-calling to go God knows where, with God knows whom.

Susan rolled on her side. She was wide awake.

Maybe they needed a family counselor, Susan decided. Perhaps if Dory found some kind, sympathetic, tweed sweater sort of psychologist—no psychiatrist, because she would definitely need some sort of medication—then college could be a possibility. Susan remembered reading somewhere that students that hated school always had an underlying reason. People couldn't just dislike school anymore, could they? Was that even a thing to despise these days? Maybe some specialist would diagnose Dory with a learning disability, or some sort of social anxiety.

"Or maybe, an expert would see our whole family for the dysfunctional group of misfits that we are," Susan muttered aloud. "That, plus a suggestion to give Dory a swift kick in the ass."

She stared into the fading darkness and thought about all of them. The fact that both of her parents and one uncle spent their lives as professors made Dory's decision not to finish school all the more painful. In her uncomfortable bed, Susan could see the irony of it all.

Here was her family, filled with adults who had spent their lives in pursuit of knowledge, unable to settle a local estate or compel a young woman to finish her education.

In the early blue light of morning, Susan rolled over on her other side. Sleep was impossible.

Last night, the only thing her parents were told was that there would be another meeting today. Omitting the fact that a new appointment involved yet another attorney, she promised herself that the truth would be communicated if everything went well. Her mother was still tired from the latest round of chemotherapy last week, so there was merely a nod when Susan reminded them that she would have to go out in the morning.

Getting out of bed, Susan grabbed her bathrobe and opened her door to find the house strangely quiet. Her mother would try to sleep late. Mornings were hard in the days following her treatments. Her father would be up by now, most likely already at school. He had always been an early riser, and one that perfected the art of leaving home silently.

Susan walked down the hall. Months ago, Dory had taken over the guestroom, which remained dark. Peeking around the half-opened door, Susan knew that her cousin was either sleeping late, or she'd never made it home.

Against her better judgment, Susan stepped inside the bedroom. Clothes covered the entire space, at least six inches deep, obscuring the furniture and the hardwood floor. The bed was a rumple of blankets with a depression in the middle.

Dory was gone. Susan smiled. She was secretly glad, which conjured up slight feelings of guilt. But she knew her own limit. Daybreak with her moody relative, who would most likely be dressed in some ridiculous outfit leaving for the animal shelter, would set her teeth on edge.

Susan stepped back into the hallway. During the holidays, the family had lived through too many mornings with Dory. If the young Miss Upton wasn't grumpy and complaining as the day began, then she was talking endlessly as the master of all information.

Listening to Dory was the most exhausting part, Susan thought. She always claimed to be the resident expert. Anything that Susan tried to say was dismissed because her millennial cousin knew everything.

"We don't need the internet in this house," Susan had told her mother dryly one evening over the Christmas dishes as she was clearing the table. "If we want any information—any piece of data in the world—we just need to ask Dory."

Susan headed for the bathroom. The quiet of the old house was soothing as she walked down the hall. Her delight at the solitude ended when the light switch flipped to illuminate the room. More clothes from Dory and wet towels covered the floor, sink, even the shower curtain. Susan swore under her breath. This was yet another reason to have everything settled and send Dory out on her own. The mess was the last thing her mother needed to see. Susan would have to pick up everything and get herself ready to meet Craig Cartwright.

After a quick shower, Susan quietly walked into the kitchen in her bathrobe with her hair in a towel. She microwaved coffee that had been left in the pot earlier that morning by her father.

"The dawn is the best time of day," her father always said.

Long ago, Susan came to the belief that his schedule usually had more to do with the birds he was studying than anything else.

"Look, Susan," her father would say, staring into the backyard, if she'd gotten up early in the morning. "Look how the birds come together, in social order, with the early light."

Opening the cabinet, Susan rummaged for the oatmeal. She thought about her day. Hopefully, Craig Cartwright would offer help, or at least some sort of direction. There wasn't much choice except to tell him everything.

Susan wrapped her robe tighter around her waist. The winter was as cold in Mount Robert as it was in Tennessee. She decided to dress warmly before leaving the house in the frigid air.

Back in her childhood room, her heaviest clothes were unpacked. She brought a skirt or two from Germantown. It was better to appear professional. Selecting her outfit, she remembered a few old things, namely stockings and scarves, that were left in the old bureau in the guestroom. She wondered if Dory had taken over every drawer. Susan recalled an old pair of warm navy tights at one point in the extra bedroom. Maybe they were still there.

Dressed in a soft blue skirt and a white top, Susan looked in the mirror. Her reflection appeared hopeful. Maybe her meeting would yield some answers. Did she look like a client Craig Cartwright would want to help? That wouldn't matter to him. She knew that much. It would be all about the money. Lawyers were all the same in that regard.

She chewed her lower lip while putting on a bracelet. The problem was just that her family history would have to be discussed. She would end up telling this new lawyer about her uncle and aunt, living everything over again, during their meeting. If Mr. Cartwright didn't already know the whole story, Susan would have fill in all the facts.

With her heels in her hand, she pushed open the door to the guestroom. The shades were pulled down and the dim room had a stale smell of old winter clothes. Susan kicked piles of garments apart to get to the dresser.

Dory's clothes were shoved into giant balls of fabric in the top three drawers of the bureau. Only after Susan pulled on the bottom knobs did she recognized some of her old things mixed among her cousin's sleepwear.

She reached to the back of the drawer and searched until the tights emerged. That was when her fingers hit something hard. A solid shape, yet soft-feeling to her hand. Susan pulled out a small square.

It was a green box. Susan remembered the jewelry. Standing there confused, she didn't remember leaving anything valuable in the guest room.

"What the heck is this?"

Susan opened the top and found a locket. It was her necklace, the one that her father had given her when she turned ten. But what was this doing here? Didn't she have that in Germantown? Had valuables been forgotten at her parents' home? She tried to remember the last time that she had worn the golden heart.

Standing there puzzled, her phone rang in the next room. Maybe the call was Ryan. They hadn't spoken for few days, and she missed talking to him.

The lid snapped shut on the velvet box as her hand enveloped the small heirloom. Moving to the doorway, Susan shrugged her shoulders. She couldn't remember leaving the gift, but if her treasured piece had been forgotten once, it wasn't going to happen again.

CHAPTER 10

C raig Cartwright took a sip of hot coffee and looked at his calendar for the day. He would be reasonably busy for most of the morning. Staring at the appointments spread throughout his working hours, the usual addition began. Mental calculations reviewed what each case should generate in income. Checking his bottom line was becoming a hated obsession. Even though he chafed at the idea of being motivated by money, the reminder to himself always stayed the same. There were no guarantees for small-town lawyers when they decided to hang out their own shingle.

Quickly, he looked around his office. New clients were coming in today, and Craig always felt self-conscious about the appearance of his business. He was painfully aware of his small space. His office resembled a glorified box with walls. Even the reception area, separated from his desk by only a partition, had a small, minimalist feel. As the aroma of roasted beans filled the well-lit but slightly barren workplace, Craig put down his cup as he turned on his computer. At least this office was clean, he noted. And the coffee was good. He took another sip. It needed to be, since he refused to pay for drinks from any of the local shops.

The reception desk sat empty for the moment. Craig Cartwright was not a man to spring for a full-time receptionist. He hired a Mount Robert student to cover his front desk on Tuesdays and Thursdays only. This was Wednesday, so it was his day to be alone in the office. The lessons from the last few years had confirmed that law remained a feast-or-famine business, and he worked relentlessly to cut his overhead.

With his computer on and a daily calendar in front of him, he reviewed the first appointment of the day. Last evening, Craig had been able to connect with the woman who'd left a message on his phone. He noticed that her voice sounded young, at least, youngish. And much to his surprise, she seemed better educated than most of his clients. Again, the lady told him, with a hint of vagueness, that her need centered on help with an estate. He thought about his usual clientele and looked forward to meeting this mystery woman. Maybe the case would prove interesting and possibly profitable.

Craig also knew himself well enough to realize that at the moment, he would be glad to meet a little different segment of the population. Lately, there had been nothing but a string of young DUI offenders from the college or unhappy divorces filling his days. What a welcome relief to handle something else; not to mention, the fees for estate work could be attractive.

He looked out the large window by his desk. With the thin blinds opened to the cold January morning, Craig thought about what might be involved in settling an estate. The case might require some meetings, perhaps even a court date. But a decent fee usually came at the end of the process. That made the whole idea of this new client tantalizing. And yet, he had to be realistic. Given that Mount Robert prevailed as only a rural county; the situation would probably involve some unfortunate local who passed away without a will. It was always the ones who died intestate with sketchy insurance policies that created the biggest legal headaches.

Craig logged onto his computer to check his email and start the day. Maybe he would have a few more requests for legal services filling his inbox. There would be time for a couple of quick calls in the morning, to possibly connect with some new business. Chasing future clients felt routine these days.

Organizing paperwork and his computer, Craig Cartwright reflected on his law practice. He had never intended to become an attorney that spent his days pursuing the next piece of work. In fact, he had never really intended to be an attorney at all. In truth, the decision to pursue law came a bit late for him; certainly later than most. The original plan in life was to follow his one passion: baseball. The game had been his first love. Craig arrived in town as the star pitcher on the Mount Robert baseball team. And for the first two years of college play, he'd done well. Things began to unfold for him, and dreams of success in sports seemed like the ticket to his future.

Playing ball had been perfect in those days. For the first time in his life, Craig did some traveling and saw more than the mountains of North Carolina. He desperately wanted to get out of this part of Appalachia. After growing up in a small foothill town in the Piedmont, the desire to go anywhere that his sport would take him burned through his mind.

But reality came with a swift, unforeseen jolt. By his junior year, Craig's shoulder had finally created other ideas for his life. After the second surgery, the decision was made to sideline him from pitching for the Mount Robert team. He could manage enough to keep a scholarship, but that was about all his arm could muster. So playing baseball continued, and he did what came naturally—his thoughts turned to other options.

History remained his favorite subject, and the ideas were a natural fit for him. Craig had spent years memorizing the ever-flowing mountains and studying the people who once settled them.

"Look, I found another arrowhead," Craig told his teachers at school. Delight spread over his face. The treasure was just the prize for a scrappy, skinny boy who read everything he could find about Indians.

"Stick with it," one of his older teachers said to him. "History can take you places that you never imagined."

Craig took the idea to heart, even as a youth. With his love for the past still intact by his junior year, he began to think about his life. Unsure of the future, law school hardly received a passing thought.

Only after the assistant coach on the college baseball team became the target of a drug sting, just because of his Hispanic background, did the young Mr. Cartwright change his mind. There was something about the entire lack of justice during the investigation that had opened Craig's eyes.

"Shut up," barked a police officer to the team when the senior players spoke up to support their coach.

"But if you check the practice log, you'll see he was here with the team," began Craig.

The blow struck hard and fast. Craig never felt it until his shoulders were slamming into the wall behind him in the weight room.

"I said, shut up!" boomed the officer, his breath hot on Craig's face. They locked eyes.

"What are you going say about it?" taunted the other police officer at the scene while Craig stood pinned to the concrete at the back of the room. He could feel a forearm crushing his windpipe.

The policemen both smiled. "Well, just like I thought. I guess the cat's got your tongue."

That was the day that his new journey began. Somewhere deep inside, Craig felt a fire start to smolder. Soon, his work ethic in class began to accelerate. By the end of four years, he had earned a scholarship to Duke Law School.

He vowed to himself that he would take his legal education and make the most of it. And his degree had been used to help quite a few people who needed a lawyer on their side. That part of his profession felt good. But now as a Mount Robert solo attorney— "hanging out his shingle," as he always said—he seemed forced to wonder. Sometimes it appeared as if his career just involved spinning his wheels, beating the bushes to find his next client.

Craig never intended to stay in the mountains of his youth. But on a holiday break from law school, he came back to town and attended a party at Appalachian State University. Undergraduate social events were really beneath him, but Mount Robert was painfully quiet that winter. With inches of snow on the ground that stubbornly refused to melt, Craig felt like he'd been forced to stay inside for what seemed like forever. It was such a lonely time for him. His mother had died the year before law school began. Thinking back on that night, he realized that the evening ushered in the first real meaningful romance of his life.

"Hi, I'm Ashley," she told him. He noticed her immediately. The brown eyes held his gaze from across the room.

"What's a pretty girl like you doing with a tapped keg?" Craig asked her. Over the next few years, both of them often laughed at that awful pickup line.

They were a good match in the beginning. Their goals aligned completely. Ashley was young, but ambitious. After spending hours talking, Craig thought that he finally found someone who understood him perfectly. The two of them agreed on practically everything. As a couple, there was shared determination to have more out of life than living in the sleepy mountain hamlets of their youth.

"Open it," Ashley said one day, handing Craig a small box.

Inside the tissue paper rested a coffee mug. Without much thought, he read the words printed on the side.

"World's Best Dad," he said, his brain not processing. Craig's mind went numb.

It had been a crash course in adulthood. Craig's life and plans took a seismic shift. He wanted to believe in their future. Ashley said that everyone was young and afraid when they became parents.

The ceremony took place under a large oak tree on the edge of town. In truth, Craig remembered the event now only as a blur. In his mind, the day was like trying to piece together a stained-glass window, but all that remained were a few shards of brightly colored glass.

He remembered Ashley, with her veil blowing in the wind. And he could recall the mountain flowers that bent in the breeze that day and the taste of the champagne in the warm afternoon sun.

"I promise," Craig found himself saying in a nervous whisper.

After the wedding, the two of them packed up all their possessions. Everything they had seemed to fit in the back of Craig's pick-up truck. And suddenly, the new Mr. and Mrs. Cartwright were off on their first big adventure. Moving back to Durham let Craig finish his law degree. And everything seemed happy, for a while.

"I need to get back to Mount Robert," Ashley told Craig when she was in her last trimester.

"But I thought that you liked it here," Craig answered in confusion and disbelief. "I thought we wanted to see some new places, to live somewhere else."

"I do, but not with a baby, not right now. We need to be close to the family."

"You mean *your* family," he answered with a hint of bitterness. "I only have a few cousins left."

Ashley shrugged her shoulders in response.

Somehow it was settled. When Craig received an offer for a position in the district attorney's office in a county close to Asheville later that month, he took the job. They returned to Mount Robert and back to living in their small town. In a way, picking up their life in western North Carolina felt like they had never really left. Within weeks of their arrival, Tyler came into the world in the same hospital that Ashley had been born in twenty-three years earlier. But reality began to gnaw at their lives.

"I thought lawyers were supposed to have it better than this," Ashley complained. Her words measured in tone, part of the daily sermon that she gave him. "I'm doing everything myself."

"Life is not like TV, Ashley," Craig retorted with an edge in his voice. "I have to work these hours because I'm just starting out, and I'm new in the office."

In the end, he could look at her and see that the long hours and low pay in the district attorney's office left Ashley resentful and restless.

"This isn't working," she told him late one night as they stood in their galley kitchen. "I want more out of life, more out of a marriage, than this."

The words had stopped Craig dead in his tracks. For a moment, his whole world tilted. He actually reached out to grab her arm. But looking into her eyes, he saw the truth. Behind her grimace, there was heartbreak. And for the first time, the future stood inescapably before them.

"I'm sorry," was all he managed to say.

They were silent for a long time that night.

"Maybe we could try—" Craig had begun.

"No," Ashley said quietly. "We have to stop pretending."

For the next two weeks, Craig slept on the lumpy sofa in the living room before he finally had to admit that she was right. His ambition was fully intact in life, and he would get there, but a legal career would take time to establish. Sports taught him that rewards only came after patience and sacrifice. Ashley would always take a different approach. Craig knew that the two of them could never see life the same way. Somehow, they would forever be out of step.

In the end, the split was mutual. Craig gave Ashley a generous settlement, which resulted in the the depletion of most of his savings. But the decision had been the right thing to do, and Craig knew it. He actually gave Ashley the money with surprisingly little resentment.

Now, they shared custody of Tyler. The most surprising thing to both of them was how well everything worked. After all these years, their relationship seemed more like old friends. Focusing on Tyler meant that there was mutual agreement on most of the important things.

When Craig finally decided to change jobs, he took a gamble at Ashley's urging. If he ever wanted to make more money and grow professionally, then the switch would have to yield more than his small salary from the district attorney's office. That was when the idea to take a chance with his own firm started to take shape.

Ashley encouraged him. And she had been right.

With his connections to the school, Craig found a continuous stream of college clients with enough local business to steadily round out his practice. While the hours were long and often unpredictable, his own firm became a good living that provided Tyler with all the things that his parents failed to have in their youth.

The door opened and Craig looked up from his computer monitor. He tabled his thoughts as cold wind filled his office.

Peering around his partial wall, a woman stood by the front door and lifted the sunglasses from her eyes. She was forty-something, Craig estimated. With her dark gray cape and black gloves, she had a slightly sophisticated look. The lady did not seem to be a local from town.

Craig stood up and motioned her into his office as he began to move from behind his desk.

"Mr. Cartwright?" she asked in a soft voice.

"Yes, I'm Craig Cartwright," he extended his hand. "You must be Susan Abbot."

"Yes," she took his fingers in her smooth leather gloves.

"Please sit down," Craig motioned to one of the seats in front of his desk. Often he would sit in one of the other chairs if a client looked overwhelmed or distraught. The woman before him looked neither. She was clearly not from the Mount Robert area. Craig made a quick assessment of the situation. Unsure of how the meeting would progress, he returned to sit behind his desk.

"What can I do for you?" Craig asked while settling into his chair.

His eyes took a sweeping view of his office as the question left his mouth. He always tried to imagine what any clients would notice when they came to him for the first time. Usually, his presence, combined with a legal background, could assure most of the local population that he seemed prepared to help them. But this woman was different. Craig felt sure that she lived somewhere else. A lady like this would probably notice that his desk was a cheap purchase from Office Depot, and his wooden credenza on the right wall had seen better days. The only thing of any real quality in the room was the custom-framed law degree behind his desk.

He hoped that she would focus on the diplomas if her gaze began to wander.

"I'm here to see if you can help me with an estate case," she offered.

"Is this a local estate?" Craig had decided that he'd better lead with that question. There was no use in wasting her time, or his, if this matter was not something from a local jurisdiction.

"Yes," she offered. "My aunt died about two years ago, and we're having trouble getting the estate closed."

"What kind of trouble?" Craig asked, beginning to feel his curiosity engaged.

Susan dropped her eyes and her voice. "The executor seems to be, well, stalling with finishing the things that need to happen to settle the estate. It's causing my family great distress."

"All right," said Craig. Now he was getting interested. He pulled a legal pad over in front of him to begin taking notes. "You said it was your aunt—what was her name?"

"Julia Upton."

Craig stopped halfway through writing, and looked up from the page.

"Did you say Upton? Is she related to the late Hal Upton, the archeologist?"

"Yes," answered Susan. "She was his widow. She was my aunt."

Craig put down his pen. He looked with new interest at this woman. Everyone knew the Upton family, or at least knew of them. Hal Upton was undoubtedly the most famous scientist to ever come out of Mount Robert College.

"Why don't you tell me about what is going on," offered Craig. He needed to see if this really was a case that he could take.

"My aunt died in a car wreck about two years ago, twenty months to be exact," Susan began.

Craig nodded. He remembered the news story about the widow of the famous professor.

"She left behind a daughter, my cousin, who wasn't twenty-one at the time. The executor of my aunt's estate isn't moving in any way that we can discern to close anything. It's difficult to get information, or to even see what progress is being made to get things finished."

Craig made a few quick notes about what he was hearing. Something seemed decidedly familiar with this case.

"All right," He said. "And who is the executor?"

"Peter Elliott," answered Susan.

Craig ceased writing and looked up again. "Did you say Peter Elliott?"

"Yes,"

He felt a slight tightening in his stomach. Peter Elliott was the most powerful attorney in the county. The man had ties all over the state. Craig had only a few minor dealings with Peter over the years, but everyone knew his reputation to be top notch.

"And exactly what do you need for the estate to close?" he asked. Maybe there were simple things, and it would be easy to bring everything to closure. Even as the thought flashed through his mind, the idea was almost instantly dismissed. Craig could hardly imagine that Peter Elliott was unable to quickly close a local estate.

"Well, my father, David Upton, needs a detailed evaluation of all assets. My cousin is currently living with my parents. We need to sell my aunt's home, and we have to deal with a fair number of fossils that were in my aunt's possession."

"And Peter Elliott isn't forthcoming with this? With giving you information?" asked Craig.

"No," said Susan with a frown. "I've met with him, but I can't even get a current list of assets or details for what needs to be done to sell the house. He won't discuss any plans to deal with the fossils and artifacts that remain in the estate."

"The house is in the county, correct?"

"Yes, my aunt's house is on Winder's Knob. It's technically part of the college. I believe we need an estate sale and the home needs to go on the market. There are items in the house that may be of scientific importance that require correct placement. My aunt had a life insurance policy that took care of the funeral and other expenses. She also had a few small savings accounts, but my niece has required living expenses. Also, every quarter that the estate has been open since her death has created a fee for Mr. Elliott."

Craig had been writing continuously. He put down his pen to study the woman before him. On the one hand, all the details seemed fairly straight forward. Taking the steps to settle the property and account for the assets would be fairly routine. But on the other hand, these complicated estates could take years. Peter Elliott was a legal force in western North Carolina. If Craig took this case, it would generate a nice fee. However, he could also envision alienating a major colleague in a relatively small legal community.

"Mr. Cartwright," Susan said directly, "I need your help. If not you, then I need someone else. My family needs closure. We can't go on like this. My cousin needs money for her adult life, and my parents don't need this hanging over their heads."

Susan opened the black leather clutch she carried. Inside, she had an envelope. It held $500, all the money that she brought with her from Germantown. She looked at Craig Cartwright and wondered if the deposit would be enough to retain his services. The white business packet settled onto the desk.

"This is five hundred dollars to retain your help. If this isn't a case that you can take, will you please point me to someone that you think can help me?"

Craig looked at the envelope. Before him sat an attractive woman who had just placed a hefty deposit on his desk. Closing one of the few famous cases that ever happened in Mount Robert could be fascinating.

Susan sat before him and brushed the chocolate brown hair back from her shoulders. Her deep blue-green eyes were questioning. She really was very pretty, he thought. He reached for the envelope and smiled. It was cash from a lovely lady.

"Consider yourself one of my clients," he said.

CHAPTER 11

———————

Susan dashed across the street after her meeting with Craig Cartwright. Small erratic snowflakes were swirling in the air as she opened the door of her car. She put her purse in the passenger seat and headed for the one place that she had spent so much of her childhood. All the roads in town seem to converge, in one way or another, to her destination. Her car pulled onto Main Street as the signs were followed to Mount Robert College.

Driving past the stores in the business district, with their glass fronts that beckoned coziness inside, Susan remembered how safe it had all appeared when she was growing up in the town. The whole community seemed the perfect blend of security and beauty. Approaching the stone walls that framed the entrance to the college, she never failed to appreciate how inviting the school really looked. Larger colleges and universities might loom grander in scale, but the curving white stones and hilly vistas of Mount Robert College always cast an inviting pull.

She became keenly aware that if this much beauty and charm could be shown to the majority of her real estate clients when they were searching for a house, most people would be hooked on the property right from the start.

Susan was off to find her father. If she remembered the college schedule that had ruled their lives, the first tests of the semester would be given any day. This fact would ensure that she could find David Upton in the science building. But getting to his classroom and office required taking a few extra minutes. For a small, liberal arts school that felt endless pride in its science program, the esteemed biology department was located at the far back of the campus. Her father always said that the purpose of the design involved pulling people into the most interior parts of the property. Susan held another belief: She had long suspected that the placement of the structure centered on an architectural decision.

From the outside, the science building looked like any other ordinary colonial facade at the college. Rust-colored bricks, native material to the southern Appalachian Mountains, were the foundational medium that enveloped every part of the school. But Susan knew that what made the biology building truly different lay on the inside. Once you entered the heavy doors, the hallways became a tunnel of light. The entire back wall was glass. Sunlight and the western North Carolina mountains could be seen from the ceiling to floor windows of every room.

Susan pulled her car to a stop in front of the guard house that sat perched at the entrance to the academic quad. With its pitched roof and tiny size, she always remembered the small single room as more of a playhouse than a real security center.

"Hi," Susan said as she rolled down her window. She no longer recognized the guard that emerged from the small enclosure to greet her.

"Yes," the young man said. "May I help you?" He was thin, with bony cheeks, and a hawk-like nose that made him look like a scarecrow in his puffy black jacket.

"Yes, I'm here to see my father," said Susan brightly with a smile. "Dr. David Upton. I'm his daughter."

"Just a moment," answered the guard. He disappeared into the glass door. Susan could see a Netflix movie playing inside on man's laptop next to a chair.

"Is he expecting you?" the guard had half his long body craning outside toward Susan.

"No," Susan answered almost apologetically. "I'm trying to surprise him." Now she bit her lip. It never occurred to her that she might not be able to get into the college.

The skeletal man returned to Susan's window.

"I'll need to see your driver's license, as well as your license tag number," he announced with an air of authority. He didn't smile. Susan found herself missing the way the kind, elderly guards once welcomed her when she was a child, in the days before tightened security.

While Susan fumbled in her purse for her driver's license, the guard walked to the back of her car and wrote down her plate number. In her rearview mirror, Susan could see an arctic gust of wind yank the stick straight hair of the security employee up to a vertical position.

"Here you go," smiled Susan as she handed her license over to the young man who was resembling Ichabod Crane more with every minute that she sat in her car. He scribbled the number down and handed back the small card.

"Thank you," Susan said. The guard nodded in response. He disappeared into the warmth of his small house before she could roll up her window and drive forward.

The parking lot in front of the science department looked fairly full. Without a college parking sticker, Susan eased her car around the driveway to the back of the building that ended in a basement level stopping point. The only spot open sat in a delivery zone. Rationalizing with fair certainty that her visit would be quick, she decided to take a chance. They wouldn't tow her car, at least Susan didn't think so. Over the years, she had learned that it was easier to ask for forgiveness than to wait for permission.

Susan remembered that the door at the back of the building rarely got locked. If she had been a current faculty member in this day and time, a lapse of security like that would have bothered her. Today, approaching the entrance, her only hope was for easy access.

Opening the old delivery door, a set of wide concrete steps rose steeply to the next floor. Deciding against the dilapidated elevator to the left, Susan took the familiar staircase to the second floor.

Walking down the long hallway, Susan marveled at the winter light that flooded through each classroom from the back of the building. It was stunning the way the sunlight and clouds played on the barren winter mountains, their sides draped only in shades of dried green and brown.

As she looked ahead, she could see her father's open classroom. The large, tiered lecture hall held a small office behind the long black-topped center table. A veranda, David Upton's unique outdoor learning laboratory, flowed out from his room beyond the glass wall. Coming closer, she noticed the intense quiet on this floor of the building. Bingo. She managed to hit the lunch period before the next class would arrive. If Susan was lucky, she could quickly see her father and get the item that she needed.

The tap of computer keys and the scratch of a chair over the terrazzo floor revealed her father's location. Between almost every class, Dr. David Upton went into his small office. Susan knew that he would be surrounded by a mountain of papers secured by a few bird skeleton parts that managed to act as paperweights.

"There you are," said Susan as she saw her father bent over a stack of what appeared to be lab reports.

She smiled to herself as her eyes noted the stacks of folders and writing material that littered the small room. If she hadn't known better, Susan would have sworn that they were the same papers that that had covered his desk for decades.

Her father looked up from his work. His eyes held a question about her morning progress.

"I met with another attorney this morning," Susan began. Immediately, she saw the look of surprise followed by concern that swept across her father's face. Quickly, Susan found the words tumbling out of her mouth now. "Look, I know this isn't what you really want, but just hear me out on this. I hired him. If you do hear any grumbling from Peter, you can blame me. Just tell him that I was going to have to get back to Memphis, so I hired someone to expedite the whole thing. Although, he really shouldn't have a problem with another attorney, given all the foot dragging he's done."

Susan shifted her weight from one leg to the next. She waited for her father to speak. Either he would be thrilled, angry, or relieved that his daughter had done something. She was trying to prepare herself for any response. A few seconds ticked by and her father said nothing. When he finally spoke, Susan realized that she had been holding her breath.

"Okay. Who is he?" her father asked.

Good, Susan thought. It was straight to the point. She could handle this.

"An attorney; he's local. His name is Craig Cartwright. I read his bio while I was in town. He seems to handle a bit of everything. He seems good." Susan's voice trailed to softness.

Actually, she didn't know if Craig Cartwright was really good at all. The only thing that Susan knew was that their family seemed absolutely stuck. She felt fairly sure that he was the only attorney who was local, decent, and one she could afford.

"I think I've heard the name," offered her father. "What does he charge?" Again, her father was getting straight to the heart of the matter.

"I gave him the retainer," Susan said. Her father started to speak, but she held up her hand. "Let me do this. I have to get home soon. Let's see what he can do for us, and then we'll decide how to do the money."

Susan put a determined smile on her face. Parting with $500 had caused her more than casual angst. Real estate was so slow in the winter, and every month she calculated how much longer her ex-husband would pay for Ryan now that he was in college. Time and money always felt like they were running out in Germantown these days.

"We can always take the legal fees out of the estate once it's settled," Susan offered. Her father nodded.

"Mr. Cartwright would like a copy of Aunt Julia's will to get started. He said he'd know more, and be able to start once he saw the will. He'll look at her assets and begin to see how to finalize things."

Again, her father nodded. Susan had a momentary glimpse that maybe this would all settle quickly and she could head home in a matter of days.

"So, where is the will?" asked Susan.

"Peter has it," said her father without emotion. He looked at her as if she failed to grasp the obvious answer.

Susan began to open her mouth to speak.

"But, of course, I kept a copy," her father added with an air of confidence.

Susan let out a sigh of relief.

"Okay. Where it is? Mr. Cartwright said he'd be in his office today, and he'd start if I brought it by," she asked.

"It's in my fire safe at home," answered her father.

"Well, I'm going to need it," Susan said. "Can you come home and open the fire safe for me?"

"I have a class with a lab due in here in twenty-five minutes," answered her father. "And after class, I have a faculty meeting. I won't leave here today until after five."

Susan started to protest. She could only move things along with Mr. Cartwright if she got the correct documents.

A few students starting to enter the lecture hall outside the office, their voices rising as they talked before the start of class.

Her father opened his lower drawer and pulled out a tiny manila envelope only slightly bigger than a credit card. Onto his desk, he dumped out a quarter-size metal ring with two keys attached.

"Here. Take this," he said as he handed her the keys. "I don't have time to go home right now. Just take these and get Aunt Julia's will out of the fire safe. But you'll still need to make a copy of everything you take so we still have one at the house."

A young graduate student in skinny black jeans and a flowing shirt stuck her head into the office. "Oh, I'm sorry. I didn't realize that you had a meeting, Dr. Upton," she said. "I just need to go over the lab instructions for class today since I'll be running the experiment."

"No meeting," Susan said over her shoulder. "I was just leaving." She turned back to her father. "I'll see you tonight."

Susan had the small keys in her hand as she left his office. With some luck, she could get everything to Craig Cartwright in an hour or two. Maybe the will was the beginning of the solution for her family that would even allow her to make up the deposit money that had been sacrificed. If her parents and Dory got the right help, she might get home and back to work.

Forty minutes later, Susan's father tried to reach his daughter. She never heard the endless ringing. Her phone, left in her purse, was still on silent from her meeting with Mr. Cartwright. The call rolled to her voicemail.

In several hours, Susan would get the message and hear a familiar voice. David Upton would sound urgent, ever so slightly panicked. But by then she would have already stumbled upon it. She would already have found his secret.

CHAPTER 12

Peter Elliott slowed his car onto the exit ramp to head towards downtown Charlotte. He would be having lunch in one of the old steak houses off Tryon Street. Envisioning the dim lights and the hushed clatter of silverware made him feel excited. These places catered to the bankers and movers of the largest city in North Carolina. After waking up that morning, Peter had even gone online to look at the restaurant.

"This is impressive," he said quietly to himself as he sipped coffee and surveyed the menu. Half the entrees failed to list a price. He smiled at the wealth it all implied.

The lunch and the meeting that would follow pleased Peter. If anything, the gathering was long overdue. All of his life, he had been waiting for an opportunity like this to move beyond the world of western North Carolina. So much of Mount Robert seemed monotonous these days. Peter had known for some time that his career needed a new challenge. Without a doubt, he was tired of small courtrooms, fellow attorneys that rarely wore a suit, and meetings that took place in backwoods restaurants. Most of all, he was tired of small-town clients and their local problems. Over the years, he'd had his fill of people parading into his office who needed help because of their drug use, or their insane love of firearms, or some combination of the two.

His life and his work had been dull for years while his boredom only grew. At one point, Peter even contemplated leaving the mountains and coming down to practice in Charlotte. The thought was tantalizing to him, almost like an itch. And he came close to making the move, too, except for the fact that the change would have forced him to start from scratch and build a client base. Or worse yet, work for someone who would always be pushing him for billable hours.

"This is definitely the way to go," he said out loud to himself as he pulled his BMW into the circular driveway of the restaurant. Tall building of architectural accolade dwarfed the single-story chop house. In terms of downtown real estate, Peter knew that nothing exuded wealth like a low building with a wide driveway, when the surrounding property was vertical.

If this meeting went well, he could see himself coming to Charlotte more often. Maybe his sedan would even get serviced in the city at a true dealership instead of by the grease monkey that usually took care of his car in Mount Robert.

Peter pulled to the front of the restaurant and stepped out of his car. Seeing daytime valet parking impressed him.

"Name, sir?" the uniform-clad, twenty-something valet asked.

"Elliott," he answered. A ticket went in his hand. As he placed the paper slip in his breast pocket, he ran his fingers lightly over his gray wool suit and instinctively touched the knot of his red tie. His palms were ever so damp. It was the anticipation of the whole meeting.

As he opened the heavy door to the restaurant, his eyes tried to adjust to the subtle lighting of the reception area. Even in the glaring, bright light of a winter noon, the entire restaurant felt plush with darkened elegance.

"Right this way," said the petite brunette hostess. Peter followed the all-black outfit of the young woman to the back of the restaurant. Walking by the tables, he noticed the mahogany wine closets that lined the walls. Each cubicle held bottles behind metal doors embossed with names of the owner.

"Peter," announced a voice that seemed to boom from the quiet of a corner table.

Two men rose from their seats.

"Stan, it's good to finally meet." Peter stretched out his hand to the tallest of the two. He had recognized the voice from their phone conversations.

"Peter, this is Ross Johnson," said the host, introducing a slightly younger man with thinning hair the color of fireplace ashes. Both men were in dark suits, their open jackets draped casually over the back of their seats like expensive, forgotten garments. "He's one of our partners at Grove."

More handshakes were exchanged, and Peter sank down into an oversized brown leather dining chair.

As if on cue, a small-framed foreign waiter introduced himself while he silently slid leather-bound lunch menus into their hands. Oversized water goblets were filled as only the soft sound of ice cubes hitting the insides of the glasses floated over the table. The server seemed to retreat silently back into the woodwork of the restaurant.

"Peter, we're so glad that you could join us today." Stan fixed his gaze on Peter. His eyes were a dark brown, and in the dim light of the restaurant, they almost appeared black.

"I was delighted that you called," confessed Peter. He had rehearsed sounding sincere and hopefully warm.

"I've wanted to meet you for some time, and your reputation really speaks for itself," said Stan. "I told Ross what I knew about you as a lawyer, and he's most impressed."

Ross nodded, and Peter could feel his muscles begin to relax. Flattery from a corporate attorney like Stan Norman was just the balm he needed.

"You're from the mountains," said Ross, leaning closer to the table. "Tell me about the western part of the state."

Peter felt prepared for this. He had already thought about how to frame his world, to project his own power. He spoke about the beauty and potential of the mountains, as well as the rising growth in the upper corner of the state. Both Ross and Stan seemed to follow his comments with appropriate questions.

The waiter appeared, and the lunch order began.

"I've got this," Stan said to the table. Now he addressed the attendant. "Bring us our usual starter. We'll decide the rest of the meal after the first course."

The server nodded, and wrote quickly on a small pad. He faded back and disappeared noiselessly into the kitchen.

It was Peter's turn to ask the questions, and he began with pleasantries. "Ross, Stan told me on the phone that you're from Raleigh."

"Actually, I live in Durham, but our startup company, Horizons, is technically on the western side of Raleigh."

"And your company does . . ." Peter let his voice trail to a quiet question. He had done his research about Grove Pharmaceuticals. He knew that Stan was the chief counsel attorney for the largest drug manufacturer in North Carolina. But the company known as Horizons remained another story. They were somewhat of a mystery, with little information even circulating on the internet about the organization. Peter had done his own homework to understand both companies, but he failed to learn much about Horizons.

"Our company is a new venture," explained Ross. "We're interested in cutting-edge research. Our expertise is new medication for ongoing, chronic conditions, against all age demographics."

Peter listened closely. Drug research, manufacturing, and patents were all out of his field of expertise. He pondered why Stan Norman had arranged this meeting, and he began to feel an increasingly vague sense of question. Surely, this lunch would have a purpose. Peter took a slow breath. These things took time.

The steward appeared at Stan's elbow with a bottle of wine. Stan nodded with approval at the label, and a bold cabernet was poured into the wine glasses on the table.

Stan seemed to sense the pause in the conversation as the waiter departed. He did not want the meeting to drift, and he leaned into Peter. "Grove Pharmaceuticals," Stan confided in a dropped tone of voice, "is looking to partner with Horizons. Their goal is to bring more therapies to the marketplace. Both companies can benefit from a combined effort to develop new drugs," Stan explained.

Peter nodded, still unsure of his contribution to any of this. He only knew one thing at this point. The information was possibly privileged, and would have to be treated as such.

Stan swirled the wine in his glass until it looked like a racing red river. He took a long sip and continued. "I'm sure that you're wondering what this all has to do with you."

Peter sat motionless. It was best to listen closely now. He could feel that something would happen.

"We've been watching you for some time now, Peter. You're a very impressive man who knows how to get things done. We think you're just the help we need."

Peter could feel the slight swell of his chest. Compliments were always a weakness, but he felt secretly delighted. They wanted him; he was sure of that fact. His breathing slowed down, but not his pulse.

"We understand that you're well connected in the western part of the state, and we're looking for some help with both real estate and personnel."

Peter looked confused, but before he could ask anything, Stan continued. "Do you know what Death Valley is in the drug industry, Peter?"

Peter knitted his brow together in thought and prepared to ask a question.

Stan merely noted his expression and continued in his hushed tone. "Well, it's where companies like Grove and Horizons find themselves with new therapies and drugs before the FDA approves them. We have to spend millions of dollars—and I do mean *millions*, if not billions—to get new life savings measures out to the people who need them the most. Companies like ours have to be efficient. And we often need an edge, especially given our investment. So this is where we need help."

Peter had been listening closely, trying to figure out where this was leading.

Stan continued. "You see, Peter, we need a place, a fairly quiet place to do some drug testing. We also need some help as we identify subjects for those tests."

A hush fell over the table as the two men stared at Peter. Stan and Ross seemed to pierce him with their gaze. This was new territory for Peter, but it also sounded strangely familiar.

Didn't Peter know every back country road and building between Asheville and the Tennessee line? Didn't he also know a few hundred country bumpkins that would take any drug you gave them, especially if you paid them? A smile began to spread across his face.

With his mind working in overdrive, Peter could envision the partnership. It all seemed very doable. After all, his connections stretched from Mount Robert to the entire state. This was the type of opportunity that could definitely lead to more corporate work. Instinctively, the calculation of fees from Grove and Horizons began to fill his brain. His head started to nod.

Stan had watched Peter carefully. "Of course, Grove will pay you well for your services, and of course, we'll require your utmost discretion." He slid a small piece of paper toward his guest.

Peter opened the folded slip and saw a six-figure number. He felt his jaw go slack.

"This is just to get everything started. There's more where this came from."

Peter swallowed, unable to find any words. He had never been speechless before a client, but then he had never been presented with this type of offer. Peter reached for his wine and took a slow sip, careful not to choke. "I think we can find something to your liking in the mountains and I think that you'll find people more than willing to work for you." Peter hoped that he had said all this without his voice wavering.

"Wonderful," beamed Stan as he nodded at Ross. "Oh look, here's our first course. We can celebrate together."

Three waiters appeared as if on cue. They refilled the wine glasses and put the dishes on the table simultaneously. Peter looked down. The raw egg glistened on top of the mounded marinated meat.

"For you, sirs. Enjoy," said the server. "Steak tartare."

CHAPTER 13

Peter's black BMW headed west in the fading afternoon sunlight. Lunch had proved to be more interesting than he ever imagined.

For almost three hours, Stan Norman and Ross Johnson sat and lingered at the table with Peter in the quiet elegance of the restaurant. During that time, they spoke about everything that ambitious men often discussed in protracted meetings. They were all interested in amassing money, conservative politics, and the power that the collision of those two forces could derive.

Peter's mind was already in overdrive. He felt the tingle of adrenaline running through his brain during the entire lunch meeting. Without a doubt, the Elliott Law Firm could be a valuable key partner to Horizons. The pieces of the deal would all fit into place. For the first time, Peter imagined a future bigger than he had ever known up to this point.

The Carolina winter light gave everything a dull, washed-out look in the northwest piedmont. As his sedan sped along the bleached winter landscape, the afternoon sun glowed like a blood-red orange for its final encore of the day.

He would be in the mountains by dark. Driving needed to be a concentrated effort at that point. The roads were never without the possibility of some small bit of ice left over from a shade tree that hovered above the country lanes.

Peter glanced down at his phone as it sat charging on his car's dark leather console. Messages needed to be retrieved while a response could be made, in case cell service was lost. He picked up the device as the traffic thinned and the landscape faded to rural pastureland. He decided to listen to voicemail on the speaker of his Bluetooth.

The silence in the car was suddenly broken by the words that belonged to a client who lived in Asheville. Peter remembered him as a businessman, forty-something, who had needed help with various small legal matters. The man's raspy breathing, followed by a string of four-letter words muttered in exaggeration, became apparent.

"This is about my son, Shawn."

Peter could detect the weariness and flattened anger in the man's voice.

"He's twenty-one, and he's been arrested. The police found meth. The charge is manufacturing with the intent to sell. I need you to call me at this number as soon as you can."

Peter sighed. This would require his attention tonight. He needed to call the father, and possibly stop in Asheville on his way into Mount Robert.

"What a dumb shit," Peter said out loud, as he thought about his new young client.

It was fortunate for the young man that the father had plenty of money. That would change everything for the son. Of course, Peter knew how to make sure that the results of the arrest were as light as possible, but he found himself shaking his head. Throughout his career, he had seen a legion of cases like this one. The young man would claim to learn his lesson, to clean up his act, only to most certainly be his client again before the year was complete.

The second message filled his car as he rounded a long curve. Peter caught his breath, and his mind began to instantly turn. Behind the wheel, the road before him became a rote path.

Craig Cartwright's voice came across Peter's car speaker. With greetings and pleasantries, he indicated that he had a new client who might benefit from the collaborative help of several attorneys, and he was seeking a meeting.

"I need to speak to you about a real estate holding. There's a property matter that I think may benefit both of us in terms of a meeting. Please call me at your earliest convenience. I look forward to hearing from you."

Craig Cartwright. Peter could feel himself sneer. If a lawyer ever existed who took every case in the county and beyond, it was Craig. Peter had always considered him somewhat of a bottom feeder when it came to clients. The business would probably involve some desperate person who'd retained Craig, and yet had some connection to one of Peter's more well-healed patrons.

Watching the road, he replayed all the conversations of the day. Producing everything that Grove and Horizons required would be a feat. And yet, if done properly, the payout promised to be be huge. So many details needed to be arranged. He knew that he could handle the job. It was just a matter of putting the connections together. Ideas, like puzzle pieces, were starting to fit together in his mind.

He squinted his eyes in thought as he drove. His lunch meeting offered the best opportunities for his future if only he could grab everything that was necessary and put all of it into place within a speeding window of time. Horizons needed real estate and people; he had learned that much in Charlotte. Now, he would have to be the master of both elements.

Peter glanced down at his cell phone. His mind raced through possible connections. Whoever Craig Cartwright was representing would be between a rock and a hard place. Whatever the details, this might be the perfect union of need and opportunity. His mouth started to water ever so slightly.

Quickly the cell phone went to his ear to call Craig Cartwright as the afternoon light folded onto the distant mountains. He was suddenly eager to arrange a meeting.

CHAPTER 14

S usan pulled into the driveway of her parents' home and noticed the quiet emptiness of the space before her. The economy box on wheels that defined the Puritan ideals of her family was absent from the small single carport. Her mother had left the house.

Before cancer, Sylvia Upton was a fast-moving bundle of energetic ideas and resolve. As an assistant professor of history at Mount Robert College, she maintained an armory of clear facts on most periods of American history. Rarely were her opinions passive on any subject. With her small frame and bright eyes, her mother always reminded Susan more of the quick, darting birds that her father loved to study instead of a degreed historian. Hardly ever bothering to wear makeup, Sylvia Upton instead preferred the natural exterior of the Woodstock generation that she embodied. Only after the disease had begun its relentless assault, did Susan realize how vulnerable and frail her mother had become. In her unadorned face these days, a roadmap of pain often seemed imprinted.

It was Wednesday. Her mother now got her hair done every week on the same day. Her short bob didn't really get "done", not in the old-fashioned sense of curlers and a dryer. Rather, she just had a nice wash and style. The medical port that still inhabited her right side made things tricky. A standing beauty appointment meant that her mother didn't have to do more then gently brush her now close-cropped silver hair for a week.

Susan let herself into the practically silent house. Only Toby heard the key in the lock, and lumbered from the den into the kitchen. Anyone coming into the back door might provide an opportunity for petting or a treat.

Aware that Dory might be asleep, Susan entered the house as quietly as possible. With a hushed pat to Toby's shaggy fur, she hung her purse on one of the hooks by the back door. With as little noise as possible, her feet tiptoed down the hallway.

Surely, she was alone. After all, the driveway had been vacant. But there always remained the outside chance that Dory would be in her room. These days, her cousin either worked odd hours, or slept late after being out all night. Her boyfriend, Dan, sometimes dropped Dory off at home in the morning, her car left in some unknown locale.

As Susan approached the guestroom, she saw a bedside lamp glowing softly. Pushing the door completely open, she shook her head. It was a dim mess as usual. But unless Dory had decided to hibernate under the ten pounds of clothes strewn on her bed, Susan felt fairly certain that her cousin was gone. More than likely, she'd left hours ago for the animal shelter.

"Well, you're either at work, or sleeping with your boyfriend, or out doing God knows what," Susan said out loud.

The sound of her own words surprised her. She had that of-course-you-are tone of voice, like an old, stern school teacher. Susan cringed at herself. Only Toby, who followed at her heels, heard the verbal complaint. He gazed up at her lovingly and wagged his tail, as if in agreement.

"Come on, guy," Susan softened her tone as she looked down at the dog. "We have work to do."

Heading into her parents' room, Toby trotted close behind her. As she turned on the overhead light, the dog headed for a familiar spot on the carpet near the end of the bed. He frequently slept with her parents. Making only two circles with his body, he flopped to the floor and shut his eyes.

To the right of the room, Susan moved into the small alcove that housed her father's home office. The area was really more of an extended bay window bumped out of the square bedroom that her parents shared. Her father had always been quick to claim the few feet of space he called his "study," as if staking the claim to the yardage somehow enhanced his head-of-household status.

The blinds were partially drawn around the roll-top desk that rested against the window. In the weak winter sunlight, Susan could see the dust that floated casually in the air. The entire small area gave Susan a memory of earlier times. Everything about her father's desk felt familiar. When she was young, she hid underneath it almost weekly. The small space beneath the writing surface had been the perfect refuge for a lonely girl and her private thoughts.

Pulling the keys out her pocket, Susan wondered where to begin. She opened a few desk drawers. At first, the usual culprits of old check registers, pens, and various file folders seemed to be the only residents of the desk. But in the back of one drawer, Susan spotted something hard and luminous. Reaching into the most hidden spot, she touched the smooth glass front of a bottle. She knew immediately what it was.

"Of course," she said quietly as she pulled out the half-empty fifth of scotch.

It was her father's secret stash. Susan had known for years that spirits were hidden all over the house. Scotch remained her father's private little affair. She knew that he drank quietly when he could, away from the eyes of Susan's mother, who hated all alcohol after growing up in a family steeped in booze. The underhanded way that her father drank always made hard liquor look risky and sordid to Susan. It also made drinking irresistible.

She licked her lips. The thought of the amber liquid passing warm down her throat gave her a swooning sense of temptation. Hesitating, she held the bottle up and reviewed her options. It had been quite a week. But she lowered her hand, and despite her sudden longing, put the scotch back in the original resting spot. If all went well with getting the paperwork to Craig Cartwright, Susan could visit the hidden treasure later that evening. She made a mental note of the exact location.

Susan now stepped back and put her hands on her hips. The desk was proving to be relatively empty, except for the scotch. Where was the will? She spied a large wooden chest resting on the floor. The lock on the front looked ancient. Susan wondered if the fire safe, by chance, rested inside the oak box. With the two keys in her hand, Susan would have to play a game of elimination. One key might open the chest, and the other might open the safe. She picked a key. The latch of the box clicked with the first turn.

As Susan lifted the heavy lid, she could see something dark inside. Immediately, she knew that the item was the object of her search. Filling almost the entire area, a black case looked wedged tightly against the wooden sides of the chest. Her fingers barely had room to move down the walls of the square. She tried to pull, but the safe was incredibly heavy. With one hand working its way under the dense, smooth side, her other fingers were grabbing at the handle. Susan heaved upward.

"Well," she grunted aloud. "If a fire comes, I guess this is the heavy protection that you need."

With a grunt, she hoisted the safe up to waist level on the desk. A thudding sound echoed in the bedroom.

"Let's see what's here," Susan whispered.

She inserted the remaining round key into the safe's lock, and turned. Nothing. The key made a few twisted movements as she went back and forth trying to open the latch. The mechanism held, like some sort of a clenched fist. It wasn't until she realized she needed to push down on the safe's upper side, that she heard a pop. The security lid gave way and opened under her hands.

As she raised the lid, a shifting stack of documents came into view. On top of everything, small blue books created a top layer. They were passports. Most of them appeared ancient and worn. Susan guessed that some of them dated back more than a few decades.

Out of curiosity, she began to flip open the old documents. Staring back at her were the early travel photos of her parents. The free-flowing hair styles of the 1970s framed their smooth faces. On the bottom of the pile, sat the oldest books, containing pictures of David and Sylvia Upton when they'd still been doing graduate work. They had traveled the world to study birds, or history, or both, at any given time. Susan shook her head and smiled. Their photos looked more like the soft images of two teenagers setting out for far-flung places than the pictures of a pair of serious academics. As she looked at the dates on the oldest passports, Susan realized that her parents must have been twenty-something in their earliest travels. She marveled at their youth. How was it, she wondered, that young people feel older and more fully prepared to live than they really appear to the world?

Underneath the passports, Susan found two large envelopes, one white, and the other that had softened to beige through the passing of time.

"Got it," she said delightedly to herself. Toby heard her voice and merely stirred in his sleep behind her.

Susan dug out the thick packets and spread them on the desk. Surely, one of them would be her Aunt Julia's will. She began by opening the first envelope, the one with the freshest-looking paper.

From under the flap, a clearly legal document meant her gaze. Reading the wording, Susan knew that she held the deed to her aunt's home. As something that Craig Cartwright would need, she set it aside on the floor.

The next envelope contained the characteristic blue backing of legal pages. With her eyes scanning the paper, she realized that this was, in fact, exactly what she had wanted to find. Two wills, one for her aunt, and another for her father, had been stuffed together into one folder.

Susan pulled the worn wooden chair on rollers up to the desk. She would need to sit down to look at both wills. Realizing that she had never seen these documents, she wanted to read through everything.

She started with her father's will. It was surprisingly thick. Susan had always assumed that all property would automatically pass to her mother, and then to her. Making a quick mental note, she needed to remember where she'd found all the papers. The day was coming with her parents when Susan would need to put her hands on all their legal information.

As she unfolded the long sheets, she knew the details should be fairly clear. In the afternoon hush of a still house, Susan turned on the green hooded desk lamp and started to read.

The shrill ring of the house telephone made her jump. She looked up from the desk and turned her head to see the blinking light on her mother's nightstand. Should she answer? She really didn't want to talk to anyone, and her cell phone was in the kitchen. If she got the records in hand, then she might be able to get them to Craig Cartwright this afternoon. Let them leave a message, she decided.

Susan looked back at the papers in her hand. She turned the page and followed the names typed into the blank spaces. First, her mother's name, and then she read the rest of it.

"And to my two daughters, Susan Ann Upton Abbot and Dory Lynn Upton, I leave . . ."

Susan stared. Two daughters. No, one daughter and a cousin. How was this wrong? How had this been written so wrong?

The answering machine clicked to project a familiar voice that was leaving a message. The tone was clipped and anxious.

"Susan, this is Dad. I know that you're going into the fire safe today, but we need to talk first. There's something that I need to tell you."

CHAPTER 15

Peter Elliott tackled the long, winding two-lane road that framed the Mount Robert community. His headlights now stabbed the darkness like a pair of illuminated fangs. Ringing from his cell phone filled his car.

He picked up to answer and a slow smile crossed his lips.

"Craig, how are you? Thanks for returning my call. I'm sorry that we have been playing phone tag."

"I'm fine, Peter," answered Craig carefully. He was surprised to hear from the all-powerful Peter Elliott so quickly after he'd left a message.

"Craig, you originally called about a client who has some needs. I'm not sure how I can be of service, but we should most likely meet and discuss the matter."

"That would work well for me. Do you want to come to my office at ten tomorrow morning?" Craig held his breath for a response. It would be so much easier if Peter Elliott came on his turf, in his office.

"That's fine." Peter's voice had a smooth flow like honey being poured from a bottle.

"Then I'll see you at ten and we can discuss the matter in my office," Craig confirmed.

"That's fine. I'll see you then," Peter responded, hitting the button to end the call.

Craig stared at the phone in his hand as the voice went silent. Sitting on his leather couch, the only decent piece of furniture that he owned, he looked around his small three-bedroom house. Maybe working with Peter Elliott would not be so hard after all. If Craig could just help the Upton family settle their estate, then a nice little bit of change might possibly come his way. One thing could lead to another for his business.

After a lifetime of taking every scrap of work available in order to build a client base, Craig wanted to finally start attracting larger cases. Maybe it wouldn't be so hard to make this work for everyone, he thought.

In the dark, Peter tossed the now silent phone onto the passenger seat. Craig Cartwright had a needy client. This was the perfect beginning for putting the parts together for Horizons Pharmaceuticals. Now all Peter needed was some real estate, preferably large. He smiled again. Everything would all come together.

CHAPTER 16

David Upton balled his fists around his office telephone and wondered if he should say more into the answering machine. There was no way that his wife needed to hear the message, not a single word or the frantic tone. His stomach dropped when a voice came on the line.

"Dad," It was Susan. "I...found...something..."

By her strained tone, David knew immediately what she had found. How could he have forgotten that the documents were all together? Air caught in his throat. Swallowing became impossible. Guilt. He felt nothing but the rushing waves of shame. Clenching the end of the phone with one palm, he worked the fingers of his other hand around the desk edge in order to stop shaking.

The one emotion that haunted him over the years was washing over the moment like an ocean wave. For decades, the secret had taken up an uneasy residence in the corners of his life, eating away at him in private. He tried to master the art of ignoring the pain, of keeping it at bay, for the most part. But now the feelings were threatening to envelope him.

Now he was talking to his daughter.

"Susan," he muttered. He would have to face her. His mouth felt like a dry oven.

She said nothing.

"Susan," he said again.

Both eyes shut when her name slipped out a second time. So many thoughts fired through his mind all at once. In an instant, almost without effort, he began to calculate a plan.

"Dad?" she repeated.

"Susan, listen to me. You need to listen. I need to talk to you. It needs to be alone. Is your mother home?" There was anxiety in his voice.

"No." Susan spoke as if she couldn't think clearly.

"All right. You need to meet me. Come out to the Quarry Road, the one that we used to take to go fishing in Miller Pond."

"Dad, what are you talking about? It is almost dark soon."

"Meet me there in twenty minutes. Don't tell anyone where you're going," her father spoke quickly in a low tone.

"I don't understand," Susan began.

"Just drive to the Quarry Road. I'll be there. I'll explain everything."

David hung up the phone. From his small office, he could look out to his lecture hall and see the room growing dim, as the bleak sunlight from the windows started to fade on the mountains.

At the end of the almost deserted hallway, he heard the distant voices of students floating towards him from another part of the building. A faculty meeting was scheduled to begin in a few minutes. He would just have to miss it. This was an emergency.

Grabbing his keys, he moved towards the door. The sound of quick, determined strides echoed through his classroom.

All the secrets, buried for so long, were finally all around him. As a family, they had been on a trajectory of lies for years. But he needed to handle this, once and for all, before everything got any worse. This time, he knew how to finish it.

CHAPTER 17

Susan pulled onto the Quarry Road and felt the gravel crunch under the tires of her crossover. The sky was darkening, a casualty of the short winter afternoon.

She came to a stop. Other than the low hum of her car's engine, silence filled the air.

A rap on her window made Susan jump. She had expected to see her father's car, but instead he stood beside her. Where did he come from? She rolled down her window.

"Are you alone?" he asked.

"Yes," she answered.

"Well, come sit in my truck. We need to talk."

Susan turned off the ignition, grabbed her purse, and opened the door. Light spilled from the inside of her car onto the dusty rocks at her feet. She had not been out to Miller Pond in a decade or two, not since her youth when she used to fish with her parents in the reservoir at the end of the road. Her eyes tried to adjust to the twilight all around her. She followed her father. Her wedge heels made walking feel unsteady as she stumbled after him.

The doors of David Upton's old red pickup truck opened as they both pulled the handles. A dim light shone from the roof, revealing the worn black interior.

For as long as Susan could remember, the truck was the family work vehicle. While never fancy, the ancient cab and flatbed had carried her father for decades into the woods to hunt for his bird specimens. The smell of damp earth permeated the front of the truck. A single eagle feather hung from the rear view mirror.

"Susan," her father began. He sounded tired, and stopped.

"What's going on?" Susan asked pointedly. "Why is your will written with Dory listed as your daughter? Was this something that came about after Aunt Julia's death? I don't understand."

The interior lights of the truck were now off and they sat in darkness. The sky was moonless and cloudy. Her father swallowed. His eyes looked out through the cab window.

"I should have told you sooner," his voice began.

He sounded spent, Susan thought as the words fell from his mouth. She had so many questions, but she said nothing.

"I should have told others, maybe everyone, sooner. It was a choice made years ago, one that I agreed to. I kept quiet. At the time, I thought it was the best idea. Honesty would have hurt so many people."

Susan stared past the dark outline of her father. She had never seen him so distressed and yet also calm. It a strange way, she could feel the pieces of their family beginning to fall together

"What about Dory?" Susan asked.

"Dory," said her father. "Dory was a surprise, at least to me."

Susan shot her father a narrow sideways glace. There was a sound in his voice, almost like a cliché. This was never going to work unless she got a real, honest answer from him.

"What are you talking about?" she asked.

"Uncle Hal was on his final dig in Zaire back in the early 1990s," her father told her. "When he left, he and Julia were having problems. It was nothing too serious; I mean I feel sure they could have worked things out between them. At the time, I think they both wanted different things. Hal wanted more time to travel and lead expeditions, maybe even leave Mount Robert. He wanted a larger school, a true university, for his research. Julia was ten years younger than Hal. She wanted children. She was hoping that he would take his career in a different direction, one that included a family."

"How did you know all this?" asked Susan. She had never heard this family history.

"We were brothers," her father answered quietly as he stared out the darkened windshield. "I knew all about this because Hal asked me to keep an eye on Julia while he was gone."

Susan could feel her neck stiffen as her chest rose in anger. A slew of accusations and sarcastic comments formed in her mind. She opened her mouth and then closed it. She was willing herself to listen; she needed to hear everything. If this was going to be some sort of confessional, a place to lay out your sins, then she wanted to hear the truth directly from the source.

"On the night we got word about the accident involving Hal, Julia was the first one to get a call. She phoned me and I went over to be with her. Your mother taught a section of history in the evenings. I went to Julia's house, and your mother finished her class and then went home to see if they would possibly call us with any news."

Susan was listening carefully, trying to remember the awful day that she'd lost her uncle. How old had she been? It all happened when she was in college, her sophomore or junior year.

"Late at night, we got the call from Zaire. Hal passed away before they could get him to a hospital, not that he would have had a good chance in any African clinic." Her father sounded as if he was back in time. His voice faded with the memories that were before him.

"Julia and I wept together. We had both lost so much. Julia suddenly lost a husband she needed, and my only brother was gone." Her father stopped at this point.

"And then? What happened then?" Susan asked. She felt calm now, but she needed to hear everything to understand it all.

"I held Julia. She had been waiting all night; against hope, really. We were both suddenly so lost, so empty, so alone." Her father's voice was softer now. He turned to look at Susan. "Julia and I never meant for anything to happen that night. It just did. We both lost a part of ourselves when Hal died."

Susan let out the air out of her lungs that she had been holding. "And Dory?"

Her father looked down at his hands as they gripped the steering wheel.

"Julia found out that she was pregnant a short time after the funeral. At first she wasn't sure, but I think that we both suspected the truth. Hal was gone, and I had your mother and you. It was just better that way."

"Better for who?" Susan demanded. "For you? For Julia? For Mom?" Susan was bitter now, angry. "Didn't you think the truth would eventually come to light? Good God, what were you thinking?"

David Upton was quiet for a moment. "Julia wanted everything the way it was. Hal was gone, and Dory needed to love the father that she never knew. I wanted to tell her the truth as she got older, but by then it was too late. Both families were settled in the lives we had."

"Does Mom know?" Susan asked, her tone sounded flat, almost without emotion.

"No," he admitted. "I thought about telling her a few years ago, especially after I added Dory to my will, but your mother had been diagnosed with cancer by that point. I left it alone." He ran his hand through his thinning gray hair. His voice cracked. "I left it alone for everyone. That is the truth."

For the first time, Susan sat in stunned silence. None of this seemed right, but somehow it all made sense. It was a truth that made the parts of their family fit together, completely, for the first time.

Suddenly, Susan thought about the locket in Dory's room. The same gift that she'd once received had also been given to another daughter.

They sat quietly in the dark until Susan spoke. "So, what happens now?"

"That's where I need your help," her father answered. "I have a secret. And now you do, too."

Susan shifted in the old, frayed seat of the pickup truck. Why did it almost sound like there was relief in his voice? This was nothing that she wanted.

He turned his head slowly toward Susan. His gaze was penetrating, even in the dark. "I have a plan, and now you're going to help me."

CHAPTER 18

Peter opened his eyes before his alarm started to beep. He stretched his tall frame under the smooth sheets of his king-sized bed and turned to face the oversized windows of his bedroom. His sleep had been amazing. Despite all the details of the day, he felt ready to take on the world.

The early gray light caught his eye. A cloudy winter sky predicted a cold morning. The taupe silk comforter rested lightly across his legs, creating incredibly warmth. He typically hated to get out of bed and stand on the chilly hardwood floors, but not today. With a full schedule of important activities, his mind felt ready. He decided that he would forgo making his own coffee. That was one thing that could be picked up on his way into the office.

Strolling into his tile bathroom, he turned on his shower heads. There were three of them. Together they rained steaming water against the the oversized marble walls.

The master suite remained one of the best parts of Peter's home. When he first saw the house with his real estate agent, it had been one of the key selling features. He knew his residence was unlike any other in the

Mount Robert area. On his first visit to the sleek modern dwelling on the edge of town, the property seduced him. Built by a doctor and his artist wife, they'd left North Carolina only a year after it was completed. Peter desperately wanted to have the house, but he had only feigned interested in the premises at the time.

"Wow, this is really modern!"

That was the typical comment people said whenever they stepped inside his home. The expression of amazement always made Peter smirk.

For the vast majority of the local population, the house was deemed too contemporary. Peter knew that, and found it delightful. Sleek urban styling created exactly the statement that he liked best. The beauty derived from the unadorned, angled lines left exposed like the bones in a model's face. In the kitchen, the room he most enjoyed flaunting, the stainless-steel cabinets shone like glass. Peter's taste kept the furnishings scaled to perfection. The monotone palette was the ideal neutral backdrop for his streamlined interior.

But Peter adored the other important aspect of his property. Solitude enveloped his residence. Tucked among hills at the end of a rarely used country road, he reveled in his ultimate goal: tranquility.

"Privacy is for rich people," Peter could still hear his mother say those words from his childhood. And privacy was the one thing that he most craved.

Years ago, when Peter came to Mount Robert to clerk for an elderly lawyer, he made a critical decision. Leaving the tiny hamlet of his youth forever, he chose never to return. At the time, the option had been a gamble. But his determination was like an itch under his skin that propelled him forward. He felt destined to have the things he always wanted, away from his hillbilly family.

After his law partner died, leaving him with a lucrative practice, Peter bought the house. Having spent his youth in a shotgun cabin with four siblings, he'd always wanted real estate. Peter swore that if he ever got out of the drafty, crowded shack, with its sagging floors, he would live in a place that reflected more than the generational poverty of Appalachia.

These days, if he brought a woman to his residence, it was only after a few dates with her in the hotel on the edge of town. The ground rules had to be strictly understood. This was his home, after all. He refused for his house to resemble some sort of fancy dessert in an overpriced restaurant, one that could be shared by two people and enjoyed. Peter always slept alone at night.

Adjusting the sleeve of his custom suit, he smiled at his reflection in the large mirror of the living room. With his keys picked up from the wine bar, Peter moved towards the door. His cell phone rang as he walked into the two-story foyer.

"Elliott," he said smoothly into the phone.

"Yes, I'm prepared," Peter answered in a confident voice as he heard the caller continue to speak.

His walking slowed down to a standstill by his front door as he received a quick outline of meetings for the day. The words were like listening to a verbal tsunami.

"Of course," Peter added as he smiled. "Consider it all taken care of today."

The rapid-fire voice on the other end of the line eased to a normal speed. Within a minute, the call had ended. Peter readjusted his jacket and smoothed his crisp, white shirt with his free hand. Placing the cell phone in a front pocket, he walked out the double steel doors and climbed into his sedan. The motor purred as he turned the car toward town.

He had several clients to see and phone calls to return. Now there were added appointments that would have to occur. There was nothing like being gone for the better part of the previous day to force his morning into a compact schedule.

His thoughts turned to Craig Cartwright and their meeting. Everything that Peter would do today was essential. Actions would have to be step by step, going forward. What better way to begin with Grove Pharmaceuticals than by putting needy people in a position to help themselves? Of course, Peter knew that this reeked of a serving advantage. That really was the beauty of the whole thing.

As he pulled onto the main road, he began to smile. The weak winter sun broke through the clouds over the mountains. It was going to be a great day.

CHAPTER 19

Susan rolled over and stared at the dull chrome light seeping beneath the lace curtains of her old bedroom. After returning from the Quarry Road, she'd complained of a headache in order to avoid her mother. The story was not a total fabrication. Dealing with her father clearly left her with the beginnings of a migraine. But the decision to stretch the truth meant that she was in her old room for hours. It had been an incredibly long night.

Every time she shut her eyes, Susan was back in her father's old truck. In fitful sleep, she could see the silhouette of his face against the darkened windows, his large weathered hands opening and closing around the worn steering wheel. In her dreams, his mouth was always moving, omissions of his life in a continuous flow. As she tossed and turned chasing sleep, Susan could only picture herself immobile in the passenger seat, her mouth agape like some sort of horrified Kewpie doll.

Awake, she threw back the antique quilt on the bed. She just wanted to let herself scream. It would feel so good to roll her head back and release every bit of frustration. The problem was that if she began ranting, then tears would soon follow.

For the tenth time that night, she reached over and grabbed the cell phone on the bedside table. Illuminating the screen gave her a sense of normalcy. She desperately wanted to make a call.

"Hi, Ryan," she could almost hear herself saying. She knew that her voice would be shaky as she spoke to her son. "I'm okay. I just needed to call. I'm still at Mom and Dad's house, helping them deal with everything." Susan wanted so badly to say those words to her son.

Ryan would inevitably ask, "Mom, are you okay?" Then he would hear her strained tone and with his voice still thick from sleep, he would want to know what was really happening. "Mom, are you drunk?" That would be the typical thing for him to ask, of course.

Susan knew she would laugh nervously. Then, she could start, the ugly truth erupting like some sort of spewing bombshell. "Of course, I'm not drunk, honey. It's just that I spent last evening learning that your cousin is really your aunt, or half-aunt, because my father couldn't keep his pants zipped. But other than that, I'm fine."

Susan stared at her phone again. Maybe she was grateful that the clock read only half past five. With Ryan on central time, it would only be four thirty in Mississippi. She knew that she couldn't make the call to her son.

Loving Ryan, her only child, meant more to her than the desire to unburden herself. Just last month, Susan had cringed at the conversation they shared at home in Germantown. Ryan spent the day with her looking at his tuition, scholarships, and expenses for the semester. She agreed to put money in his checking account every month, never letting him know how tight her own situation was during the slow months in real estate. She would do anything for him.

In her childhood bedroom, Susan stared at the soft rosebud wallpaper that appeared with the first light of day. She was far too old, too ancient and exhausted, to deal with the problems of her family. The events from the previous day had left her drained. She felt like Alice in Wonderland, falling down a dark hole, waiting to hit the bottom. As the white painted iron bed creaked beneath her, Susan tried to reposition herself by jabbing her pillow in search of a cool spot.

That was when it hit her. Everything about her parents and Dory involved some sort of crisis. Secrets and lies were all tangled around everyone. As she stared at the window and heard the furnace of the old house click on to erase the morning chill, Susan realized the problem. Drama seemed to continuously follow each member of the Upton family. Every one of them was such a mess. How did she manage to find herself here? She only returned home to help her parents. Was it really like some folks said: no good deed goes unpunished?

Susan rubbed her eyes and then her neck. The decision to come back to Mount Robert started out to be so relatively simple. She merely came home to assist her parents with a fairly straightforward piece of family business. People settled estates, even complicated ones, every day of the week. But now it was so much more.

As she stared at her phone again, she realized that she would forever carry a secret. If the truth emerged, the facts would hurt her mother, maybe killing her faster than the cancer. And if Dory were to find out about her paternity, her whole world would be destroyed yet again.

With a slight groan, Susan sat up and dangled her legs over the edge of her former adolescent bed. She'd hardly slept all night. Every time she managed to close her eyes, she heard her father's voice: "It was better for everyone. Julia wanted it this way."

During the last hours of the night, Susan tried to review her options. She was incredibly angry, but she also needed to decide if she would hide the secret.

"Take my will back to Memphis. Keep it in your safe deposit box. I don't want it in my study anymore," her father implored her in the truck.

"And what if something happens to you?" Susan asked, dumbfounded that her own parent couldn't see the potential pain for everyone with his plan. "What do I do then? How am I going to explain all this?" She heard her voice rising, the words spitting from her mouth.

"I'm sorry," he said, on the edge of weeping. "I trust you. You would know the right things to say."

His solution meant that Susan would need to hide his documents. She was furious that he thought it could be so simple.

"After all, only two people know the truth," he said. "It needs to stay that way."

But now she found herself wondering *How long do things ever really stay hidden?*

Susan stood up and felt the exhaustion settling in her head and shoulders. In addition to all the family revelations, she found that her thoughts had turned to Craig Cartwright during the night. He was the first helpful, interesting person she had met in months. Without meaning to, she looked forward to meeting with him again. She chewed her lower lip. Surely, Mr. Cartwright wouldn't figure out the truth about Dory. And what if he did? That piece of information couldn't possibly influence the outcome of Aunt Julia's estate, could it? Wasn't he bound by some sort of attorney-client privilege? Susan shook her head, trying to relieve the dull pain that was starting to pound in her temples. She just didn't know if her mind could handle all of this.

Without making any noise, she moved to the closet and opened the door. Her hand pulled on the top of her suitcase. Before she fully formulated any thoughts, her clothes were silently nestled in layers of color in the open bag.

She quietly tiptoed out of her bedroom. With the house completely dark and every door closed, Susan gambled that Toby was asleep with either her parents or Dory. The last thing she needed was any barking.

She looked towards her parents' room. She imagined her father, his mouth dry from the scotch that he'd most likely consumed late last night. He would be positioned in bed next to her mother, his wife for the last forty-odd years. Susan realized that he had never even tried to share his dark secret with her. His sin against the very woman he called his own had rested between them for decades.

In near silence, she padded down the hall and into the bathroom. If she was quick enough, she could leave before her father's fleece slippers hit the old wooden floorboards. The need to get out of the house motivated her rushed activity. There was no way that Susan wanted to see him this morning. She was still incredibly angry. His choices threatened so many people.

She was more concerned with seeing her mother. Facing her felt unbearable. This past week had been her mother's brief respite, her break between chemotherapy treatments. The thought of seeing Sylvia Upton wrapping her robe snug against her gaunt, sleepy frame as she insisted on making a family breakfast, would be more than Susan could bear.

Back in her childhood bedroom, she made a thorough sweep of all her things. The suitcase clicked shut under her hand with a soft sound. Susan quietly hoisted the bag up, careful not to roll the toy-sized wheels over the floor. With her purse on her shoulder, she stopped and listened. Everything was quiet. She headed out the door and down the hall to the back of the house.

When Susan reached the kitchen, she placed her luggage on the floor as silently as she could. On the counter by the kitchen wall phone, sat a note pad and can of pens. Such old-fashioned staples had been there as long as she could remember. Rarely, did Susan even show a home these days with a land line, let alone a wall-mounted telephone. But now she was grateful for the old familiar items. She crossed the room and reached for the paper. She wrote a note and hoped that it would be good enough.

As she put her vaguely written goodbye in the center of the worn kitchen table, she took a long look around the room. Her childhood home used to seem so simple and safe. Now it just felt suffocating.

Susan grabbed her bags. The back screen door hit the wooden frame with an almost silent thud.

Her motor hummed quietly as she warmed the car in the driveway. Susan could not wait to leave. She needed to go home, back to Memphis, she told herself. The most important thing was her life in Tennessee. She wanted to look forward now, and not backward. Her father could handle settling the estate, or not. It was his choice. After all, Susan had used her money for a deposit for Craig Cartwright. David Upton had thrown enough on his oldest daughter. Keeping his secret and paying an attorney's retainer made Susan feel like she'd done her father's dirty work, and then some.

The weak morning sun barely filled the windows of her crossover as Susan rubbed her hands together and turned on the heater. With the car in gear, she backed out of the driveway and went down the street.

She thought about her work and friends in Germantown. Her son was just a few hours away in school. Maybe she would surprise him with a visit in the next week or two. The exhaustion settled into her shoulders as she shifted to find a more comfortable position. She needed to do a final thing before leaving. There was only one last place that she had to go.

CHAPTER 20

Craig Cartwright pulled to a stop in front of his office. Typically, he parked his slightly scratched, faded green hatchback behind the building. It was better if people didn't always associate his car with his practice. Some of his best surveillance happened because nobody could ever easily identify his old car. Also, any image of success that he hoped to create was hardly enhanced by the sight of his vehicle.

But he felt a bit hurried this morning. With cold weather, he knew his building would be chilly. He couldn't believe he'd scored a meeting with the Great Peter Elliott at ten o'clock. Grabbing his battered briefcase, Craig approached the doorway as the condensation of his breath hung in the frosty air.

Once inside, he turned on the lights, bumped up the thermostat, and started a pot of coffee. Only after he'd headed back to the turn on a lamp at the receptionist's desk, did he spot it. On the carpet, almost behind the door, lay an oversized white envelope. The placement of the letter indicated an early arrival through the mail slot. Bending down to retrieve the enclosed letter, he wondered. Mail delivery occurred in the afternoon. That meant that the correspondence must have come late last night, or early this morning. He moved to the front desk and opened the top flap. Hopefully, this wasn't some crisis that would require immediate attention during the morning. His tight schedule already crowded the entire day. Everything would have to wait until after his meeting with Peter.

His brow furrowed, then relaxed when as he examined the contents. The Last Will and Testament of Julia Upton sat before him. Good. Susan Abbot had obviously delivered the envelope as promised. A small hand-written note rested on top of the papers. He leaned over to read the neat, perfectly spaced penmanship.

Dear Mr. Cartwright,

Please find enclosed my aunt's Last Will and Testament. I'm leaving it with you as requested. Hopefully these legal papers can help our family find closure to this matter.

I'm heading back to Memphis. My life and work are there, and I don't think there is any more that I can do to help my family. Feel free to call my father, David Upton, with additional questions.

Susan

Craig folded up the will and the note. He poured a cup of coffee from the pot that sat on the teacart in the reception area. Before his meeting with Peter, he would need to study the document thoroughly.

Heading back to his office, he pondered the Upton situation. Hopefully, the meeting with Peter Elliott would be fruitful. He wanted to have good news for the family on this matter.

Memories of Susan Abbot sitting in front of him the other day filled his mind. The brush of her brunette hair on her shoulders and her interesting face had stayed with him. He'd actually thought about her more than once in the last few days. He could always reach out to her father, but he really wanted to see her. Technically, David Upton had not hired him; Susan had. It was a fine point that played to his favor.

He unlocked the file cabinet and pulled out the case folder for the Upton family. He opened the top flap and searched his notes.

Got it. She did leave her cell number with him. It was only a matter of time until he would call. He felt determined to see her again.

CHAPTER 21

S usan crossed the state line into Tennessee when her phone rang for
the first time. Bending to the left, and then right, around the curving
mountains, she pressed forward as the highway stretched westward
over the Blue Ridge Parkway. In the morning light, her driving required
her concentration.

She chose to ignore the ringing. Paying attention to the road was more
important. Trucks clogged the interstate in single-file determination to tackle
the terrain. Besides, she assumed that the call would be from her father. Let it
ring. They needed some space, some air between them right now.

Traveling home to Germantown, she realized that her whole life felt
like a big, fat, distorted lie. Everything clearly seemed off course. Her forty-three years were like some sort of misguided GPS system that took her
farther from the life that she'd dreamt she would have as a child. Her
parents—the one part of her past she'd believed she could take at face
value—had been living with secrets for years. In one evening, the pieces of
her family came apart, and were put back together in an entirely different
arrangement, like familiar mechanical parts that suddenly shifted to create
something entirely new.

Her cousin was her half-sister. Ryan had been born when Dory was just eighteen months old. They played together as small children whenever Susan and Neil came home to visit. People always remarked how cute Dory and Ryan were together. "Two peas in a pod," they would say.

The problem was, in a weird way, the truth made a strange kind of sense. Nobody embodied stubbornness quite like David Upton, except for Dory. And Susan had always noticed that they shared the same piercing brown eyes, the same forehead. "It's the Upton family face," her mother remarked over the Christmas holidays when Susan's father had mimicked Dory with an identical expression.

They all laughed about the resemblance around the dinner table one night. Now Susan wondered how her father could smile; even find it all that amusing. The laugh had really been on Susan and her mother. The lie was right in front of them the whole time. Why had Susan not seen it? How did her mother miss the obvious? Maybe Sylvia Upton knew deep down inside, or at least suspected the truth, about Dory. Don't most women ignore the pain, the facts about their own men, when it's too hard? Susan thought about all the deceptions. She had certainly done that in her own marriage. Maybe living with dishonest men was some sort of family curse.

"This is so fucked up," Susan said aloud to herself.

She shook her head as she accelerated. The new reality of her family left her bone weary. An entirely new picture of the four of them emerged with the facts about Dory. Susan looked out at the landscape as she drove along and thought about the alterations to their family. It was like the rocks that lined the side of the mountain highways. They were wet and dull most of the year from underground springs, but changed in the coldest months into glistening, frozen stalagmites that sparkled like thousands of diamonds in the weak winter sun.

By the time Susan arrived on the eastern side of Knoxville, she could hardly think beyond her hunger and pounding head. At the Dandridge exit, she pulled off the interstate and headed toward a diner. She got out of the car and slowly stood in the chilled air to unbend her stiff legs.

In the hard molded booth, Susan studied her breakfast options. There was a normalcy to sitting and just thinking about food. It felt good to be in Tennessee, in a warm restaurant made ever so slightly humid by the flat-top grill bellowing smoke from the pickup window. She was just starting to relax when her cell rang again.

Her father's name flashed across her phone screen. She decided to let it roll to voicemail again. Maybe she would feel differently after coffee and food. Maybe she would call back tonight, or maybe tomorrow, or maybe next week. She sighed and studied the menu as the server shuffled over to her table.

"You know what you want, sugar?" The waitress poured dark coffee into Susan's upturned mug.

"How about a number three, eggs over easy," Susan answered.

The waitress pulled a small order pad from the blue pocket of her apron and retrieved a pencil from behind her ear. She nodded as she dropped her glasses onto her noise from their perch in her beehive hairdo.

When the food arrived, Susan forced herself not to eat too quickly. The breakfast tasted somehow perfect in its simplicity. Butter pooled in small drops on her plate, flavoring everything that the liquid touched. Eating in silence, she welcomed the momentary peace and quiet.

Susan began to calculate time as she paid her check. If she filled her car with gas, there remained the chance that possibly, just possibly, she could pick up Harvey from the vet before they closed for the night. It was worth a try. Being at home with her cat would make life start to resemble a routine again.

Back on the road, Susan felt more settled than she had all week. She rolled down her window and took a deep breath. The Tennessee air, combined with a plate of eggs, grits, and biscuits, began to work magic on her.

This was a second wind. Her energy would last until somewhere between Nashville and Jackson.

Five minutes before closing, Susan pulled her crossover into the nearly deserted animal hospital. She grabbed her purse and walked quickly towards the door.

"I'm here to pick up Harvey, Harvey Abbot," Susan said a bit breathlessly.

The high-school-age vet tech put down her cell phone and faced her last-minute client with an obligatory smile. Her name tag said Brittaney, with a little heart over the *I*.

"Your baby's name again?" she asked as she wheeled her chair closer to her monitor.

"Harvey Abbot," Susan repeated. "He's a cat."

"Bring up Harvey Abbot," Brittaney called into the intercom. She studied the screen in front of her, frowning. "Did we have your cell phone number?"

"Is everything okay? Yes, you have my number on file. It hasn't changed. Is my cat okay?" Susan asked.

"Oh, now I see," said the receptionist. "I guess they decided not to call you. Harvey is fine, but he did refuse to eat for a day or two, so they had to give him special food. It's all on your statement. Just sign here. We billed your credit card."

The printer behind the counter was busy spitting out several sheets of account information as Susan was handed a pen.

Looking at the bill seemed surreal. There was something wrong with the fact that the cat had eaten better than she had this last week. She signed her name. *Well,* Susan thought, *the time to go home and sell some real estate has arrived.*

Her crossover turned into the neighborhood as the sun was setting in dusty orange light. Harvey emitted a low growl as Susan pulled into her driveway. The house, with its shuttered windows, looked silently back at her. The yard, dormant and bleak in its winter top layer, appeared remarkably undisturbed by her absence. She pushed the remote to open the garage door and said a silent prayer of thanksgiving to be back home.

Within an hour, Susan sat in her oversized soaker tub. She leaned back and became immersed in a sea of scented bubbles.

Harvey rested with his eyes shut on the bathmat, his legs tucked under him. The position reminded Susan of some sort of compact, rectangular, feline loaf of bread. Placing a washcloth over her eyes, the warmth of the water began to transport her into a dozing sleep.

The shrill ring of her cell phone made Susan jump. Her heart pounded as she reached over the side of the tub to grab the intrusion and answer the offending caller.

Sylvia Upton's name and mobile number appeared on the screen. Susan stared. Rarely, did her parents use their cell phones in the evenings, except in emergencies. Reaching to answer, Susan could just imagine her mother, still weak from her last round of chemo, needing to talk to her.

"Hello, Mom," Susan tried to sound cheery and light.

"I'm so glad to talk to you," Sylvia Upton sounded tired and worn.

"Mom, I—" Susan began, but her mother cut off her words.

"Susan, we had some news today. I needed to share it with you." Her tone was tense.

Susan was wide awake now as she sat up in the tub. Water sloshed back and forth like like an angry ocean.

"What is it?" Susan asked, almost fearful of what she would hear.

"I didn't want you to hear it from anyone else, so I needed to call you." Her mother took a breath.

Suddenly, Susan felt sick. She shut her eyes, afraid of what she would hear. Could her mother have already found out about Dory? Did her father have some sudden change of heart and decide to come clean after decades of dishonesty? Susan didn't know how she should respond. Surprised? Shocked?

"An announcement was made today," her mother said weakly.

Susan caught her breath. She knew what was coming.

"The board of directors at the college announced that Mount Robert College will close at the end of the semester," her mother said.

"Oh, Mom," Susan began. "What?" She was shocked. The unexpected words hit her brain.

"It's incredibly sad. Your father and I are heartbroken. But it seems that the decision has already been made." Sylvia sounded despondent.

There was a pause on the line. Susan knew her mother must be fighting back tears. She could hear sniffling.

"Enrollment has been flat at the college for some time. Your father knew about this, but he was still surprised. Many small liberal arts schools are struggling, but we didn't see closure for the college. Mount Robert has a small endowment that we both thought was sufficient to keep the school going, but the board of directors decided to close. It's too little, too late, they said."

"Mom," Susan repeated. "I don't know what to say."

Where had this news been the last few days? Just yesterday, Mount Robert had seemed like a vibrant college community to Susan. This was so shocking.

"Your father and I'll be all right. He'll get a small pension. I was given a tiny honorarium because I only taught part time the last few years. Of course, we'll lose our health insurance. Both of us now have to move to a state plan and Medicare. My treatments are all experimental, so who knows if I can continue with my doctor in Asheville."

Susan heard the words and tried to take in all the information. Her mother's voice continued.

"Of course, your father feels devastated. He's seventeen years into a twenty-year bird study for the state of North Carolina. Without the school, I don't know how he can finish and publish the results. This was to be his crowning research in his field. He committed to a book deal with the results of the analysis. It would have been a nest egg, so to speak, for our retirement."

"Mom, I . . . I'm so sorry." There was silence on the phone. "Mom, what do you need?" Susan's voice sounded level. Her emotions, so wild over the last two days, suddenly flattened. She could feel herself coming back to her center. This was her family.

"Oh, I don't know." Her mother sounded tired again. "You did so much to help your father with Julia's estate. We are so grateful."

"Mom, Aunt Julia's estate isn't settled yet," Susan confessed.

Silently, she wondered what this new bombshell added to the process. No one would even pay attention to an unsettled estate with a college closing looming over the community.

"Well, we'll sort it out." Her mother sighed into the phone. There was bravery and resolve in her voice. "Until then, Dory can just continue living with us. I don't want you to worry about this. I just felt I had to let you know. You have your own life to live in Memphis. You can't lose sleep over our situation. We'll work it out the best way we can."

Susan grabbed a towel from the wall behind the tub. She stood, bubbles dripping.

"Don't worry, Mom. We'll figure this out. We can figure out the best thing to do." Susan wondered if the words sounded false.

Her mother sighed wearily on the other end of the line. Susan felt a sudden wave of guilt for offering platitudes, for throwing nonexistent hope between them.

"I love you, dear," Sylvia said, the weight of her emotion coming through the phone.

"I'll call you tomorrow," Susan promised. "And I love you, too."

Susan hung up and wrapped a towel around her body, then put the phone down and stepped out of the tub.

Mount Robert College. How many decades had the school been a part of their lives? This would change everything for their family and the town.

And Dory—what would become of her? First, as a young woman, she had lost her mother, and now this. With the closure of the college, Dory would lose another chunk of her life forever.

As Susan rubbed her shoulders with the towel, Harvey stood up on his tip toes to stretch. His paws moved vertically until he rested only on the pads of his feet. Arching his back, his head turned toward Susan.

"How do you feel about a road trip?" Susan asked him. "Do you think that living in a house with a dog for a while might work?"

Harvey opened one eye, then the other, looking suspiciously towards Susan. They stared at each other. With a flick of his head and tail, he turned and walked away indignantly towards the master bedroom.

"You don't get a vote!" Susan called after the cat as he sauntered around the corner.

She moved to the closet and grabbed her robe. Whatever upheaval happened during the last visit was separate. Susan would have to compartmentalize it, to hold the drama for another day. But the college closing was bigger than any secret. Her family would need her help to get through this. Susan glanced in the mirror and saw the determination in her face.

It might take a few weeks or more, but one thing remained certain: She was going back to Mount Robert.

CHAPTER 22

The sun faded into purple evening light as Dory finished sorting the last of the pet adoption papers on the reception desk. From the back of the building, she heard the yapping of the kenneled dogs, restless before they surrendered to sleep. Teenage voices floated and called out to the animals throughout the building.

It was the sound of Thursday, the day every week that ended with a group of youth volunteers. Bess set up the weekly schedule with adamant zeal. There was a clear expectation that Dory would be the one in charge, left alone with extra hands. In exchange for her weekly departure, Bess made sure that the local 4-H club came and worked with the animals. The real truth behind the altered staffing emerged for Dory only after having worked for several months.

"Okay, Bess," Dory asked. "What other life do you lead on Thursday nights? Why do you always leave early?"

Bess merely shook her head and shrugged her round, soft shoulders.

Dory only put everything all together one day after reading *The Mount Robert Gazette* as she lined cages with newsprint.

"Wow, it sure is raining hard," Dory remarked seriously to Bess one Thursday morning as she studied the sky from the front desk. Swollen dark clouds unleashed pelting drops against the front window.

"I hope that it won't ruin your 'plans', you know, for your secret other life."

Bess looked up from her desk. Dory smiled.

"It won't," Bess said calmly, shaking her head. She noticed the mirth along the edges of Dory's eyes, and refused to smile.

"Of course it won't." Dory laughed, certain she knew the truth. "Because your Thursday nights are spent inside the Mount Robert Bowling Alley!"

"I don't know what you're talking about," Bess said flatly, with a tone of mocked indignation.

"Oh, come on," pleaded Dory. "Why didn't you tell me about your bowling league?"

"Okay. You got me," Her boss confessed with a smile. "Guilty as charged."

"Is that the extent of your loyalty?" Dory questioned. "After all, are you, or are you not a proud member of the Mount Robert Pink Ladies Bowling Team?" The whole thing was so old school that she could not stop laughing.

"I didn't tell you because I knew you would laugh," admitted Bess. "See, you're doing it now."

Without meaning to, Bess began to chuckle. Dory rarely even smiled, and just seeing her so amused made everything funnier. But after a moment, Bess lowered her voice.

"Besides, we have a situation on our team."

Dory was wiping her eyes from tears of giggling.

"A situation? Really? What's the problem? One of the Pink Ladies can't keep her ball out of the side gutter?"

Bess raised a finger to her lips. "No, that's not it." Instinctively, she looked sideways to make sure no one was listening, even though they had been alone together in the shelter since breakfast.

"We have a good time on the team, if you know what I mean," Bess said in a hushed tone.

Dory raised her eyebrows in question.

"One of our Pink Ladies is a Baptist. And after we bowl, we always get some, you know, *refreshments*," Bess confided.

She looked so serious. Dory was laughing all over again, ready to roll out of her seat.

"We drink wine coolers," Bess said slowly in confession. "But don't tell anybody. We put them in Styrofoam cups so nobody can tell."

Dory tilted back her head and howled with delight. This was hilarious.

"Wine coolers?" Dory asked as she gasped for air. "Seriously? What are you, ninth-grade girls?"

They both laughed now, their heads thrown back, their roller chairs swaying.

"Bess, I drank that stuff in middle school!" Dory said between giggles.

"Shame," Bess responded, wagging her finger and laughing so that her whole upper body shook like Jell-O in a bowl.

Dory wiped her eyes to catch her breath.

"Well, who knew I was working for such a badass?"

Bess looked at her and raised a warning finger in Dory's direction.

"Don't tell anybody. I let you in on a little private business about the Mount Robert Pink Ladies. Remember, I sign your paycheck."

"Your secret is safe with me," Dory said as she held up three fingers in a promise. "Just don't tell me anymore, or I may wet my pants!"

Now the fading light from the window surrounded the lobby, and memories of that day with Bess filled the room. They had laughed until they couldn't breathe. It was Dory's favorite moment with her boss.

Her eyes glanced at the television at the far end of the reception area. The noise in the back of the shelter began to fade. From where she was sitting at the front desk, she could hear the top news story. But even if she moved, avoiding the familiar images and words seemed impossible.

For two weeks, Dory had turned off the wall-mounted set. Leaving the local channel on for the volunteers, she decided to just ignore the head-lines. But it was impossible. The lead story, once again, centered on the closing of Mount Robert College. Dory clenched her jaw as the newscaster talked one more time about the pending future of the school and the town.

Glancing at the television made Dory glad that Bess could still go bowling. Life was shifting enough in Mount Robert, as the news story an-nounced to the world. Having some things remain constant and normal felt like a godsend.

The past two weeks had been ripe with fear and uncertainty. Ever since the story first aired, Bess had worried about the changes that the college closing would create for the city services. The future of the animal shelter looked uncertain. Gazing out the darkened window, Dory wanted Bess to take a break from the unsettling reality of their community, even if it was only for one night a week.

She took a deep breath. Looking down at papers in her hands, she knew that she needed to concentrate on the positive. The past week had been a good one for dogs, better even for the cats. Four families visited the shelter to find pets. Three of them wanted cats, which was never surpris-ing in winter weather. No feline ever demanded to be walked on a cold mountain night. One older couple adopted a dog. Everyone filled out their paperwork, and all the families appeared aboveboard. Dory had a sixth sense about that sort of thing. When someone came into shelter, she could always distinguish the would-be good pet owners from the people who were just looking for an animal they might later abuse.

"Hey, Dory," said one of the high-school girls as she pushed open the heavy door to the reception area. "I fed everybody in the back, and all the dogs have been taken outside for the night. Our group also made sure there was clean litter for all our cat friends."

Dory looked up from the papers and gave a grateful smile. She could always count on these kids.

"Thanks, Sam," she answered.

The young woman put her hands on her hips as she gave a troubled stare at the television set. She grabbed the broom that was propped against the far wall and started to sweep, her arms pulled back in angry jabbing motions.

Dory looked up at her. She could read the frustration all over the teenager's face.

"Sam, it's going to be okay," Dory assured her. "Even though the news can't stop talking about the sale of the college, we'll be okay. This town is going to be okay, and the shelter, too." Dory hoped that she sounded convincing. The words made her feel like a parent trying to tell a child that it really wasn't so bad, when everything looked completely bleak. Her own mind had been swirling ever since the news stations broke the story.

Sam leaned on her broom and faced Dory. Her expression clouded with worry.

"Do you really think so?"

"Sure," answered Dory. "We're tough mountain people. We've been through more than just a college closing. Our entire community has faced lots of hardships in the past."

As she spoke, Dory had a fleeting memory of her mother's funeral, and the way it felt like the whole town turned out to pay their respects.

"Both my parents are contractors at the college. Besides their jobs, we just have a small farm. I don't know how our family will pay the bills without the school," confided Sam as she pushed the hair framing her face back towards her long French braid.

"Look," responded Dory as she rose from her desk, "you need to go home. Go see your folks, have dinner."

"Oh, I don't want to leave you here. I mean, it's dark and everything," said Sam.

"I'm fine. And really, I'm five minutes behind you," assured Dory.

"No. I'm not leaving you here. Even though we have the dogs, I mean, they're in cages. The others already went out the back door. They were leaving as I came up front. It's just us. I think we should walk out together," decided Sam.

Dory smiled. There was nothing like being cared for by a girl five years her junior, pulling on a varsity letter jacket. It tugged at her heart.

"Well, I'm not going to refuse an escort," Dory responded with a smile. She grabbed her old olive Army coat and brown fringed purse, and headed to the door with Sam. Quickly, the security alarm was set. They both went out, turned the lights off behind them, and locked the doors.

Outside, the sunset had faded to a velvet black night, filled with stars. The only light came from the large moon and the glowing street lamp on the edge of the shelter driveway.

Dory walked Sam to her old truck and gave her a hug.

"It's going to be okay. Send me a text after you talk to your parents."

Sam hugged her back with the force that only an emotional sixteen-year-old could thrust into an embrace.

"Thanks," she whispered.

Dory nodded and smiled as she headed to her own car. Sam hopped up into her old truck and started the engine. She waved as her tires raked over the gravel.

With her motor running, Dory wiped her eyes. The tears had been there all day, just under the surface. As she searched in her purse for a tissue, thinking about everything that was happening, her crying continued.

Everything just felt so shitty. It wasn't enough to lose her mom and have the estate in limbo; now she had no idea what would happen to her aunt and uncle, or even her town. Mount Robert College had been the one constant in her life. Even though she had dropped out, she'd always known the school was there. She wiped more hot tears from her eyes. She guessed this was what her garage band friends would call ironic karma.

As her car eased out of the parking lot and headed to the end of the driveway, she could practically see the news story that dominated their lives playing in her mind. The television streamed the same constant pictures of the college. Beautiful brick buildings with blooming azaleas in May, followed by videos of students and professors. In some of the news clips, there was even a shot of her uncle giving one of his bird lectures. Finally, the footage always ended the same way. Every new cast had a picture of the president of the college, joined by Peter Elliott and the rest of the board of regents. The final image looked sad, except for the fact that Peter Elliott never appeared very somber.

She pulled her Honda onto the now deserted winter road, and headed back towards town. With the shelter on the edge of the city, the trip would take a good twenty minutes. Dory drove slowly, hoping that her teary eyes would be dry by the time she reached her aunt and uncle's home.

Her mind turned to Peter Elliott as she drove along the two-lane road. He was supposed to be settling her mother's estate, and now he seemed to be consumed with closing the college. Dory had always disliked him. Long ago, he'd been her father's attorney, and her mother had also adamantly insisted on using him to write her own will.

Dory could remember the first time she saw Peter. She was young, maybe six or seven, and the Upton family had attended one of the lectures at the college. When she met him, he smiled at her, but something about him felt off somehow. He reminded her of a chocolate Easter bunny, all dressed up on the outside but hollow, with nothing underneath. His fake smile made her instantly dislike him.

For the past decade, Dory watched him around Mount Robert. He was odd, always out of place. She had never changed her opinion of him. And if she staked money on one thing, it would be on the obvious: Peter Elliott only cared about himself.

As Dory mulled over her concerns, she suddenly saw the headlights. Up ahead, a car raced over the hill. It flew past her, speeding in the opposite lane.

"Where are the cops when you need them?" Dory asked out loud.

In her rearview mirror, she recognized the car as a dark model BMW. It seemed to be going back towards the shelter. Dory slowed down and watched the sedan accelerate behind her. Where was a fancy car like that going in the dark? And why was a BMW speeding out here, in the middle of nowhere? She only knew one person in town who could afford a car like that one.

Dory made a quick turnaround on a dirt road. Maybe Peter Elliott was coming to the shelter to talk to her about settling the estate. But why not just call her or her uncle? Why drive all the way out here in the dark?

When she reached the shelter, Dory could see that the gravel parking lot was abandoned. The building remained dark. She puzzled over the oddity. What was the Great Peter Elliott doing on the edge of town at this hour? And if it wasn't Peter's car, then who else could it be?

Dory sped up, passing the shelter as her car headed in the opposite direction from town. She knew a few winding turns that could get her back to the square. Rubbing her neck, the fatigue hit her. Maybe she was just imagining things.

As she turned left just beyond the shelter, it happened again. The same car appeared ahead of her, farther down the road. Dory looked closely. Either Peter's car was moving in front of her, or one exactly like it.

The sedan headed toward a rural trailer park that sprawled in dingy rows. Dory knew the locals nicknamed this part of town the "Crack and Track Alley." Drugs and a railroad track were the only things that ever seemed to leave this part of Mount Robert. In fact, most of the illegal activity in Robertson County seemed to either originate, or end up in the squalor of the twenty mobile homes clustered in that area. The black BMW slowed down as it approached the first trailer.

Instinctively, Dory dropped her speed, careful to stay back from what was likely to unfold. What was a fancy car like that doing in this part of town? Everything about it looked like a drug deal to Dory.

"So this is where the fancy Peter Elliott goes after the sun goes down," she whispered to herself.

To her surprise, the car didn't stop. As it came to a crawl, Dory saw a door open from the second trailer. A young girl stood in the doorway. *Did she shout something to the driver of the BMW?* Dory wondered.

Suddenly, the sedan ahead of her sped up and then made a right turn at the end of the road. Dory was confused. If a fancy car wasn't out here for drugs or sex, what would that type of vehicle be doing? Only warehouses were scattered across the landscape beyond Crack and Track Alley.

Dory drove quickly past the trailers and turned right. The taillights of the sedan were only small circles up ahead of her. In the dark, she noticed that a few farms dotted the hills on this side of town. She knew that the emergency shelter of the Children's Home Society was also somewhere out in this part of the county. Losing sight of the BMW, the car seemed to pick up speed, heading for a well-lit building just beyond her view.

As the import disappeared around a curve, Dory took the last familiar road to the left that would lead back to town. In her seat, she felt a prick at the base of her scalp. It was her sixth sense, the same instinct that she used at the shelter.

Her mind raced. If Peter Elliott had driven out to the edge of town, then the question was why? Dory looked out her car window into the night and made a decision: The time had come to find out what Peter was really doing.

CHAPTER 23

———————

S usan pulled the white fleece robe around her body and tightened the belt around her waist. With her relaxation vanished, she stood over her lamp-lit desk in what was once the guest room. She looked with dismay at the mess in her office.

A stack of old mail, about a week old, rose like a hill on her work area. Her answering machine, connected to her home telephone, blinked wildly on the corner of a shabby-chic table. Housing tracts that had been tossed in a heap before she departed, littered the room.

She gave an inward shutter. Her house and her office were disaster zones. After hardly sleeping the last two nights and driving nine-plus hours, she felt weariness deep within her joints. Standing in the middle of the chaos and rubbing her eyes failed to erase her pounding head.

Susan had a sudden realization. The late hour created a stroke of good fortune. It was out of the question to return phone calls tonight. If she got up early, she could attack all of this, hopefully with a mug of coffee in her hand. She grabbed a small hotel pad of paper from the edge of her desk. What she needed was a plan. Her mind raced, and her pen flew, as a list formed. So much needed to be done before returning to Mount Robert.

Looking down at the page, she saw a three-column list of tasks. The work to leave Germantown again would require days of effort. She dropped the pen with a weary shake of her head, and turned off the lamp.

Back in her own room, she marveled at the sight of her bed. Turning down the covers, she could feel her weary body yearning to roll into the soft gray sheets. As Susan stretched on her side, there was a familiar jump on the end of her bed.

"Harvey," she murmured as he padded his way to the small of her back.

The cat kneaded the thick comforter with his paws as Susan turned out the light. With her eyes heavy from exhaustion, she sighed as she drifted off to sleep with Harvey nestled beside her.

Late that night, Susan woke with a start. She stared in the darkness and wondered for a full minute where reality stopped and started. Her dream had felt so sharp, so clear.

She was back in Mount Robert again, but as a young child. Standing in the quad between the academic buildings, she waited for someone; yes, she was sure she needed to be patient. Her father had told her he would come for her. Maybe her mother had said the same thing, too. Except that in her dream, she walked all alone on the reddish-brick walkways that lined the square patches of green grass. Suddenly, a large dark bird appeared along one of the pathways just ahead of her.

But her family never came. Susan remained all alone, chasing after the bird that had long since taken flight.

CHAPTER 24

S usan pulled close to the carport and let her wipers continue their rhythmic swaying. Earlier in the day, the precipitation had started as she'd approached Knoxville. For the last two hours, her car thermometer read thirty-three degrees. Heavy, wet clumps of February snow made the drive into Mount Robert both beautiful and treacherous.

Her childhood home sat silently before her. Susan put her crossover into park and turned off the engine. Opening the car door, she placed both hands around her purse, her overnight bag and Harvey's cat carrier. She had already decided that her big suitcase in the truck could wait until tomorrow. Susan only wanted to take inside what she absolutely needed for the night. The last thing she intended to do was wrestle heavy bags up the back steps that might already be slick with ice and slush.

Trudging through the snowy backyard towards the house, a warm yellow glow spilled onto the concrete patio from the back windows. The kitchen light had been left on for her, no doubt, as a welcome sign.

For the last two weeks, Susan had called her mother every day; relief had filled Sylvia Upton's voice when Susan had finally confirmed a date to return to Mount Robert. It took three weeks of careful planning for her to figure out how to temporarily leave her life in Germantown. Susan had spent an entire week in the office arranging for properties to be represented by other agents. She hated walking away from the commissions but she knew the decision best served her clients. Long ago, Susan learned that forthright service payed for itself in the long haul. She told everyone that she was on an extended vacation to help her family, and closed up her house.

Before she left, she managed to spend almost an entire day with Ryan. She had driven down to Mississippi State to see his rental house, and they'd had lunch together. The time with her son felt like an idyllic reward for everything she would be facing in North Carolina.

As she struggled up the snowy back steps with her arms full, Harvey made a low growl. It had been a long day for him in the car.

"Hang in there, buddy," Susan said to the carrier that swung back and forth in her hand.

Halfway up the steps, the back door opened. Susan stared up and saw her father standing above her in the doorway. In the soft kitchen light, she noticed immediately how stooped he appeared to be. His hair looked even thinner than Susan remembered, and it seemed unkempt, standing on end in the halo of light behind him. Susan thought immediately that he had aged ten years since she'd seen him in his truck on Manning Road just three weeks earlier.

"I thought I heard you," he said softly. "Here, let me help you with your things." He reached out to take the carrier and her canvas overnight bag.

"Who do we have here?" her father asked as he peaked at the cat.

"That's Harvey," Susan answered as she reached the top step. "He's probably desperate to get out and have some water, maybe explore the house."

Her father backed up to the kitchen sink as Susan entered the warm kitchen. Taking off her coat, she turned around to see him stooped on the floor. He opened the the door of the carrier as Harvey emerged wide-eyed into the unfamiliar room. His hand gently stroked the frightened cat.

On the kitchen table, she noticed a small glass of what looked like scotch. It rested in front of her father's usual spot.

Harvey stood tentatively on the kitchen mat, basking in his newfound attention. Suddenly, he shot out of the space and down the hall.

"I guess he figured out that we have a dog," her father said softly as he rose from his squatting position.

"Where's Mom?" Susan asked. Silence filled the house.

"She went to bed to read," he answered. Glancing at his unfinished drink on the table, and then back at Susan, he continued. "I checked on her about thirty minutes ago and she was asleep."

Susan nodded. The air between them was tense and tentative. She wasn't sure what to say.

"Where's Dory?" Susan asked as she smoothed her hair.

"She had to work late at the animal shelter," her father responded. "After work, I think she was going to try to see Dan, her boyfriend."

He moved toward the table.

"Will you sit with me?" he asked.

"Sure," Susan answered, stepping over to the worn pine table that was old enough to be considered an antique. "Why not?" she added blithely. Their talking, sooner or later, seemed inevitable.

The ladder back chairs scrapped across the old vinyl flooring with a dull pull as both father and daughter found their usual places. On any other night, gathering in the kitchen might have felt like some kind of assigned seating, but now it was a relief just to sit in a familiar spot at the old table. Susan found herself praying that their conversation would not turn into some verbal landmine about the family.

"You left without saying goodbye," her father said quietly. His hands were on the table, one folded over the other. He looked down at his entwined fingers.

"Yes, I know," Susan admitted, taking a deep breath. "I just couldn't stay—I mean, I needed to get home. I just couldn't—"

Her father raised one hand slowly upward. "It's all right. I understand."

They looked at each other. There was a pause between them, long enough for discomfort.

"Thank you," Susan finally replied. "Thank you for understanding."

Silence expanded in the room. Susan could hear the ticking of the old wall clock.

"Dad, I've come back home to help," Susan began. Her slow words projected into the empty void between them. She paused and studied her father. Her voice became softer. "I wanted to come back to help Mom and you. I'm so sorry about the college, truly sorry." Her voice faded with sadness. "The college was your life; it was all our lives, for that matter. I can't really remember a time without Mount Robert College."

Her father nodded slowly. His shoulders slumped as if he had been carrying a heavy burden. Susan decided to keep speaking. She had been rehearsing the conversation in her head for weeks.

"I'm here to try to help all of you with this transition. You and Mom will have a lot to do. I can help look at insurance changes and retirement plans. Also, Aunt Julia's estate is still not closed. There may be some things I can do to get some of the paperwork done, maybe even help move items out of the house."

Her father sat motionless, listening to her. He studied his drink in front of him.

"You both have decisions to make," continued Susan. "But once the dust is settled, so to speak, I think you should both consider moving to Germantown."

Her father raised his eyes that had suddenly widened with surprise. Susan could tell from his expression that he had never considered leaving Mount Robert. She decided to press just a bit more, to get everything out in the open.

"We can decide all that in the next month while I'm here. I can afford to stay until the early part of March."

Her father nodded in thought.

"Maybe," Susan added her final interjection, "a move would even be good for Dory. Perhaps finishing college in Tennessee could be a fresh start for her."

The words hung in the air between them, full of the weighted choices they faced.

"Susan, there are some things I need to say," her father began. His voice was tired. "Things I should have said to you before you left."

"All right," Susan said. "I'm listening."

"I should have said more to you the night we were out on Manning Road." Her father looked back down at the drink he cradled in his hands.

Susan let out a long sigh of fatigue and rubbed the back of her neck. The last thing she wanted was a heavy conversation about the past. The future had more than enough obstacles for everyone.

"Dad," Susan began, "let's not do this. I mean, what good does it do? It's not going to change anything, not for you, or me, or anyone. What's done is done." As the words fell out of her mouth, Susan hoped she had blunted the conversation.

"I know all that," answered her father. He looked at Susan again, his eyes, red-rimmed and moist. "We can't change the past. Believe me, I've often wished we could undo our mistakes. But we can't. That's life. We do things, and we have to live with the outcome of our choices." He looked down and tilted his glass in front of him. "Trust me, I'm not letting myself off the hook." He paused, lost in honest reflection. Softly, he continued. "I know what it is to make mistakes, and maybe that's why I always loved teaching at Mount Robert. So many of my students were in need of a second chance, some sort of clean slate, if you will. I always tried to be a teacher who could give someone another shot."

"You gave grace," Susan said.

"Yes, I gave grace," her father agreed with a rueful smile. He hesitated before his words got quieter. "Maybe you can never really know grace until you're in need of it yourself." After a moment, he spoke again. "But there are some things that you need to know—things I need to say."

"All right," Susan responded. She sensed this was a different kind of moment for both of them.

"I just want you to know that I love your mother deeply," her father said, his words full of confession. Susan noticed his labored breathing. He paused and instinctively lowered his voice. "I've died a thousand deaths over what I did. My guilt at times has all but consumed me."

Susan stared at him. She could never remember her father talking like this. His voice was halting and genuine.

"And yet, I want you to know that I have never stopped loving your mother, you, and yes, Dory."

The words were out between them. Susan studied her father. He was a man she had known all her life, who was transforming before her eyes.

"I never meant to hurt your mother. Really, I never did. I've struggled with this for years. I don't know if I'll ever tell her the truth. At this point, I don't know if it even matters. All I care about, even more than the college, is her beating this cancer."

Susan nodded, remaining quiet, trying to give him room to speak.

"But you and Dory," he continued, staring at her intently as he spoke, "both of you are my blood. I love you both, and I just want you to know that."

Susan nodded, her face softening.

"I want us to be a family, to get through all this together," he added.

"I want us to be a family, too," she said.

For the first time, maybe in years, Susan realized that she wanted to hold on to her parents and Dory.

"We'll all need each other if we're going to get through all this—if we're ever able to move forward," her father spoke with conviction. "There'll be things we'll all need to do for one another."

Susan nodded again. His words were the bridge between them. Now they were both quiet again at the table.

"Well," Susan said at last. "If you want to begin, I could use one of whatever you're drinking." She looked at her father with a tired smile.

His worn face broke into a pleased expression as he sat up straighter and said, "Absolutely."

His chair scraped across the old green floor as he rose and moved to the sink. Pulling the side cabinet knob, he opened the cupboard to produce a juice glass.

"Pardon my barware," he said with a small laugh. Out of habit, he shot a quick glance down the hall. "And let's not trouble your mother with any details about our evening beverages."

Susan chuckled. "Your secret's safe with me."

From his brown fleece vest, her father produced a flat pewter flask. He unscrewed the top and poured the amber liquid into Susan's glass.

"A flask?" Susan questioned amusingly. "One would think that you work college students!"

"The flask is a wonderful invention," began her father in his teaching tone of voice. "It has unfortunately been hijacked by those younger adults who are not always capable of appreciating the fine art of portable alcohol."

He sat back down in his chair and raised his glass. "What shall we drink to this evening?"

Susan thought for a moment. "How about to better days ahead?"

"To better days ahead," they both said as their glasses clinked together.

CHAPTER 25

Craig Cartwright leaned back in his leather chair and tapped his pen onto the file in front of him. He surveyed the stacks of folders strewn all over his desk.

Ever since the announcement was made about Mount Robert closing, his workload had been incessant. Any collegiate client he had helped with anything, from a parking ticket to a school infraction, had been in contact with him. Even though it was still February, every single one of them wanted the same thing: to make sure their name got cleared to squeaky perfection before the great unknown of a college transfer came into the picture.

It was a Tuesday afternoon. He glanced at his receptionist sitting at her desk near the front door. Between photocopying and filing, she had plenty of work to do. At the moment, the pixie-cut political science major stared at her computer screen as she pushed her glasses into place. From his chair, Craig could just see her tucking her hair behind her ears and leaning towards the monitor.

She's probably looking at social media, Craig thought with a shake of his head. He intended to say something about her constant use of Facebook, but then he reconsidered. Remembering his own youth, he knew how hard concentrating felt in a chaotic world. And Mount Robert was nothing if not chaotic these days. Besides that, both Craig and the young woman knew this was a short-lived job. By May, the college would close, and his office would be all but desolate.

"Oh, Mr. Cartwright!" his receptionist called out to Craig. "I meant to tell you that a package came for you while you were out. It's a large white legal-size envelope. I put it on the corner of your desk."

"Thanks, Melinda," Craig answered. He glanced at the mess in front of him. He dropped his pen and tried to clear space on his desk.

While he had been at lunch, he'd managed to miss two phone calls, and now a delivery. His eyes fell on a teetering stack of folders on the far edge of his work space. He finally spotted the envelope.

"I see it!" Craig called back.

He realized that if Melinda had failed to mention the package, the envelope could have easily gone missing among the mountains of paperwork that seemed to be accumulating. As he moved his white Styrofoam takeout box to the top of his keyboard, he grabbed the letter to take a closer look.

"It was like a special delivery," Melinda told him from across the small office, her eyes still glued to the screen in front of her face. "Some messenger guy came in and wanted to make sure you got it."

"Okay," Craig answered distractedly.

He reached out to grab the packet. Only a few people sent him documents by special courier. Smiling, he felt silent pleasure to see that the envelope originated from the law offices of Peter Elliott. Because Craig had only one current case with that firm, he felt sure the contents involved the Upton estate.

As he opened the envelope, Craig found himself hoping that the paperwork might contain material that would necessitate a phone call to Susan Abbot. She was back in town. He had seen her once in Mount Robert, and he secretly hoped to meet with her again.

She'd stopped in to see him one afternoon. He'd noticed her the minute she'd walked into the office. She had on black leggings, simple boots, and an oversized sweatshirt. With her hair in a loose ponytail, she looked more like a thirty-something-year-old town tourist than a client in her early forties. She breathlessly told him that she and Dory had been working all day, cleaning out the remaining personal items from her Aunt Julia's home.

Ever since that day, her image remained stuck in his head. Susan Abbot looked like the girl next door, and yet there was something fascinating about her. The high cheekbones of her face gave her features interest, and her eyes were a color he had never quite seen. They were blue but mostly green, with a depth that hinted at her personality.

When he opened the envelope, the contents surprised him. The Peter Elliott Firm was making an outright cash offer from an anonymous buyer to the Upton family. Craig raised his eyebrows as he read the proposal. This was not what he'd expected.

He and Peter had clearly understood, even agreed, about the tasks at hand when they'd met. Craig had been waiting for Peter to outline a proposal for the sale of the house that included the acreage, as well as a plan for the fossil collection. Now, he held an offer that appeared to cover everything in full.

His eyes narrowed as he studied the figures in front of him. From the recent date on the paperwork, he saw the buyer had offered $100,000 for the home of Julia Upton. He read the documents carefully.

To most of Craig's clients, a cash offer would have seemed like a godsend. But he knew the Upton family differed from most of the town, both in educational background and community position. Susan clearly understood the value of the property. The house and land that adjoined the college appraised at twice the offered amount, or more. Craig rubbed his chin as he continued to pour over the pages.

Studying the offer before him, the details of the case raced through his mind. On the surface, the offer seemed low, clearly less than the family had anticipated. And yet a completely cash offer was valid and forthright, to be sure. He quickly flipped through each page, searching for additional facts.

As he continued to read, no mention of the fossil collection appeared. That detail would be important to the family, Craig realized. The rare artifacts were as much a legacy from the estate as the land. Such a unique collection would require some additional consideration. Peter would have to identify exactly what would happen to those items.

As Craig picked up his pen again, he tapped the Upton file, deep in thought. It was time to make a phone call. He glanced out to Melinda; her chair sat empty. Light seeped from under the closed door of the powder room in the reception area. Without meaning to, Craig began to smile. He realized he had been hoping for a bit of privacy.

Opening the beige folder before him, he dialed the cell number written on the front page. The call rolled to voicemail.

"Susan, this is Craig Cartwright. I have some news about the estate we need to discuss in person. I was wondering if we could meet, either at my office, or over dinner, if you're still cleaning out your Aunt's house. Please return my call at this number, or the office."

Hanging up, his cell phone rested silently in his hand. For a moment, he felt a pang of guilt. Had the call sounded like a date? It wasn't a date, he told himself. He occasionally met clients over coffee or . . . Craig wrinkled his forehead as he tried to remember. Had he ever had dinner with a client?

He scratched his head, and his dirty blond curls rumpled under his fingers as his past cases flipped through his mind. He could only ever recall discussing legal matters in his office or over an occasional cup of coffee with anyone. He dropped his pen and closed the file quickly. But why should dinner really be any different? Of course, he had to admit, his clients were usually not as attractive as Susan Abbot.

Just get the Upton case settled, he told himself as he quietly put the folder in his top desk drawer. He needed to remember his priorities. But if a meal helped to settle the estate, then all the better. And, he reminded himself, everyone has to eat at some point.

Craig glanced out the window at the cold February afternoon. Having dinner with Susan Abbot sounded wonderful. After all, between the college closing and the town in flux, a nice evening with an interesting client might just be the welcome relief he needed.

CHAPTER 26

Dory stared at the shelter time sheet as she ran her blue painted fingernails over the empty shifts. She knew the importance of filing out the schedule, especially as the one in charge. It was part of her new responsibilities.

For the past two weeks, Bess had been out of the office on sick leave. Dory suspected her illness probably stemmed from the stress of the whole Mount Robert College closing. She knew that her boss worried endlessly about the future of the shelter. After weeks of turmoil, Bess finally ached to the point that she could hardly walk. Early one morning, Dory got a call.

"I'm going to have back surgery in Ashville," Bess told Dory.

"When?" Dory asked.

She felt a wave of panic. She wanted to see Bess, to be with her.

"Later today, the surgeon had an open slot. I'm sorry about this, but I'm really going to need you at the shelter, dear."

Dory understood. Without question, she made an instant decision. The shelter would run as smoothly as possible. Her leadership was the best way to help her boss.

For the last ten days, Dory had been in charge. The good news was that Bess had returned home to convalesce after the repair of a ruptured disk. The bad news was that Dory, the right-hand staffer to the director, had quickly realized the shelter remained woefully understaffed.

She looked up and down over the work schedule. It really wasn't much of a choice. While Dory did love to come in early in the morning, and open the building to greet all the animals, she did have a part-time staffer or two who preferred the day shift. Without hesitation, she grabbed a pen and scheduled herself for every ending shift that remained open, beginning with the next three nights.

Dory sighed as she inspected the arrangements. She understood exactly what she was doing. Marking the schedule, she wanted to tell herself that she was helping out the entire staff. But deep down inside, she knew the real reason for taking the evening shifts. If her mother had been there, she would have guessed exactly what Dory was doing. Julia Upton had always understood her daughter and her motivations. She'd have clearly labeled Dory's behavior, yet again, as obsessive compulsive. While Julia acknowledged her daughter's sixth sense, she discouraged her covert actions, nonetheless. Dory knew that if her mother were still here, everything would have to be explained to her. But she wasn't alive, Dory reminded herself as she looked around the small office. And everything was a mess.

Dory wanted to work the later shifts. Having a different schedule would allow her to look for Peter Elliott around town during the day. The evening hours also afforded plenty of opportunities to watch for his car at night. It wasn't that she had ever intended to spy on him. Personally, she still found the attorney to be arrogant and pompous, not to mention incredibly shallow. In any other situation, he wouldn't have been given a minute of her time. But ever since she'd seen his car on the edge of town that night, she'd been curious—or maybe she felt more than curious. And, Peter Elliott held the keys to the settlement of her mother's estate.

While she hated to admit it, Dory desperately wanted closure. With the future of Mount Robert College unknown, and her own world shifting almost daily, she needed the estate settled now more than ever. So what if she followed him whenever she could spot his car in town? She felt compelled to see where he was going. His presence on the wrong side of town late at night still puzzled her.

"You gotta hold your enemies close," one of her long-haired boyfriends in high school once told her. He'd said those words right before he'd gotten busted for pot possession. Dory always remembered him, and wondered if he ever thought to follow his own advice. But it was actually a good example for her. And Dory had every intention of learning from the vast number of losers that had colored her past.

But looking down at the committed evening shifts, she frowned. Dory realized that she really didn't want to spend her time this way. On some level, looking all over town for Peter Elliott felt stupid. What she really wanted was to spend her evenings with Dan. And therein lay the problem.

These days, the town bustled with visitors arriving daily due to the announced college closing. So Dan cooked every night at the inn until the early hours of the morning.

Dory smiled to herself as she thought about Dan. The one huge fringe benefit of her new schedule came into her mind. When she worked late, she got to surprise Dan in the morning. If she played her cards right, Dory knew that she could show up at his condo, steaming latte in hand, and let herself in the front door. She would always find Dan the same way, sleeping, exhausted from his late-night labor. Dory could slip quietly into his bedroom and uncover his body buried beneath the soft layers of rumpled sheets and faded blue quilts. She loved to run her fingers under the epidermis of blankets until she found the familiar smooth flesh of his arms and back, gone slack during sleep, as opposed to their usual tautness brought about by daily kitchen work.

"Hey, babe," he would sleepily offer as he started to stir.

"Hey, you," she always gently replied as she shed her own clothes to slide in next to him.

That really was the best part of her later work day. Those moments were some of the best with Dan, with talking and touching uninterrupted. Just that morning, they had been together.

"I've got something for you," Dan had said, with his voice husky as Dory left her panties and bra in a heap on the floor and climbed into bed with him.

"I bet you do," Dory purred as she reached out to take hold of Dan's bare hips, to caress his hardness.

"Yeah, that too." Dan chuckled, smiling as he enveloped her into his chest. "But that's not what I meant."

"Oh, really?" teased Dory. "What did you mean? You have more for me?"

"That guy," Dan said, sleepily.

"What guy?" Dory traced the skin on his forearms with her fingers. Her own blue tattoo of an infinity symbol on her wrist was the exact same color of the veins under his skin.

"That guy, what's his name? Elliott? Isn't he the one who's supposed to be helping your family? He was at the inn last night."

Dory felt herself tense involuntarily. Her bracelets jangled together on her arm.

Dan shifted and opened one eye, but then continued. "It was too late to call you last night when I finally got a chance and looked out in the dining room and saw them. He was entertaining some group of three or four men."

"Who were they?" Dory asked, now eager to find out what Peter had been doing at the inn.

"I don't know, not local." Dan rolled onto his back.

"You know he drives me crazy," began Dory, rising to both elbows, now fully awake.

"I know, and that's why I got the server to chat them up and get their names. I wrote it all down. It's in my car, tucked under the visor."

"You did?" questioned Dory as excitement flared in her voice.

"I did," responded Dan, reaching for her again. "Now before you go bolting to my car, my naked little jaybird, let's see if we can use some of your wide-awake energy for better pursuits this morning."

When Dory left the condo later that morning with the names of the mystery men in her hand, she smiled as she silently gave thanks for Dan. She was in such a great mood. How could he know just what she needed in bed, and also just what she needed most for her family?

As she got into her car to go to work, Dory had an ironic thought. She realized that she almost felt gratitude for all the eyes and ears of Mount Robert. While she often claimed that the provincial restraints of small-town living choked her spirit, the whispered voices that never hesitated to meet a stranger and pass on the information could be enormously helpful.

Now Dory rose from her chair and headed towards the bulletin board in the break room. She was alone, except for one volunteer in the far back. Seeing Dan later would prove impossible. His work schedule had been "manic" the last week, as he had already admitted. Dory looked around at the darkening shelter. She bit her lip and pondered her options.

Unfortunately, she didn't have an exactly brimming social life full of choices. Most of the people her age in town were Mount Robert students. All they could think about these days was where they would transfer, and when they would pack up to leave. Most evenings, Dory usually ended up driving around until she got tired and went back to her aunt and uncle's home. But the very thought of returning to their house again, tonight, made her grimace. The atmosphere at "the David and Sylvia abode"—what Dory called their residence—felt like a solemn tomb these days. Her uncle usually worked late most nights now, preoccupied with the closure of the school. Her aunt went to bed early, drained by her cancer treatments that ran together while their medical insurance lasted.

Dory stood in the break room that resembled an enlarged closet and contemplated her choices for the evening. There wasn't really much to do. Driving the long way to town at night in the dark, and keeping an eye open for Peter, made her tired. For two weeks there had been no sign of the BMW, or much of anyone else in the cold mountain darkness.

But then, two nights ago, she'd seen the same car again. She'd driven to the edge of the town square after work, and noticed the same black car, the same tinted windows, speeding in the opposite direction. It was headed, once again, on the same road that went out to the animal shelter. Dory turned around as quickly as she could, but she still managed to lose the sedan within a few minutes.

She grabbed a pin and tacked the work schedule up on the bulletin board in the tiny break room. The last worker nodded to Dory as he went out the front entrance, leaving the shelter silent. She glanced out to the reception area, surveying the video monitor that showed the back row of dog kennels. She was definitely alone now. With one last look at the shift assignments, she went back into the office.

She pulled out her cell phone from the back pocket of her skinny jeans and started to search for the names of Peter Elliott's dinner companions. As she sat down in the black mesh swivel chair and stared at the screen, her eyes narrowed. There was more than one way to find out about anyone, even the Great Peter Elliott.

CHAPTER 27

Susan stood in front of the long oval mirror in the corner of her childhood bedroom. The dull, slate-colored dusk of evening gathered outside and washed through the lace curtains, making the room seem gloomy. She reached over and turned on the bedside lamp. Standing in the light made her frown at her reflection. She was going to dinner, but she had no idea if she was wearing the right thing.

"So what do you think?" she asked Toby.

The dog stretched out on the colorful braided rug next to her bed. He raised an eyebrow, and his tail gave a firm thump on the hardwood floor.

Her dinner would be with Craig Cartwright. He'd suggested the mealtime meeting when she'd stopped by his office. Susan had practically rushed over to see him after he'd called her with news about the estate. Not only did she hope to hear some sort of good progress, but she found that she looked forward to seeing Craig.

"It's a cash offer," he explained as he settled into a chair in front of his desk next to her. "It's from an anonymous buyer. I think the settlement might be worthy of your family's consideration."

Susan's face clearly fell when Craig read the details of the proposal. Typically, she would never be so open with her expressions. After selling real estate in Germantown, she'd mastered the art of a composed face. But this wasn't the suburbs, where she maintained the role of an unbiased agent bringing deals to clients as she worked on their behalf. This was different. It was her own small hometown, and her own family property. The estate represented the legacy her uncle and aunt had built. But even more important than any hopes and dreams, this offer held the financial future for Dory, and to some extent, her parents.

"Go home and discuss the details with your family. Take a day or two to think about it. Today is Wednesday. Why don't we talk again on Friday? In fact, why don't you let me take you to dinner on Friday and we can discuss it?" Craig asked.

The words were out of his mouth with incredible ease. He tried to smile nonchalantly.

Susan looked up and realized that she had been pouting in thought while reviewing the paperwork. Craig sat smiling at her.

"Um," she said, trying to say something, but her thoughts were tumbling too fast. The offer in front of her, the cash, the selling of Mount Robert College; it was all swirling around in her head.

"There are now far more restaurants here than there were twenty years ago," Craig continued, aware he was trying to sound smooth. "Asheville and Mount Robert have really jumped off the map. It's become quite the foodie scene. But there are some very quiet spots, where we could talk about this offer after you've had some time with your family."

"Okay. I mean, all right." Susan smiled. Dinner sounded lovely, and typically she would have been flattered, but she felt preoccupied with the paperwork in her hand.

"Fine, I'll pick you up at six," Craig finalized.

Susan rose to leave and smiled at Craig as she held out her hand.

"Thank you for working on this for my family." she met his gaze with her hazel eyes. "We were hoping for more money, for Dory's sake, but the town is in flux right now, I know. This is a lot to think about for us, but I'll let you know something on Friday."

Susan pulled her soft, small hand from his fingers, and bent to retrieve her purse. She walked out the door.

Now in the fading afternoon twilight, Susan looked at her reflection. She gently bit her lower lip and wondered about dinner with Craig. It was a week past Valentine's Day, and she stood there wearing a red dress. The cabernet-red color could not be mistaken for any other shade. Synched at the waist, the dress hid the softness her stomach had developed since she turned forty. With lace sleeves that came to her elbows, it flattered her arms that were still toned, but barely. She hoped the outfit was fun without being flouncy. The dress was the only one she'd brought with her from her closet in Germantown. She packed it hoping to go to dinner one night with her parents and Dory, thinking they might have something to celebrate.

With simple sheer pantyhose and nude pumps, she checked herself in the mirror. Her hair pulled gently back, loose and low, off her neck, highlighted her small gold earrings. She straightened the skirt and touched her neckline, and wondered again if she was overdoing it with the dress. Maybe a business outfit would be more appropriate, she thought. But honestly, it had been such a long time since she had gone out to dinner, especially with a man. And Craig seemed more interesting than anyone she had met in a long time.

She glanced at the clock on the bedside table and realized that the time had arrived. It was almost six. She really hated changing clothes. The dress just needed a necklace, she thought. Remembering the locket that still rested in her suitcase made her shake her head. That would be overkill, she decided, not to mention ironic, given her family secrets. No extra jewelry, she finalized. Less was more. Hadn't Coco Channel said something about taking off an extra accessory before you left for the evening? Well, her neck would be bare. She grabbed her long black wool dress coat and headed for the door.

Outside her bedroom, she noticed the quiet of the house. The dog was at her feet, following, as she saw the two glowing lamps in the living room. She slipped on her coat and peeked into the empty room. She knew her father wouldn't be there. Hoping for an extension for his migratory bird project, he had driven to Raleigh earlier in the day. Dory had left hours ago, presumably to go to work, and that meant only Susan's mother remained in the house. Down the hall she now noticed a dim light in her parents' bedroom.

She walked to the door and gently tapped on it.

"Come in," her mother's voice said, tentative from a full week of treatments.

Susan pushed open the door, and wasn't surprised to see her mother already in bed with Harvey curled up in a ball by her side. Ever since Susan had returned with her cat, he had become incredibly attentive to her mother. It was as if he could sense all the anxiety, and was constantly trying to soothe the situation by his presence.

"I'm leaving in just a minute. I won't be late tonight," Susan told her mother.

"You look so pretty." Her mother smiled.

Susan could feel herself blush. Maybe the dress was a mistake.

"This is the only dress I brought from home. I probably should have worn something else, but I'm tired of business clothes. And the only other things I brought were clothes to clean out Julia's house."

"Well, you look lovely. Do you still have a key to the front door?" asked her mother.

"Yes, and don't you worry. I'll lock the front door as I leave," she responded.

"Do you think we've made the right decision about the offer?" her mother asked, lines of worry etched on her brow. It reminded Susan of her father's care-worn face these days.

"Yes," Susan answered as she moved across the room to kiss her mother on the forehead. The doorbell rang and Toby let out a bark. "I have to go." Susan turned to leave the bedroom. "I'll check on you when I get home and say goodnight."

The dog trotted to the foyer and wagged his tail as the heavy oak door opened.

Craig smiled and their eyes meant. Susan could feel herself start to smile, too. She noticed he was wearing a navy blazer and dark tan pants. His white shirt opened at the neck, free of a tie. He looked handsome, Susan thought, before she chided herself silently. This dinner centered around the offer for her family. Their future was at stake. She needed to remember that.

She took her purse from the hall tree by the front door, patted the dog's ear, and headed out into the night with Craig.

CHAPTER 28

As Craig Cartwright opened the car door for Susan, he felt the chill in the night air for the first time that evening. For the last hour, he had been lost in thought, too preoccupied to realize much about the weather. But as he gently closed the passenger door, the dropping temperature cooled his skin. Eagerly, he put the key in the ignition. The heater began to warm his front seats as he slowly eased his hatchback towards town.

His car, although simple, was at least warm and clean. He had actually run it through the car wash and then used the oversized vacuum hose at the gas station to perfect the interior. Very rarely did he wish for the trapping of a nice sedan, but tonight was one of those times.

"We could eat at the inn on the square, but it's the only nice restaurant in town. Usually that means it's incredibly hard to have a private conversation," Craig began. "I thought that Asheville would give us a bit more privacy, plus there are some interesting places to dine."

As he spoke, he hoped that getting out of Mount Robert would be agreeable to Susan. Asheville promised to be a better destination, he had already decided, for many reasons. Finding new and exciting restaurants remained only one, relatively small, consideration. What he really thought—and didn't tell her—was that eating local meant the inevitable. Any restaurant, coffee shop, or café in town, not to mention the bars, employed the people who usually sought out his services. Staying in Mount Robert would be one continuous parade of his former, if not current, clients. And while most of his cases involved good, hardworking people who got caught up in poor choices, he needed a break from them, especially with Susan. Craig liked most of his clients, but tonight he didn't want the intrusion of seeing them.

As the road darkened and twisted on their way out of town, the mood in the car relaxed. Craig had learned years ago that there was nothing like a small hatchback with two people stuck inside to induce conversation. It was a trick he often used with his own son. Some of their best talks happened in his small car as he ferried Tyler around on the weekends Craig had visitation. And now, as the vast nothingness of the darkened landscape enveloped the two-doored vehicle, the couple started talking as they traveled towards Asheville.

Days ago, Craig had reserved seating in a small, intimate dining room, at one of the new hotels that lined Biltmore Village. Gas lamps glittered in the winter evening as they drove into the quaint tourist-lined streets.

As Craig pulled the car into the wide circular hotel entrance, he sensed the familiar pang of embarrassment once again. It was bad enough to pick Susan up in his very plain, very clean subcompact, but he knew what awaited his arrival. The hotel and restaurant would all but require valet parking. For the second time that evening, he felt a longing for a sleek, polished luxury car.

Directed to the dining room, Susan and Craig stood at the entrance of a softly lit series of rooms, tucked away behind the lobby fountain and front desk. The restaurant embodied hushed elegance. The tables, heavy in linen, could seat no more than four people, giving the room a feel of individual privacy. The atmosphere was a polished mixture of contemporary dining set against the rustic mountain backdrop of the elegant Biltmore House.

Craig held her seat, and Susan slid into a rustic chic dining chair. As they settled into the table, a waiter appeared with menus in hand.

"Wine tonight?" asked the neat, small-statured waiter.

Craig raised his eyebrows at Susan in question, and she nodded.

"Red, please," Susan requested.

"Two glasses of Turley, Old Vine," Craig ordered.

He rarely allowed himself to have good wine, but this night was different. He wanted something special, and he remembered the deep red wine as fruity, peppery, and above all, interesting. He usually drank cheaper selections, but he was tired of standard table offerings.

He smiled at Susan. For the third time that evening, he longed for more than he had. The first two wishful thoughts had involved cars, and now he wanted more opportunities to drink nice wine with someone special.

As Craig studied the menu, he noticed that the seafood selection was extensive. While they both chatted about the dishes offered, Susan confided that she loved to cook.

"I took a French cooking class in east Memphis when my son was young," Susan offered. "I loved it. It was really wonderful, but then my son only wanted homemade croissants for breakfast after that."

Craig let out a low laugh, trying to envision anyone ever caring enough about his palate to bake for him. Over the tiny covered tea light that flickered in front of them, Craig gazed across the table. He knew they should talk about the offer, but he was determined to get to know Susan Abbot. He decided that the business of the evening could wait.

"So tell me about your life in Tennessee," he began as he sipped his water.

"Well, I actually live in Germantown, which is a suburb of Memphis. But my office is right on the edge of east Memphis and Germantown," Susan said.

"And you sell real estate, as you said in the car?" asked Craig.

"Yes, I've been an agent for about ten years. I mostly sell residential, but I do represent some commercial properties."

Craig studied her as she spoke. She really was lovely, he found himself thinking.

"That sounds very interesting. So how did you decide to become an agent?"

Susan's face gave a small twitch, almost a slight smile.

"It was after my divorce," Susan admitted. "My son attended middle school and I contemplated what I should do. I had been at home with my son for years." Susan paused, sipped water, and continued. "I always enjoyed people, and I found the real estate market fascinating. By becoming an agent, I could do something interesting that gave me flexible time with my son, Ryan."

The waiter noiselessly appeared with a wine bottle. Showing the label, a small amount then went into one of the oversized goblets on the table. Craig tasted it and nodded.

"Very good, sir," the waiter said as he tucked one arm behind his back and poured the burgundy liquid into both glasses.

"So what about you?" Susan asked. "How did you come to Mount Robert and your law practice?"

"I came to town for college about twenty years ago," Craig admitted. "I guess that makes me sound old."

"Not at all," said Susan with a smile. "Remember, I grew up on the campus as a child."

"Well, I came to play baseball, but my shoulder didn't have enough longevity to make it a career beyond college. I always loved history, so law was a natural fit for me."

"I wanted to be a lawyer when I was young," confided Susan with a wisp of nostalgia as she took a sip of her wine.

"You did?" questioned Craig, slightly surprised. "So what made you change your mind?"

Susan dropped her eyes.

"I fell in love my junior year in college and I got married the week after I graduated." she confided. "Neil was in the Air Force—he flew—so we moved often. We lived in five different states, courtesy of the US Air Force. We had our son when we'd been married a year."

Craig nodded. He had represented enough military clients to understand the frequent marching orders.

"And his career took you to Memphis?" Craig asked. He was intrigued to think about everywhere that Susan had lived.

"Yes," Susan said, with a small shake of her head. "Neil accepted a job flying for FedEx when he left the service. Memphis is the headquarters with the huge hub, so that's how we ended up there."

"FedEx is a great company," nodded Craig thoughtfully. "Did he enjoy flying for them?"

"Well, he never had a package that complained." Susan laughed.

Craig felt himself laugh also. Looking across the table, he realized that their conversation seemed to flow effortlessly.

"And your son? Tell me about him," Craig said as he sipped his wine.

Susan's face softened as she thought of Ryan. "He's such a good young man," she gushed. "He's twenty, and studying engineering at Mississippi State."

Craig nodded as he listened. "That sounds great. Engineering is a wonderful field."

"He already had an internship with Nissan," added Susan with a smile. "So I'm really proud of him."

"And is it just your son?" asked Craig.

"Yes," she said slowly. "Ryan is my only one." She took a breath and continued. "I always hoped to have more children, but my husband was not . . ." Her voice trailed off quietly.

"Are you ready to order?" The waiter appeared at Craig's side again. "Allow me to tell you about the specials tonight." From his small note pad, the dark-haired man read a list of choices, each one a contemporary twist on a traditional dish.

"And for the lady?" the server asked.

"I'll have the petite fillet," said Susan.

"Make that two," added Craig. "And a small Caesar salad to start." Craig looked at Susan questioningly.

"Yes, a small Caesar for me, also."

"Perfect. I'll get your order in, and I'll be back with some bread." The waiter seemed to evaporate into the kitchen as Craig smiled at Susan.

"So where were we?" he asked.

"You need to tell me about your family," Susan said.

"I have a son also," Craig began as he sipped his wine. "He's ten, almost eleven. He loves baseball, which is lots of fun for me. He lives with his mother, but I have him most weekends, which works well because my ex-wife is a nurse. She works the weekend shifts, so we can both work and both be involved with our son."

"That's wonderful," said Susan.

"And he's in Mount Robert?" she asked.

"He and his mother live about twenty minutes outside of town," Craig told her. "They have land that was in my ex-wife's family."

Susan nodded.

"Your salads," the waiter said with flourish as he appeared and placed the chilled plates in front of them. A second server appeared from behind with bread in a large basket that hung from his arm by wicker handles. He placed a roll on each bread plate with small silver tongs.

"Thank you," Susan replied.

They both picked up their forks and began to enjoy the crisp tanginess of the shaved parmesan cheese mixed with the lightly dressed romaine lettuce.

"So, I reviewed the offer with my family," Susan began.

Craig took a long sip from his wine glass as his eyes focused on Susan. He didn't want to interrupt or rush her words.

"Craig," Susan began, "I did as you suggested. We had a family meeting about the offer. It's certainly worth consideration, but we're going to decline."

"I see," Craig answered slowly.

"I know the college will close, and the future of the town is uncertain, but if we take the offer, my family faces being shortchanged."

"It's a cash offer," said Craig, feeling the need to remind her of the benefits. "There would be no need to do anything more to the house. It takes the uncertainty out of selling all the property."

"Yes, and that seems tempting," agreed Susan. "But one hundred thousand dollars is not enough. The house alone appraises at twice, maybe three times that amount, not to mention the value of the several acres of land that adjoin the college. The fossils that are still in the house also have value."

Craig nodded. He understood, but he felt he must say more. A good attorney should always want their clients to fully appreciate the deal before them.

"Susan," he began. "It really is an uncertain time. When the school closes, property values are likely to plummet. You understand this as a real estate agent. I say this so that you and your family won't have any regrets."

Susan gave Craig a rueful smile.

"I appreciate your objectivity," said Susan. "And I would say the same thing to any client of mine in the Memphis area, really, I would. But for us, it's so much more complicated."

Craig said nothing more. He waited for her to continue.

Susan took a big breath and exhaled, seeming to make a decision.

"Whatever settlement we get, we'll first have to pay two attorney fees, both for Peter and you," she said. "My mother also has cancer," Susan continued, her voice softening. "She uses an experimental treatment that's probably her only hope for remission. When the college closes, the insurance my parents currently have will end. They need to budget much more money to cover her care."

Susan reached for her wine, sipped, and continued. "And while this settlement is really for Dory, she's been living with my parents for almost two years. Her health insurance, her car payments and insurance, and even her cell phone have been taken care of by my father and mother. The small amount of cash my aunt left behind paid for her funeral and the annual taxes on the house. Everything else for Dory has been done by my parents. While they would never want to take Dory's money, they should be reimbursed—at least in part—for what they've spent." Susan stopped and took a drink from her water glass. "And then there's Dory," she added. "She lives with my parents, and she still needs an education. With the college gone, that means she'll no longer have a family tuition discount, like she had at Mount Robert."

Susan stopped again.

"I understand," Craig said quietly.

"When the college closes, my father's research grant will end. He only has a small pension. My mother never had tenure, so her retirement is only a modest IRA. The three of them—my father, my mother, and Dory—will live on the pension, social security, and the estate settlement of my aunt for the rest of their lives."

Craig nodded. This was not a surprise. He had surmised that the family would be pressed for money, more for the future than any immediate need.

The waiter approached with their plates. The aroma of butter sauces and herbs arose from the deconstructed dishes before them.

Susan and Craig each picked up a fork and savored the first entree bites. After a few moments of quiet, Susan looked directly at Craig.

"I'm sorry about the offer. I hope you can understand."

"Family is important," Craig agreed. "You have to do what you think is best for everyone. In the end, you're all in it together."

CHAPTER 29

Dory rolled Dan over and straddled him with one continuous movement. She arched her back, her dark hair tumbling in her face, sticking to her red lipstick. Dan moaned. They were grinding, pumping a continuous rhythm. The two of them moved as one, with hips and flesh intertwined as the bed rocked against the beige wall. Dory was on fire.

He reached for her firm breasts as Dory sat up and raised her hands above her head. She danced as she could feel ever part of him inside her. As she lowered herself onto his chest, she could see his sweat. His heart thumped and his breathing intensified. They were groaning in climax.

"Yes! Yes!" Dory called out.

With a final inaudible cry from Dan, she rolled off him and onto the damp sheets beside him. The room remained silent except for their labored breathing. Dan made low noises.

"Good God, Dory," he managed to say between ragged gasps. "You're amazing."

Dory let a coy smile spread across her face. Being close to Dan felt wonderful, so right in every way. And blowing his mind with great sex was the icing on the cake.

"You're not so bad yourself."

"I'm so glad," muttered Dan, as his breathing started to return to normal. "I'm so glad that I had the night off, and so did you."

Dory stared at the ceiling, trying to steady her own racing heart. Dan was right, and she knew it. Having a night away from the inn and the animal shelter gave them the time they needed.

As her muscles began to relax, she rolled onto her side away from him. She started fumbling in the purse she'd left on the floor next to the bed. She wanted a cigarette. She was going to quit, she had already decided, but not right now. Great sex made the craving to smoke more compelling than ever.

"I need this," Dory replied out of the side of her mouth as her lips pursed the smooth white roll of tobacco. "Usually I would go outside, but not now, you know. You're just going to have to smell it."

Dory lit her Marlboro, taking a deep drag, before she sighed. Punching the two pillows on her side of the bed, she flopped back and pulled the rumpled covers across her bare thighs.

This was good, really good, between them. Dory's thoughts ran like lightening as she stretched out in bed. She had been realizing a lot of things about the two of them lately. Not one person in her life could match Dan. Of course, she'd dated plenty of boyfriends in her past, and she certainly hadn't been a virgin when he'd asked her out six months ago. After all, she was twenty-one.

But most of her other "dates" had involved a steady string of what turned out to be inevitable losers. All of the men she had ever been with were young, restless, and more than anything, immature. Not a one of them had finished any kind of schooling, and most of them enjoyed smoking pot daily.

All those other people made Dory appreciate how differently Dan lived. He was the only guy she ever knew who'd risen above his background. He had grown up fifty miles away from Boone on the wrong side of the tracks. Living in a mobile home with his mother, there had never been a dad in the picture. In that way, life without a father, both he and Dory were identical.

He'd actually told her that his mom didn't know who his father really was. It could have been a coin toss between several characters. And yet his mother had loved him, really loved him. She'd taken good care of him as he'd grown up, and pushed him to find his passion. After high school, he won a scholarship to a culinary institute in Charlotte.

Dan confided to Dory that while he liked the kitchen work in cooking school, he hated the big city. The traffic and the endless crowds left him feeling drained. When he finished the program, he desperately wanted to get back to the mountains. He said that being back in the Appalachian hills felt like coming home, like connecting to a part of his blood. So he was thrilled when he became the chef at the inn in Mount Robert. It was a perfect fit, he'd told her. In addition to complete creative license in the kitchen, he loved being in the western part of the state again. He and Dory had met each other within a few months of his arrival in town.

They both said their relationship was really good. It felt right, for each of them. As she puffed on her cigarette, Dory came to the conclusion that her own mother would have liked Dan, had she lived to meet him.

Julia Upton and her daughter had often had heated arguments, almost coming to blows on more than one occasion, because of Dory's boyfriends. But Dory smiled as she tapped her ash into the mug on the bedside table. Her mother would have approved of Dan; she was sure of it.

"I have to pee," Dory said as she glanced over at Dan. His eyes were shut in relaxed sleep.

She got out of bed and grabbed an old T-shirt from the chair by the widow. Dory could tell that his breathing was deep now, slow and steady as he rested on his back.

In the bathroom, she turned on the light and glanced in the mirror. Smudged mascara made her eyes look like those of a raccoon. She surveyed her surroundings. Urine spotted the floor, and bottles lined the small sink that practically begged for a cleaning. Dory shook her head. He was a typical guy. Dan's kitchen might always be spotless, but his bathroom looked like a mess.

When she returned to the bedroom, Dan rolled onto his side, facing the wall.

"Scratch my back," he muttered.

"What do I get if I do?"

"Scratch my back for a few minutes and I'll get up and cook."

Dory lifted the sea of covers and climbed back in bed, still wearing the T-shirt. No more sex for the moment. Now she could relax. Rubbing his back a bit meant that she could have another cigarette, and then a gourmet meal. It was a no-brainer.

As her nails drifted across the expanse of his slightly olive skin, she took a puff of her second Marlboro and let herself unwind. Her legs and lower back felt heavy, finally unknotting from her interlude with Dan, as well as all the stress of the last few weeks.

Things really were a mess right now, she thought with her eyes shut halfway. Dory ached from never knowing her own father, and then she'd suddenly lost her mother two years ago. Nothing had prepared her for the crash.

Sometimes, when she was absolutely alone, she would drive to the place where her mother had lost control of her car. A winding stretch of old mountain road, Julia Upton had not been the first fatality on the isolated hairpin curve. For the longest time, Dory refused to even drive on the county road where her mother had lost her life. Only after her boyfriend at the time had given her some pot and let her smoke it while he drove the fateful course, had Dory actually arrived at the sight of the crash. When she'd gotten there, she'd cried without stopping.

Her boyfriend had slung his arm over her shoulders and said, "Yeah, man, it sucks."

Dory became furious. All the anger that she felt about her mother simmered just underneath the surface as she looked at her boyfriend with his scrawny shrugging shoulders in his AC/DC T-shirt. He should have been the one person who understood Dory, but he was too stupid and insensitive.

When she got back in his beat up old truck, Dory took his bag of weed from the glove compartment and slipped it into her purse before he could open his door and start the engine. After dropping her at home, she deleted his number from her cell phone. She never went out with him again.

That was the one thing that made Dan so unique, Dory thought as she rubbed her fingertips against his back. Certainly, his age made him more mature than her other boyfriends, but he also proved to be someone Dory could trust. He was the first person she had come to depend on, to really need. She let him into her life, and it had been such a long time since she'd done that with anyone.

As she settled under the warm rumpled covers of his bed, she knew that she could talk to Dan about anything. He was probably the first person to really listen to her since her mother had died. He would face her, completely silent, hearing everything and anything she had to say. She even tested him once to see if he had a limit with her, a place he would not go.

"My cramps are a bitch," Dory said when she came over to his condo one day.

Dan said nothing. He simply got up and went to the bathroom. Dory heard water running. She wondered if that was her clue to leave. Instead, Dan emerged carrying a pink hot water bottle. He gently placed it on her lower abdomen and reached his other hand around her lower back to start a massage.

Dory finished the end of her cigarette and opened her eyes fully. She stamped out the butt in a coffee mug that rested on the nightstand. *Yes, Dan,* she concluded to herself, *you're a keeper.*

As he started to stir, Dory gave him a gentle nudge.

"Hey," she said. "How about that gourmet food? I'm starving."

With a long stretch, Dan rose to his elbows. He swung his feet to the floor. Dory loved his tall, muscular frame. Dan used his body as a chef. Whatever extra calories he ate in the kitchen, he burned off with constant activity.

"I'm thinking it's time to have breakfast for dinner," Dan spoke, pondering his culinary options. "How about omelets, a rustic potato hash, maybe some fried apples?"

Dory could feel her mouthwatering. She was hungry, and she knew it would be divine.

"Sold," she answered.

Dan slipped on a pair of long basketball shorts and a dry-fit shirt that hung on the doorknob of his closet. With his feet in his beloved Crocs, he headed out of the bedroom.

"Come down when you're ready," he said over his shoulder to Dory. "I have some good wine you'll enjoy while I cook."

Now Dory sat up and studied the task at hand. She had to find all her clothes left scattered across Dan's bedroom like a road map of their earlier passion. As she reached out to put on her panties and shirt, the familiar banging of kitchen pans filled her ears.

Within fifteen minutes, Dory sat perched on a high stool at the bar that framed the small kitchen. She watched Dan cook and held a glass of crisp, light pinot grigio. They didn't talk now, and Dory realized that they didn't need to. Sipping wine and staring into the pale yellow liquid, she knew that she was falling for Dan. It was odd, Dory thought. She wasn't scared like she'd imagined. She only felt happy.

As Dan plated the beautiful omelets, Dory moved to the bistro table that took up the small dining area of the condominium. Joey, the one-eyed cat that Dory had begged Dan to take from the shelter, awoke from his nap on the sofa. He jumped down from his spot and came over to the table. His short black fur rubbed warmly against her leg. He could obviously smell the food, and hoped that his dinner might be next. Dory instinctively stroked his head as he purred.

With a small flourish that made her laugh, Dan delivered the plates onto the table with a bow. As they savored the rosemary potatoes and steaming omelets, Dory's mind wandered to all the things that had happened in the past week.

"So, you never really said what you thought about what I told you. You know, about Peter Elliott," Dory began.

"Yeah," Dan replied, forking his omelet, cheese running onto the plate. "I've been thinking about that."

"So, what do you think? I mean, his friends, the ones you saw at the inn, are from Charlotte, some big-time lawyers. And then some guy the internet says is a pharmaceutical startup CEO. What do you think it means?"

Dan took a sip of his wine.

"Babe," replied Dan slowly. "I'm honestly not sure what it means."

"But don't you think it's odd?" asked Dory as she studied her potatoes on her fork. "He shows up in town, entertaining people from all over the state."

Dan silently moved his food around on his plate. His expression told Dory he was somewhere else.

"What?" Dory asked him.

Dan looked up from his eggs. "We need to talk."

Dory meant his eyes. Her stomach gave a slight lurch. "Okay," she muttered.

"Dory," he began as he held her eyes. "I don't know what your lawyer Elliott is doing, or not doing. I know I'm not an attorney or anything, but it seems to me he's never really done much for your family, and I'm sorry about that. It really hasn't been very fair for you." His words had taken on a softer edge. "But there's something else we need to talk about," Dan continued.

Dory could feel heat on her face. As she stared at him, she could taste vomit in the back of her throat.

"Dory," Dan started again. "The town is really in a mess. Ever since the college said it was closing, there's been a sense of panic all over the place. People don't know what's coming next, if anything. I've been meeting with

George, who owns the inn, and he doesn't know what the future of the town will hold. He's not sure if the inn itself, or even the restaurant, will survive."

Dory could feel herself nodding, sensing there was more to come.

"I wanted to talk to you about me putting out feelers to some restaurants in Asheville," Dan said.

"Asheville?" Dory asked. She tried to follow what he said as she watched him pick up his wine glass.

Yes," he nodded slightly as he took a quick sip. "I don't really want to look for another job. I love what I've been doing. George and I work well together." He set his wine glass down. "I think both of us wanted the inn at Mount Robert to someday be written up in publications all across the state, maybe even in *Food and Wine* magazine." There was a slight longing in his voice. "But Dory," Dan continued as he looked at her, "I don't want to have a gap in employment. I think it's best if I at least look for other opportunities."

"But I don't want you to go somewhere else," Dory said. Her voice sounded small, almost immature, in her ears.

"I know," agreed Dan. "And I don't want to go anywhere else, either. But I think I should be prepared. And I didn't want to do anything until I talked to you." He smiled at her.

Dory felt herself relax slightly. He was asking her permission.

"I want a future with you," Dan said. He seemed resolute, solid in his intent. "I just feel that we should be on the same page. I think that's important, that we always talk about everything."

Dory smiled. *So this is what it feels like,* she thought, *to be together—really together.*

"I want that, too," Dory agreed. "I want a future with you."

Dan put his napkin beside his plate. He touched her hand. "I love you, Dory," Dan said.

Dory felt her breath catch. It wasn't the first time he had said the words; they talked like that in bed to each other. But things always happened in the heat of the moment. Now just the two of them sat at the table in his condominium.

Dan was so sure, so intent. It suddenly reminded Dory of the way he cooked. Add flour, add milk, and I love you, Dory.

"I love you, too," said Dory with a smile. She moved towards him and brushed her lips across his.

Dan smiled and rose from the table.

"I have fried apples that should be about ready," he offered. He began to clear away the plates. "I'll serve you, ma'am," he said, in his best French accent.

Dory smiled. From his spot by the stove, Dan stirred the fruit that perfumed the kitchen. He looked over his shoulder at Dory.

"I didn't mean to cut you off earlier," he said. "You know, about Peter Elliott and everything."

Dory took a sip of her wine. *How could it be,* she wondered, *that life is so good with Dan, and so unsettled in so many other ways?*

"I just don't know what to think," Dory said contemplatively. "I just don't know what to make of him. Our family just needs all of this settled."

"It sounds to me like these guys might want to do some sort of business in Mount Robert."

"You're probably right," Dory replied. After another sip of her wine, she added, "He just ticks me off."

As she reached down to pet the cat, she remembered the many dinnertime conversations with her aunt and uncle. David Upton had never ceased to complain about the cavalier attitude Peter displayed towards the college, its budget, and enrollment. Lately, the rejected offer on the estate only added increased tension to her family.

"You know, I told you that Susan went to Craig Cartwright, the lawyer she hired, and said we wouldn't take the initial cash offer," Dory added from the table, shifting the conversation back to something that they had talked about last week.

Dan nodded.

"Susan said that maybe if we wait, the offer would be increased, especially since we have a lawyer working on our behalf," Dory said.

The presiding sentiment of the senior Upton family members involved waiting for a better offer, but as Dory spoke from her seat now, the words did not sound convincing, or even likely.

Dan remained silent. Only the sound of a pan moving back and forth on the stove filled the kitchen.

"What?" Dory asked.

"I don't know, babe," Dan responded slowly. "Your family has to do what they think they should, but the town is in chaos. Nobody knows what's coming next."

"You think we should have taken the offer?" Dory asked him.

"Not my call," Dan said looking over his shoulder at her. "Your family has to do what they think they should."

"You know, it's mostly my money," Dory said as if she was reminding him. "I mean, I have to pay the lawyers and all, but most of the cash is mine." For a moment, she thought about what the settlement could mean for both of them. "It's money for us," she added.

"I know," said Dan in agreement. "But I can do pretty well as a chef. I think your family has to do what they think is best."

Dory felt her shoulders relax as she sipped her wine. She could always count on Dan to be a good guy.

"Maybe these men with Peter Elliott want those warehouses out by the shelter as a place for some sort of new venture," Dan offered as he stirred that apples that were beginning to stick to the pan. "Didn't you say that you saw Elliott out that way? Maybe they want to get into growing medical marijuana or something." Dan laughed. "The locals would love it—they would line up around the square for a chance to get paid for that kind of job."

Dory laughed at the idea, but then said thoughtfully, "But if they had a big plan for the Mount Robert, why not announce it?"

Dan reached for two square white plates in his cabinet and shook his head. "I don't know, babe. It seems weird to me. I mean, if I had big news for the town, I would put it out there like a big announcement."

Dory went silent. She had been thinking about this all week.

"Every day I go into the inn, I see him," Dan added as he began to serve the cinnamon apples. "I always find Elliott coming out of the coffee shop on the square with some police officer or politician. It's like he's running for office, or something."

Dan brought the plates to the table, the steam rising from the fruit like a smoke signal.

"I know all of this bothers you," he said as he sat down next to her. "I just don't know what you can do about him, or if his choice of companions really changed anything for your family." He tasted the apples and nodded his approval. "But for what it is worth, I think he's a jerk, too."

Dory laughed, but as she picked up a spoon, the smile faded from her face. She stared into her dwindling wine glass. Maybe Dan was right. Maybe none of these facts really mattered. The information about Peter Elliott made sense but only if she forced it. The pieces went together, in a way, but something was missing.

Peter Elliott, Dory thought. He was at the root of every problem her family had faced since her mother's death. She slowly felt her skin tingle, ever so slightly. Her sixth sense kicked in again as she sat there. Peter Elliott. What was he hiding?

But as she tasted the apples, she pushed everything out of her mind. She looked up at Dan and smiled. He was such a wonderful man, and now he would have to begin looking for another job. He needed her support. Dory savored the subtle spice on the fruit and nodded. She intended to focus on what was right in front of her.

CHAPTER 30

———————

Craig Cartwright had been at his desk for about fifteen minutes, when he heard the front door open, and felt the cold February wind blow into his office. He glanced at the clock on his computer. It was early, just after eight. His receptionist arrived at nine. He looked up from the files on his desk expecting to see one of his clients.

"Craig," Peter Elliott's greeting broke the silence. He took long strides into the small business.

"Peter," Craig answered unexpectedly. "This is a surprise. To what do I owe the pleasure?" He stood and offered a hand.

Peter moved in the front of Craig and returned the handshake with an even firmer grip of his palm. He quickly settled into one of the seats positioned in front of the desk.

Years ago, Craig had learned the value of armless chairs for his office. The simple seating forced his clients to face him during meetings, forgoing the distraction of nervous hands on furniture. Watching how people used their bodies during a meeting proved to be a good gauge of their honesty.

"Well, I wanted to come by, hoping to catch you in this morning, and talk about one of your clients," Peter began. "I hope I'm not keeping you from court."

Craig noticed that Peter was surprisingly comfortable as he sat down and placed a non-descript white bag on the carpet by his foot.

Reaching for a pen and his legal pad, Craig gave a polite smile. His visitor was not a complete surprise. After his dinner with Susan, he had placed a call to Peter, leaving a purposefully vague message indicating the two of them should speak.

"Not at all," responded Craig. "I left you a message," he added, reclining slightly in his leather chair to get a better view of the man in front of him.

"I came by to see what the Upton family had to say about the offer," Peter said, looking him squarely in the eye.

By the force of Peter's words, Craig sensed a possible hint of resentment. He assumed that Susan's decision to hire an attorney to represent the interests of the family irritated Peter.

"I did take your anonymous offer to Susan Abbot. She reviewed the details with her family, and we've spoken. You're aware she's acting on behalf of her parents and niece?"

"Yes, I've known Susan for years," answered Peter smoothly. "Her family has been in Mount Robert for decades. I've been the attorney for every member of the Upton family. I even knew her uncle before he died in his accident during one of his digs."

"Well, unfortunately, Susan and her family have declined your offer." Craig decided it was best to get to the point. He had a feeling that Peter Elliott could play the name game all morning.

Peter's eyes darkened, and he made a slight frown that creased his eyebrows and forehead. "You did explain that it's a cash offer?" questioned Peter with an undertone of annoyance. He sat motionless and stared directly at the man before him.

"Yes," assured Craig. "I gave them the offer in its entirety. They did discuss everything, and I believe they did consider all aspects of the proposal, but they've chosen to decline."

"This is surprising to me," said Peter curtly. He picked a speck of imaginary lint from the front of his pants. Lifting his eyes back to Craig, he continued. "Did you explain that it was in their best interest to take the offer? That the future of property, especially with the closing of the college, is highly uncertain?" His words were clipped as he spoke, and Craig detected anger.

"Yes, I can assure you that we covered all the details of the offer. And while they understand that the potential buyer made a full and legitimate bid, they're going to decline at this time," stated Craig again.

This was as much information as he intended to give Peter. Susan's explanations for her decision fell under attorney-client privilege. Besides, Craig had a gut-level feeling that a simple rejection might bring an increased offer to the table.

Peter carefully eyed Craig. The meeting stalled into a silent standoff as he seemed to weigh his options before speaking.

"Craig, I'm extremely busy right now, as are you, I'm sure. I've been doing my best to facilitate those involved with closing the college, as well as trying to finish any remaining cases before this town changes forever."

Craig nodded, but said nothing, letting Peter direct the negotiations.

"What do you intend to do after the college closes and your client base has left town?" Peter asked.

The question surprised Craig. Was he asking about his personal plans for his law practice? What did the future of his own business have to do with the Upton case? Craig studied the figure before him, unsure where Peter was going with his question.

"Craig," Peter continued, "I intend to help this community through this transition. After the college closes, it will be a different landscape for all of us. I'm thinking and focusing on the future these days."

Craig studied Peter intently now. Where was this going? How did this relate to Susan Abbot and her family?

Even as he felt uncertain about the conversation, Craig could feel his jaw tighten ever so slightly. The pit of his stomach began to twist. It was true. Ever since the college had announced the pending closure, Craig had known that after the flurry of spring client activity, his business would face an inevitably slowdown, if not stoppage. He would have to practice law somewhere in order to provide for his son. His own future was less clear by the day.

"Well, right now, I'm incredibly busy," Craig bluffed, forcing a smile and waving his hand towards the stacks of legal folders that lined his desk.

Peter nodded and spoke slowly. He leaned closer to Craig's desk now. "I ask all this because I'm involved with many clients who will be affected, in all sorts of ways, by the closing of the college. What comes next for the campus and all the assets? Most likely, the future will be orchestrated by people outside of Mount Robert."

Craig sensed that something was about to be offered. He could feel it. He folded his hands now, noticing that his palms were ever so damp.

"Craig, I hope to be of service to people who will create great change for this town. I also believe that the closing of the college can be a new beginning—a phoenix rising, if you will. This change has the potential to propel Mount Robert into a new era. I realize that it sounds like a big vision, and it is. I need people with vision, people like you, who might be interested in this journey forward."

Peter sat back in his chair now. He let the words hang in the air between them.

"And how would I—how did you say it? —propel Mount Robert into a new vision exactly?" Craig was confused but he held his expression purposefully blank. How was a future for the town going to affect the case they had started to discuss?

"Come work for me," answered Peter Elliott.

Craig was stunned. He wasn't sure he'd heard correctly.

"What?" asked Craig.

Come and work for me," Peter said again, aiming the pointed words slower.

The last thing Craig Cartwright ever expected was a job offer from Peter Elliott. He sat quietly and stared, trying to make sense of the idea.

Peter smiled. "I need someone here in Mount Robert I can trust. I have clients who may require more of my time away from this town as I help to create a new future. I need someone I can depend on moving forward, someone I can partner with as things change."

Craig broke his intense gaze with Peter. He leaned back in his chair and swiveled his seat as the air left his lungs. What an absolutely surreal morning.

"And you're looking for a partner?" Craig asked slowly as he studied Peter.

"Yes," Peter answered, his dark eyes locked on Craig.

"And you came here to ask me this?"

"Yes."

"So you didn't just stop by to confer about Susan Abbot and her family? About the offer that you extended?"

Peter smiled. There was an all-knowing look in his eyes. Craig was suddenly aware that Peter looked exactly like a chess player before he called check mate and finished off his opponent to win the game.

"Craig," he began slowly. "As I said, I'm a busy man. I try my best to serve everyone, to multitask, as you might say. My job offer to you is sincere. I could use—and value—your help. I believe this type of future could be in your best interest, as well."

There was silence again in the room between them. Peter had a knowing upturn of his lips as he let the words swirl in Craig's head.

Peter leaned closer to the desk again and cleared his throat to continue. "Julia Upton's land, and thus home, adjoin the school property. I need the college closed, and all land as part of the college legally disposed of ownership. I've made a fair offer to the Upton family."

Craig sat absolutely still now. He felt heavy in his chair, as if he couldn't turn away, even if he wanted to. He sensed where this was going, but he couldn't help but listen.

"Make the offer—the exact same offer—to the family again. And when they've signed—and I'm sure you can get them to sign—the deal will be done. You'll then no longer be their attorney." Peter stopped speaking. His words filled the space between them with layered implications.

Craig said nothing, unsure how to respond.

Peter continued. "At that point, you can come and work for me. My offer to you is the same one I offered to the Upton family. I'll pay you one hundred thousand dollars on your first day with me. It will represent half of your annual salary."

So there it was. Clean. Legal. Out on the table between them. It was unlike any proposition that Craig had ever received. The money tantalized him, but he couldn't help but feel the words and the offer had slithered into the room like a snake.

"Think about it. You could have a valuable place in the future of this town. Doors can open for you, Craig, all sorts of doors." Peter took a quick glance around the office and smiled. "Both professional and personal ones."

Craig remained silent. He felt motionless in his seat.

"Oh, I almost forgot." Peter stood to leave, then bent down to retrieve the bag he had placed on the floor. "This is a token for you, my friend." Peter put the gift on Craig's desk.

The top of the bag was open, revealing the weight of the object within the edges. Craig willed his hand to stop the tremble in his fingers. He reached between the white paper layers and felt a smooth object, hard, like glass. He eased it out of the wrapping.

"It's Pappy Van Winkle." Peter smiled.

Craig stared in open amazement at the amber bottle. The Kentucky bourbon was the most coveted in the country. He had only tasted Pappy once, and had found it memorable beyond measure. He felt his mouth go slack in disbelief.

"This is just a foretaste of what's to come," Peter said charmingly as he headed towards the door. He looked over his shoulder at Craig. "Remember that. The future can belong to us."

CHAPTER 31

"I put birdseed out last evening, but you would never know it," announced David Upton, stepping into the kitchen from his backyard in the early morning light. "Today may be the first of March, but spring is certainly not in sight."

He shed his old worn canvas coat by the back door. The bucket of birdseed dropped into the corner with a small thump.

The morning dawned cold and drizzly. As he moved to the kitchen sink and washed his damp, earth-covered hands, the air from the back door felt chilled and raw, as if winter refused to exit the mountains of North Carolina.

Around the kitchen table sat Susan and her mother. They gathered together, warmed by the old wall oven that heated the room and the steam that arose from the coffee pot.

"I have your favorite in the oven," Susan said to her father as he draped the towel he used over the range handle. "It's apple pan dowdy."

Early that morning, while her father was still outside, Susan had mixed the old family recipe and placed the batter into the hot oven. The coffeemaker on the counter filled the room with the familiar roasted smell of morning, which mingled together with the baking.

Dory had yet to emerge from her room. She'd arrived home late last night. Susan knew that she'd worked the evening shift, and had probably spent time with Dan in the wee hours of the morning.

Everyone agreed that Dory needed to join the family for the scheduled meeting. She could sleep for now, but someone would have to wake her when Craig Cartwright arrived.

Sylvia Upton sat quietly at the table sipping tea. Coffee no longer appealed to her. She wore a green fleece jogging suit with a paisley scarf around her head. The clothes that once fit her petite frame now hung from her bony shoulders and hips as if they mocked her past health.

"What time is Craig Cartwright coming by?" Susan's mother asked.

"He said he'd be here by ten," replied Susan. "He didn't want to come by too early on a Saturday."

"Do you think he has another offer?" her father asked, a hopeful look in his eyes. "Did he say any more about why he wanted to meet?"

"He really didn't say," responded Susan. "He only called me at the end of the week, and said we all needed to talk. I told him that Saturday worked well for us due to Mom's appointments in Asheville, and your class schedule before spring break."

A dull buzzing sound resembling an A-flat drifted from the hall. The ringer on the door bell had long ago ceased to chime, a casualty of the years in their older home. Susan moved to the foyer while Toby emerged from the family room to follow at her heels. Her father headed down the hall to wake Dory.

Susan opened the door and caught Craig Cartwright's eye. She immediately thought that he seemed ever so slightly nervous, but then they both smiled. Stepping inside, he unzipped his coat in the warmth of the house.

"This is Toby," Susan told Craig as she closed the front door behind him. The shaggy dog sniffed the newcomer's pant leg as Craig reached down to pat his head.

"We are back in the kitchen. I hope that's okay with you, it just seemed like a good place to meet and talk," Susan said as she led Craig toward the back part of the old house.

The dog, satisfied that he had surveyed the character of the visitor, followed the pair down the hall. At the family room, he departed in order to reclaim his oversized dog bed.

"The kitchen is fine. I'm sorry I've come to your home so early," offered Craig as he followed her.

"No, don't be silly. This worked well for us. I mean, Mom has been with me most days in Asheville, and Dad's teaching calendar is crazy until spring break."

Susan's parents rose as Craig entered the kitchen. He nodded a greeting to them.

"Dr. and Mrs. Upton," Craig said, extending his hand.

Focusing on Sylvia Upton, he smiled, "I never had the pleasure of taking one of your history classes at Mount Robert College, but I always wanted to be one of your students."

"Did you like history?" she asked him.

"I was a history and political science major," he admitted. "But the baseball field dictated my class schedule."

"And this is Dory," introduced Susan, as a yawning, hastily dressed young woman stood in the doorway. She had on black spandex leggings and a Mount Robert sweatshirt. Her chocolate-brown hair rested on top of her head in a greasy topknot.

Craig shook Dory's hand.

"Let's sit down," Susan offered. She showed Craig to a chair around the circular table. He unzipped his coat and spread it over the back of his seat. Susan opened the oven and pulled out a steaming apple puff cake. Instinctively, everyone turned to look at the square container as Susan quickly cut pieces that slid out of the hot greased pan. She placed them on small, stacked floral plates, and poured cups of coffee, then began ferrying the food to the table.

"Thank you," said Craig as Susan handed him a plate of cake and a mug of dark coffee.

Dory said nothing. She slumped in a chair, with one of her knees drawn up to her chest. Susan gave her a cup of coffee, cake, and a fork.

"Cream and sugar are on the table," Susan directed to everyone. Dory began to fill her mug with cream and sugar, stirring with her fork before Susan could hand her a spoon.

"This is wonderful," said Craig as he enjoyed a bite of the fluffy browned coffee cake. It was warm and sweet. He took another delicious bite, and pushed the plate aside to talk.

Susan's father sat silently as he studied the man in front of him. His concern about the estate radiated in his wary eyes.

"Tell us what you have for us, Mr. Cartwright," said Dr. Upton.

"Please, call me Craig," he responded as he opened a beige folder and set a thin stack of papers before the family.

"What I have for you all is an offer. The buyer is still anonymous."

He raised his eyes and surveyed the hope and concern mixed across their faces. Craig took a sip of coffee, swallowing the bitter hot beverage before he continued.

"The Peter Elliott firm offers you cash for the house and land, the same amount that he previously presented to you." Craig took a breath and exhaled.

"I don't understand," said Susan's father. "We've already declined that offer." There was an edge in his voice, a pointed jab of his words.

"I'm aware that you initially declined the offer. I think I understand how you feel. However, the proposal has been made again, and I needed to bring it to you and discuss the matter."

Susan's mother bounced worried glances off everyone's faces. The telepathy of her expression gave fuel to the rest of the family.

"Craig," Susan began, concern etched over the forehead. "We discussed this at dinner. One hundred thousand dollars is too low. My aunt's home easily values at twice that, or even three times that amount. The lot alone measures close to two acres, not to mention the fossils."

There was silence in the kitchen as Susan continued. "My father will be retiring; my parents will have new insurance costs. Dory still needs an education." Her voice sounded flat and insistent in her own ears.

"I'm aware of your situation and your expectations for the settlement," responded Craig, more quietly now. "However, this is the offer on the table, and I think the cash is worthy of your consideration again."

"Did you counter?" asked David Upton, his brown eyes smoldering and his jaw muscles working in anger.

"I did meet with Peter Elliott," answered Craig.

"This is the offer presented. I need to remind you that it's a cash sale. Also, what will happen to land and real estate after the college closes, remains unclear. I think you must consider that, as well."

Dory had been silent through the entire meeting. She sipped her coffee and quietly studied Craig Cartwright's face.

"This is bullshit," Dory said loudly as she smacked her cup down on the wooden table. Beige coffee sloshed out of her mug and spilled on the pine surface. All eyes turned to look at her.

"Susan hired you to represent us," Dory spit out the words as her caramel eyes flashed in fire. "She said you were the best, that you fought for the underdog, for people like us. This offer is bullshit. It undervalues everything we have."

"I understand how you feel," began Craig.

"You don't understand shit," retorted Dory, her voice rising louder with each word. "I lost my parents already, and now I'll have almost nothing to move forward. That's almost nothing after we pay you and Peter Elliott." She tossed her words at Craig like javelins. "My aunt and uncle will have almost nothing for their future, as well, thanks to you!"

Her words hung in the air. The atmosphere of the kitchen seemed to crackle with emotion. Craig looked at each of them.

"Craig, this was not what we expected, nor what we hoped for," Susan said, trying to sound calm. She looked at him with disappointment.

Dory placed her legs on the floor and shoved her chair back from the table.

"I've heard enough," she said, her voice angry and irritated as she stood. "You did nothing for us. You're just like Peter Elliott. You lawyers are all the same—out for yourselves. Anything for a buck. You're just a shithead. Maybe the next time you bring an offer to someone, you'll remember to bring your conscience!"

She stormed out of the kitchen, her furious steps followed by a slam of her bedroom door.

"I'm sorry for Dory," began Susan's mother. Her voice sounded weary, even as her tone conveyed disdain for their visitor.

Craig quickly held up his hand and shook his head. "I completely understand. I know this is not what you wanted. I'm sorry."

Susan's father looked at all of them. His dark, stony expression revealed the anger and resignation of a man losing his options. He rose from the table.

"If there's nothing else, I need to get back to work." He grabbed his coat from the hook on the wall and opened the back door of the kitchen. Cold, damp air rushed again into the warm room. The door banged closed as he stomped down the concrete steps and out to the yard.

"I should be going as well." Craig stood to leave. "Don't worry, I can see myself out."

Susan followed behind Craig to open the front door for him.

"Thank you for at least trying to help our family," she told him as she leaned against the old oak entryway. "You did your best, and we appreciate it."

She looked at her feet, her eyelashes sweeping down. "I know that I paid you a deposit, but I do realize that I still owe you for your services."

"Don't worry about that," said Craig softly as he walked onto the front porch. "We can talk about that later."

As Susan closed the door, her hand rested on the smooth surface of the wood as she thought about Dory. Did she always have to be so rude? Shithead, really? Dory's manners were appalling. It made Susan sometimes just want to slap her.

But lowering her hand, Susan felt a lingering doubt beginning to form somewhere in the back of her mind. Surely Craig had done his best for them. Yet, having a meeting to reconsider a clearly rejected proposal seemed like a lack of any real progress on the estate. Susan shook her head. Maybe this really was the best offer in an uncertain market.

Turning around, Susan passed Dory's closed door as she headed back towards the kitchen. The dishes weren't going to do themselves and she could forget receiving any help from the young Miss Upton. Susan put a determined smile on her face. She just needed to believe in Craig. He was on their side, after all. Her family would have to just have some faith.

CHAPTER 32

C raig Cartwright twisted as the bands tightened around his torso. He was miserable. The thin blue sheets of his bed felt like a vise grip around his chest, trapping him like a taunt cocoon. After hours of tossing and turning, he'd only managed to chase sleep.

He rolled over with an angry punch to his pillow. For the fourth straight night, Craig restlessly wandered in and out of dreams. Like the mist on the Carolina mountains in the spring time, his sleep began heavily only to soon evaporate. He found himself constantly awake in the middle of the night, staring at his indigo-ink ceiling.

He tried everything. Yesterday, he had gone without caffeine and then risen early in the morning to jog. The insomnia left him exhausted. The more he thought about not sleeping, the worse it became.

Throwing off the covers, he swung his legs over the side of the bed and pushed himself to a sitting position. His clock glowed a menacing 2:14 a.m. in red digital numbers. He stood up and went into the hallway.

The door to the left of his bedroom opened when he silently turned the knob. A silver moonbeam fell across the floor from the only window in the tiny bedroom. The light illuminated the sleeping huddle of his son, curled up in his twin bed.

The middle of the night—part of Craig's scheduled visitation with his son—should have been relaxing. He and Tyler had been having a great time, but then they always had fun together. Video games and pick-up basketball gave way to to their standard dinner—pizza and tater tots. There was only one rule for their time together: no vegetables.

Craig silently closed the room and stepped back into the hallway. With the round, hollow knob of the door still in his hand, he suddenly became aware of a subconscious thought.

It was something that he had known for years, something that he harbored as a small resentment, indicative of everything that was wrong with his life. As he stood in the hallway, Craig realized how much he really hated the cheap, smooth doors of his small house. What he wouldn't give for something decent looking, more solid and paneled. As he looked around, with his eyes adjusting in the darkness, he knew that he had always hated all the millwork in his house. Everything about the plain trim made him feel like he had never graduated out of a starter home.

Silently, he padded down the hall and turned on a small lamp by the sofa. Moving to the kitchen, he rested both hands on the counter and leaned forward for support. He felt bone-weary. As he stood there with his taut, muscular arms leaning over the lower cabinets, his hands began to grip the edges for support.

Craig glanced out the kitchen window at the blackened sky. He knew what was wrong. It had been wrong for days. Everything in his life had collided together. Peter Elliott had offered him the job of a lifetime. It was more money than Craig could ever make on his own, especially with the college closing and an uncertain client base. The offer was outstanding, and he should have been thrilled.

He considered his own skills too mundane for a man like Peter. Somehow the Elliott Firm always managed to land all the biggest clients in town, while Craig made a living from the local residents and college crowd. The proposition could be a career-building opportunity. Being a partner would allow Craig to give his son everything that he had never had in life, whether it was a bigger house or a better education. It seemed wonderful, but it wasn't. Somehow, it was all wrong.

Craig thought about the job offer continuously. No matter what he'd done the last four days, the idea sat in the back of his mind. At first, he told himself that his nervousness stemmed from the process of switching from his own independent practice to a partnership. But even now, he knew that teamwork was not the problem.

Everything felt too cozy, too much like a back room deal. His worst moments had been with the Upton family. Craig winced as he remembered making the same shortchanged offer twice to Susan. In his office, he didn't even try to propose a counter amount with Peter. For the first time, he'd entangled the client's interest with his own self-preservation. And Craig had ultimately won. Or maybe it was Peter who had won.

Of course, he had advised clients to take lesser deals in the past, but only after Craig had tried everything to arrive at the best possible solution. For him, it had always been about the people he represented, even if the clients ultimately hadn't gotten all they wanted. Now he stood in the dark and realized he was a sell-out. He'd traded his integrity for financial gain.

"What am I doing?" muttered Craig as he stared out the darkened windows.

He left the light on, and crept back down the hall in hushed footsteps. His clock silently read 2:36 a.m. in red demonic numbers that seemed to mock his exhaustion. He got into bed again and rolled on his side.

If only he could rest until the first light of day.

The next three hours involved endless attempts to sleep. Craig would find himself drifting off, only to jerk awake from the same dream. He was always walking in Mount Robert, all over town, only to find that the sidewalk would suddenly disappear as he fell into a dark sinkhole. With each dream, he opened his eyes as he grabbed his sheets and gasped for air.

At five thirty, he sat awake in his bed. Silently, he shuffled into the tiny bathroom that opened like a closet off the master bedroom. Softly, he shut the door. With only the dim overhead light, he marveled at the small distance between his toilet and sink. At that moment, Craig realized that he hated something else: He hated tiny bathrooms.

Within ten minutes, he stood in his kitchen as he filled his coffee pot with water. Early March light, with its periwinkle-blue streaks of color, edged the eastern horizon outside his kitchen window. It was still cold in the mountains, but the chill had a lightness that hinted to a warmer day of sunshine.

Watching his coffee drip into the pot, Craig paced the floor of his kitchen. He knew what he would do; he was just waiting. With the early hour, he needed to be a bit more patient.

Craig poured himself a cup of coffee. With his cup in his hand, he strolled over to the glass door at the back of the house and unlocked the deadbolt. He walked onto the wooden deck. The cold air seemed to clear his head as the steam drifted vertically from his cup, forcing his blue eyes to open fully. He stood outside until the wet chill of the morning chased him back into the warmth of his house.

At six thirty, Craig picked up his cell phone and began to flip through his contacts. Finding the right name, he pressed the number and waited. He glanced at the clock on the microwave oven. Part of him couldn't believe he would call anyone at this hour, and part of him knew he couldn't wait a moment longer.

The number rang three times. A steel-edged voice answered on the end of the line.

"Yes?"

"Roger, it's Craig. Craig Cartwright, from Mount Robert," said Craig steadily into the phone. His heart thudded in his chest, and his palms were sweaty.

"Hey, man! I thought that was you, but I wasn't sure." The man on the other end of the phone brightened at the sound of Craig's voice. "In my line of work, you can't be too careful. You always want to really know who's calling you. To what do I owe the pleasure of your call at this ungodly hour?"

Craig felt himself relax as he listened to the familiar voice. He quickly glanced down the hall, making sure that his son still slept, before he continued.

"Yeah, about the hour, I'm really sorry about that," began Craig. He ran his hand through his thick dirty-blond hair that had curled even tighter during the night.

"Craig, it's all right," assured his friend, his voice tinged with concern. "I was just messing with you. What's going on in your part of the world?"

"Roger, I need some help."

"Well, I figured as much. Why don't you tell me what's happening?"

Craig could hear muffled movement on the other end of the phone.

"Roger, is this a good time? Would you rather I called back later?" Craig asked. There was a delay, followed by a sleepy voice, and then what sounded like a door closing.

"No. I just stepped out of my bedroom. I didn't need to wake my, um, friend," Roger added with a good-natured drop in volume.

Craig shifted his weight from one foot to the other. He felt enormously stupid for calling so early. What had he been thinking? After being alone for so long, he'd forgotten that not everyone made the choice to live as he did, focusing on work and his son, with an occasional workout thrown in for good measure.

Back on the line, Roger asked, "Are you still in Mount Robert?"

"Yes," answered Craig. "I don't know if you've seen the news from up here, or read the papers, but the town is in flux. The college is closing, and the future of everything seems uncertain."

"Yes, I heard about Mount Robert and all the town changes from my aunt who lives in Elkin. Sounds like a bit of a mess," offered Roger.

"Are you still in Fayetteville at Fort Bragg? I should have asked if you're even stateside." questioned Craig.

"I'm always stateside." Roger laughed softly. "At least, that's my official designation. But as you know, we're special forces. We 'play' all over the place. Right now, I'm in Fayetteville—at least for the moment."

Craig listened to his friend and felt another wave of guilt for the phone call. He let the line go momentarily silent.

"What's wrong?" Roger asked quietly. "You called me for a reason. What is it?"

"I need someone and something checked out," answered Craig with a low tone of determination. "It's more than I can do on my own."

"Tell me who and what you need," Roger said, his voice calm and alert.

"I need to know about a lawyer here in town. His name is Peter Elliott. You might remember him from your time up here in school. He's prominent, well connected. I need to know who he's involved with professionally, even personally. I also need to know what you can find out about the sale of the college."

"Are the two connected?" asked Roger.

"My gut says yes, but my facts are scant," confessed Craig. "Everyone, even the press, is very hushed about the sale of the college."

"All right," said Roger with the calmness of a man merely gathering facts.

"Is this information you think you can help me find?" Craig asked.

A soft sound came through the phone, almost a laugh. "Craig, don't worry. I can help you. This is just a matter of knowing the right way to dig. Besides, I owe you one. You were the only lawyer in town who got my sorry youthful butt out of trouble when I was a teenager. You gave me a job doing your surveillance, remember? Because of you, I kept my military scholarship and made it into my unit of the special forces."

"I really appreciate it," confessed Craig, sudden relief washing over him like a cold shower on a hot day.

"You need to give me a few days. I may have to go about this a couple of ways. I'll call you back at this number when I have all my information," assured Roger. "But let me ask you one question—what did this guy do to make you so suspicious of him?"

"He offered me a high-paying job," answered Craig flatly.

"Well, I'll be damned." Roger laughed again, louder this time. "Well, this is one way to know who you're in bed with, so to speak. Don't worry. You're right to trust your gut. After all, what do they say? 'Lie down with dogs, get up with fleas'? If he's clean, then he'll check out clean."

Craig hung up his cell phone and looked out the small kitchen window at the sky coming to life in the morning sun. In a matter of a few days, he would know all there was to know about Peter Elliott.

He grabbed his coffee cup and felt his shoulders start to unknot. Slowly and quietly, so as not to wake his son, he stepped back over to the glass door of the living room. He marveled at the beauty of his hilly backyard. The terrain of the small patch that Craig mowed seem to melt into the steep hillside behind his home. The grass looked wet, freshly washed from the dew. Animals were just beginning to stir. Craig smiled at a squirrel with bulging cheeks that jumped onto the railing of his deck. It reminded him of a story he used to read to his son long ago, a tale of a determined squirrel in the forest.

As he stood there, taking his first deep breath of relaxed air, he hardly noticed the shadow. Later, Craig would know that he never saw it coming. He would only remember the sound, like a punch, from the force of one object impacting another one. Craig only noted the speed, like a lightning bolt in his memory. The three-foot hawk, talons exposed, grabbed the squirrel off the railing and soared out of sight. Small pieces of fur, like shavings from a haircut, littered the deck.

Craig stood in his living room, suddenly taut, gripping his coffee cup, stunned at what he had witnessed. He turned away, sickened. He'd felt the brutality of the impact. Closing his eyes, he saw the squirrel, followed by Peter Elliott's smiling face. The images were all right in front of him. Everything looked so simple on the outside, so peaceful, until the moment it was too late.

He opened his eyes and glanced back at his cell phone on the counter. He would hope for the best with the call from Roger. But as he swallowed and tried to steady himself, he looked down. His hands were shaking, and he couldn't make them stop.

CHAPTER 33

———————

Dory wearily hung up the phone at the animal shelter as bright March sunlight filled the small office. The week of spring break had arrived, and noisy cages swamped the building. The barking echoed incessantly.

Every single day, more college students and local residents facing uncertain futures jettisoned their pets. Dory let out a sigh. For weeks, she'd worked extra hours, shouldering more of the physical work, as well as the office duties. Trying to keep up with the crushing wave of needs, the staff took in more animals than they could care for properly. While the clock read midday, she was already exhausted.

To make matters worse, the phone call Dory received came from Bess. Her boss had a request during her break from a budget review meeting at town hall. A citizen dialed her private cell phone to report a stray mother dog and a litter of puppies that were roaming out in the county. Animal control came up empty-handed when they tried to pick up the skittish dogs. Bess phoned the shelter, hoping that anyone who took a lunch break might head out to Lake Manning Road and take a look. Dory heard the plea in Bess's voice.

"I'll go and see if I can find them," Dory told her boss.

"Are you sure?" Bess asked. "I don't want to make you leave during lunch."

"No problem," assured Dory as she looked around at the mess of the office and reception area. "I need a break anyway. Some fresh air would be good for me. Besides, I have a volunteer, as well as a part-timer, scheduled all day until closing."

As Dory moved the phone back to the far edge of the desk, she rubbed her eyes. She felt weary, but she had agreed to go, and now she was committed.

She glanced out the window and took a deep breath. Only a few hours remained in the sunny, clear day. The mother and puppies might not make it through another freezing March night.

Dory grabbed a sweatshirt from the top of a cage filled with sleeping kittens stacked by her desk. Pulling the fleece over her T-shirt made her remember the praise often repeated in work meetings.

Every year, Bess flattered her right-hand employee with the nickname of the Stray Whisperer. Everyone agreed that only one person could approach a frightened pet and somehow manage to gain its trust. But Dory knew any talent she possessed came from a lifetime of feeling just like the abandoned, frightened animals that she helped.

Rising wearily from the black mesh chair, she grabbed her phone and keys from the desk. After a quick word to her daytime staffer, she headed for the door.

Once in her car, she drove slowly down the shelter driveway and eased on to the main road as empty cages rattled in the back of her Honda Element. The constant vibration made Dory grind her teeth. Lake Manning Road was on the other side of town, and her car sounded like a junkman's wagon.

Quickly, she pushed the radio to dull the shaking metal behind her. Music from a local station that played hip hop favorites filled her car. As she listened, Dory realized the theme for the day involved older hits for the Flashback Friday broadcast.

Driving through the town square, the song "Jump," by Eddie Van Halen, came through her car stereo. Even though she was tired, Dory started to laugh.

"Jump" had been the favorite song of a boy she'd dated in high school. Finding every opportunity to play the retro tune, the country bumpkin would crank up his stereo and drink beer while he nodded his greasy mullet hair to the beat. Dory always watched him and thought he resembled a chicken when he listened to music.

The same young man had mercilessly teased Dory about her car. He constantly called her green Honda Element a green Ice Cube, like the chewing gum, because the straight lines of her vehicle reminded him of the little squares of candy. Dory slowly started to hate him for his remarks, because he only drove an old farm truck.

Listening to the music, she realized her guilt. An understanding of the crushing peer pressure of high school should have made her care more about the young man, even back then. But she didn't. She knew he'd gotten what he deserved.

One night, at a high school party, Dory decided to act. When a large number of friends had gathered to drink beer at a basement party, her boyfriend quickly found the Eddie Van Halen songs and started playing "Jump" more times than she could count. Dory became incredibly bored. Her date had forgotten that she'd even come to the party with him. After he passed out in a back hallway of the downstairs, Dory went into action.

Armed with a black Sharpie, she wrote "I don't jump, I just do dumps in the toilet" on his forehead. She left him at the party, driving home alone in the car that he'd laughed about earlier that evening.

When he called her the next day, he demanded to know if she knew anything about his new temporary head verbiage. Dory did what she always enjoyed doing whenever she was confronted: She merely listened, and then she lied.

On Monday, when he came back to school, the black ink still stained his forehead. Without missing a beat, she turned her doe eyes up to his in the hallway and told him that she couldn't go out with a guy with Sharpie verses under his mullet. He stomped off in a huff, and Dory had to run to the girls' bathroom.

"Ooh, girl," her friends had said to each other as they shook their ponytails. "It's going down."

Her girlfriends looked at Dory with real sympathy. To them, the break-up would be devastating.

Dory ran down the hall of her county high school to get to the grungy bathroom. She wanted to laugh, not cry. She giggled as tears ran down her face, and she feared wetting her pants. In the end, she gained all the understanding of her friends, and her ex-boyfriend shouldered all the humiliation. It was the perfect ending to a stupid relationship.

Now, as the March sunlight streamed into her car, Dory turned her thoughts to the task at hand. Lake Manning Road ran through stretches of wide open fields. The asphalt melted into the countryside like a long black stream that flowed out from the edge of town. She straightened up in her seat. Her best bet to finding the stray dogs involved thinking like them, to get out on foot, and move like they would move.

Studying her odometer, she drove down the road for several miles. Quietly, she edged her car into a dirt driveway to her left. In front of her vehicle stood the rusty horizontal bars of a cattle gate that enclosed an abandoned field of tall grass that waved in the breeze like tan-colored ocean waves.

This would be about right, she thought as she turned off her engine. From this point, she decided to search by foot. The dogs were most likely to be close enough to scavenge from one of the few houses along the road, while able to travel without detection through the brush.

Dory got out of her car in the deep cool wind. It was no surprise that the schools of the area always went on spring break early in March. Winter in the Appalachian Mountains held onto the chilled soil and thin air with a vengeance. Warm weather only debuted in late April.

As she climbed over the worn cattle gate, Dory hoped that her sweatshirt smelled enough like the dogs of the animal shelter. Whenever she searched for stray animals, attracting as little attention as possible became the goal. It was always better to smell like another animal than to reek of human odors.

She looked carefully around her, surveying the landscape. Dory knew there were mountain people with guns, neighbors that never hesitated to shoot trespassers. In these mountains, bullets came first, only later followed by questions.

An eclectic mix of property dotted Lake Manning Road. Small ranch-style homes appeared next to larger residences that seemed to announce the presence of gentleman farmers.

She gently called, almost a clicking whistle, as she left the rusty fence behind her and walked steadily though the long grass. The fallow field looked deserted. Dory realized that she'd never spent much time in this part of the county because none of her friends had ever lived that many miles from town.

As Dory strolled the meadow slowly, she became aware of a large house that arose in the distance. Even in the sunshine, bright lights shown through every window. It looked like a gathering, or maybe a party, in progress. The smell of a wood smoke drifted faintly to her in the field.

Dory began to calculate the situation. She asked herself the obvious question: *If I was a hungry dog, where would I go? The barbeque grill, of course.* Silently, she made her way through the edge of a meadow. Looking briefly back at her car, she wondered if she should move her vehicle. She decided against going away from the house. It was better to find the dogs first. She also knew that showing restraint from riding up to the property like a party guest would be appreciated.

With the smoke becoming thicker, Dory walked steadily toward the house. As she approached, her steps began to hesitate and become uneasy.

What was it about Lake Manning Road that rattled somewhere in her brain? This area made the hair on her neck feel prickly with a clouded memory.

The large residence loomed before her. With clean lines and a monochromatic palette, the dwelling seemed out of place in a zip code more accustomed to dilapidated, unpainted barns and old weathered farmhouses. Gleaming lights radiated from the large rear windows, while a tiered deck hugged the back of the house, facing the field. Chairs and soft music on the main level looked ready for people to spill outside at any moment.

Dory shifted her approach and headed for the side of the house. Relieved to see that the north wall was free of windows, she walked along the lower brick level. The home clearly indicated wealth, but who entertained like this way out here in the middle of the day?

Dressed like a grungy teenager, and trudging through a field that she didn't own, made her nervous. This part of town was remote, even to the locals. If the homeowner spotted her, what would Dory say? "Sorry to approach your soirée, but I'm trying to find some lost dogs out here. I work for the animal shelter . . . just continue on with your barbeque."

Gray clouds from the grill drifted all around her like a fog. Dory knew that the cooking was being done on the other side of the house, most likely on an oversized black iron smoker.

From her spot by the wall, she could just make out the front of the house. Cars lined the driveway. A white van with a Biltmore catering logo had open doors, revealing trays of foil-covered food. Dory frowned. This house was at least forty-five minutes from Asheville, if not an hour. Why would the owner not use a local company, one only a twenty-minute drive from here? Dan and his staff handled all the best parties in town.

Through the overgrown grass, Dory's eyes caught a glimpse of movement by the grill. She smiled. Nothing attracted a hungry dog like the smell of meat on charcoal.

The deck rose above Dory's head like a shelf resting on stilts. She was only a few feet from the concrete slab and darkened basement floor. Dory moved quietly onto the lower patio, keeping her eyes on the smoker.

She stopped suddenly in the middle of the lower floor. As the cooking haze engulfed the yard around her, she started to feel uneasy. The grass rustled again in the barbecue area. Dory began to walk silently and slowly in the direction of the sound, but stopped again.

Anyone might see her only as a dark-hooded stranger lurking around the bottom floor of a private home. She really could get shot. The news was full of stories about people who wound up dead by being in the wrong place at the wrong time.

Before she could take another step, Dory heard the doors above her head open and heavy footsteps walking onto the deck. She froze in her spot. Her heart thumped in her chest, pulsating in her ears. Did they see her? Did the homeowners know she was right under their feet? Were they going to come down the side steps off the deck and find her? Dory slowly backed up until she pressed against the brick wall of the basement floor. She had no idea what to do.

At first the voices were low, two men talking. Dory forced herself to breath silently, trying to calm her racing heart. If ever she needed to be still and not faint, now was the time. She would have to figure a way out of her hiding spot. The dogs were all but forgotten.

"This place really is amazing, Peter," she heard a man remark above her head.

"Thank you," came another voice. "I like the privacy, and all that it affords me."

Dory knew that man and voice. Something started to click inside her head.

"Our company is enormously grateful to you for all you've been able to secure for us. Horizons had a stroke of genius when we found you."

"Well, all I really did was put the pieces together."

Dory heard the men settle into chairs. She looked up to the creaking wooden flooring above her head.

"I'm working on the finally bit of land—a technicality, really—and I think I'll be able to have the college and adjoining acreage empty by the summer."

Peter Elliott! Dory knew that voice. So this was the home of the wealthy, private big-shot attorney her mother had trusted. No wonder this place stayed hidden.

Dory had a momentary idea, a flash of herself marching out from under the deck, announcing her presence and telling her dead mother's shit-bag attorney that she was on his property looking for stray dogs. Dory could see herself sneering at him as she proclaimed that she cared about animals, and the real future of Mount Robert, not just money and power like the Great Peter Elliott.

But she didn't move. Announcing herself was a dumb idea, and she knew it. She was clearly trespassing. Peter Elliott would be within his rights to call the cops, to shoot her if he had a gun. Anyone who lived this far out of town had a firearm, if not a whole arsenal.

And what kind of men were above her head? Dory bit her lip. No one, not even Bess, knew exactly where she was. What if the men saw her down here and they were some kind of kinky weirdos? Hadn't there once been some rumors about Peter and his taste for young women? What would happen to Dory if he found her? Her mind was racing. What if he grabbed her, but she managed to run away? It would be her word against the Great Peter Elliott. Dory, the free spirit of Mount Robert, accusing the most powerful attorney in town of rape after she'd been trespassing on his property. She was stuck, and she knew it. She tightened her back into the wall behind her.

"You could have waited to host us in Mount Robert, if you had wanted the entire bit of land secure," said the unfamiliar voice. "We would have happily ventured up here this summer."

"Nonsense," answered the voice that Dory knew to be Peter's. "There's no time better than the present. All the details are practically finished. I've hired a partner, a young, rather hungry attorney by the name of Craig Cartwright. He's eager for his first big lick. He has responsibility for the final sale of land. I used the extra resources to secure his services."

Dory eyes were wide, and her ears felt like they burned with fire. Peter Elliott was talking about Craig Cartwright and the sale of land. This was about her family!

Peter continued his explanation. "Craig is responsible for getting the last family—actually, it's the Upton family, the brother of the famous archeologist—to sell the final bit of land. After that, we'll be free to empty the college and begin converting the campus to suit your company's needs."

"Have there been any problems—more than you foresaw—securing the land and closing the college?" asked the other man in a tone of off-handed interest.

"Not really," said Peter. "Your company gave me enough resources that I've been able to make this transition run relatively smoothly."

Dory hung on every word, and now grew furious. *That cheap son of a bitch,* she thought. This explained the low offer on the property. And Craig Cartwright. Who would have guessed that a guy who seemed so decent at first was really just a tool to do Peter Elliott's dirty work? Dory knew something felt off, like he was almost embarrassed at their house that Saturday morning. Now she saw her anger at him had been justified.

"Well," answered the other man, "what really impressed me—impressed all of my colleagues—was how well you really understood our vision as a company. You weren't only able to furnish us with a great campus at a reasonable price, you've arranged for us to find such a vast group of test subjects."

Dory listened in confusion. What was he talking about? What were test subjects? And how were they to be used? She strained to hear the rest of the conversation.

"The campus was the easy part," said Peter. "Small liberal arts schools, even ones with good science departments like Mount Robert, are in trouble. If they've avoided difficulty, then they're barely holding their bottom line. Take Mount Robert College, for instance. It's known as a small school, big on second chances for students from the surrounding mountain communities. The college serves a fair number of students on the GI Bill, Native Americans, immigrants, you get the picture. While the school is fine, the institution can hardly keep up with the times. Your company has a better grasp of what the real future's going to look like. Mount Robert College needs to transition into that future. The students currently attending can just as easily go on to other schools."

Dory shook her head in disgust. So that was the big plan—shut the college so the campus could pursue some for-profit bullshit. She heard Peter's voice continue, and cocked her head up to listen.

"I must admit that figuring out the test subjects took a bit of doing. But I understood your needs for subjects, especially juveniles. So it was really just a matter of convincing the people in charge." Peter stopped for a moment. He seemed to pause as if he was drinking. Ice cubes clinked in a glass before he continued. "My friends at the Children's Home of Mount Robert are delighted to have more space. The campus will be perfect for them. With the illegal drug crisis, both heroin and meth are rampant in these mountains. The Children's Home is filled with young people who will spend their youth as wards of the state. The financial cost is staggering for everyone."

There was a pause again. Dory could almost feel Peter Elliott smiling.

"And now, because of your company, these children can assist in drug trials. They'll make excellent subjects for your studies," Peter finished.

Dory's mouth hung open. Her head swirled. So this was the plan for Mount Robert College, for the kids at the Children's Home! It was surreal. And yet Dory knew it made an odd kind of sense. This explained why people had been so quiet. They either didn't know, or they had been paid for their silence.

"Well, Horizons has truly benefitted from your expertise," answered the other man. "We hope to bring new drugs to market for juvenile illness, if we can aggressively test on a large number of subjects so we understand the pitfalls before we approach the FDA."

"I can't think of a better future for us all," answered Peter.

Dory felt sick. Nausea churned in her stomach. What would become of her family? The town? The people? What about all the children who were going to be treated like lab rats? These were kids with no parents, just like herself.

"Well, let's head inside to get this moveable feast going," she heard Peter say. "We have much to celebrate, and a bright future awaits all of us."

Two chairs scraped the wooden deck as feet shuffled above her head. A heavy door opened and closed.

Dory waited several seconds, and then eased back to the north side of the house, thanking God for the architect's decision to forgo windows along one wall.

In a sprint, she ran into the thick woods, moving blindly, not sure if she would hit a barbed-wire fence before she found her car.

After ten minutes, she turned to see if she had been followed. The brush obscured the house from view. The woods were quiet, except for the hushed afternoon breeze in the leaves. Dory reached out and grabbed a fallen log. She leaned on it for support. Her head was spinning. She doubled over and vomited. Only wrenching, gagging sounds escaped her throat. She straightened up and wiped her mouth with the back of her hooded arm. With a quick glance behind her, she kept on running.

CHAPTER 34

Dory bolted to her car. With shaking hands, she fumbled for the keys in her jean pocket. She was terrified that someone had followed her from the house. Any moment now, a hand could reach out and grab her. Quickly, she opened the driver's door and slammed it shut. Within a second, the locks clicked.

Her hands were shaking so violently that she struggled to hold onto the car key. With her sweaty palm, she forced the metal into the ignition. It twisted, resisting. Her trembling hands tried again, but the keys dropped from her jerky fingers onto the floor mat. She quickly bent down, contorted in her seat, and snatched them. On the third try, she shoved the key into place and started the motor.

The car gave a dull whine. It went silent.

"Oh shit." Dory let the words escape with a sob. She looked around her, expecting Peter Elliott, or one of his men, to emerge from the bushes and bang on the car. They could easily smash the windows, drag her out of the door, do whatever to her.

Tears were streaming down her face. She turned the key in the ignition again and prayed.

"Please . . . God," was all she could whisper. The dry words caught on her shaky lips.

Dory had sworn off believing in God years ago. As a young teenager, she'd decided any deity that allowed suffering in the world, and took fathers away from their families, was dead to her. Now, she could think of nothing but praying. Dory had to get out of there, and back to town.

She turned the key again. The motor roared to life and Dory jammed the car into reverse. A fume of soft spring dirt and gravel fanned out from her back tires. She barely looked to see if there was another car on the lonely country road. Getting as far away from Lake Manning Road formed her only thought. She yanked the gear shift into drive and punched the gas pedal.

"Oh God," was all she could whisper as she sped along the isolated road.

The empty cages rattled in the back of her car, slamming into the side windows. She looked down at her speedometer; the car pushed eighty miles per hour. Gripping the wheel, she started to pray for a cop to stop her. Where were the police when you needed them? Maybe she would see the blue lights behind her any minute now. Dory decided that if she saw anything that remotely looked like the authorities, she would stop her car, jump out as quickly as she could, and run to the officer to tell him everything.

But then it suddenly hit her. Her eyes grew wide as she realized the truth. Hadn't Dan said something about the police and Peter? What if the cops were in on the deal? What if they knew, and had been paid off to be a part of the plan for Mount Robert?

She pulled her cell phone out of the front pocket of her hoodie as she raced along the road. All she had to do was call someone. But who? She started dialing home with her thumb, but she ended before she could finish the number. Dory remembered that Susan and her aunt had a doctor's appointment, and they would be in Asheville. She quickly thought about calling her uncle at school, but she stopped almost instantly. Wasn't he in Raleigh today, trying to get the last funding for his bird study?

"Ah." Frustration escaped her lips.

Dan. She really wanted to call Dan. He would help her. Dan always knew just what to do. But in a flash, she thought about what he'd said. There were meetings today with the inn's owners, and his phone was turned on silent. He told her that he would be unreachable.

"Shit," she muttered, and threw the cell phone onto the passenger seat.

Up ahead, Dory spotted a country store. Little quickmarts with antiquated gas pumps dotted Robertson County. She should have remembered the store on Lake Manning Road. Approaching the small, single-story business, Dory suddenly felt even more frightened. Should she pull over? If she ran inside and told the store owner everything, then what? Of course they would call the cops.

Dory swallowed hard. Tears ran across her checks. She slowed her car down and drove past the old store. For five miles, Dory obeyed the speed limit and tried to decide what to do. Where should she go? Who should she tell?

As the edge of the town square rose up ahead, Dory wiped her eyes with her hands. She knew where she was headed. There was only one place to go.

Only her family could stop Peter Elliott. They would have to pull together. When she stripped everything else away, Dory knew that her uncle, aunt, and Susan were all that ultimately stood in the way of Peter's plan. She was also pretty sure of just one thing: They would all pay a price.

CHAPTER 35

ory slowed down and pulled her car onto the familiar tree-lined avenue. She blinked hard, a lump in her throat. For the last two years, this quiet, well-loved turn-of-the-century neighborhood had been her refuge. Never before had she wanted to go home so badly, to throw open the front door and fall into familiar arms. She'd spent her entire lifetime frightened and alone, but now she felt terrified. Her adrenalin rose in her brain, like a buzz. Dory kept checking the rearview mirror. She still didn't know if she had been followed.

Whipping into the driveway, she gulped in relief at the sight of Susan's car under the carport on the side of the house.

Quickly, Dory parked close to Susan's car, where the brushes were overgrown. From the street, her car appeared almost hidden. Her uncle hated when she pulled her Honda into the unruly hydrangeas on the south side of the house. The shaded, patchy grass left tire marks imprinted for days. Dory rarely cared about her uncle's comments, choosing to roll her eyes instead of responding. Now, she would give anything to find her uncle coming around the corner of the house, fuming over her option of vehicle resting spots as she returned home.

Dory turned off the motor. She wanted to be as silent as possible, not sure if her engine had been heard by anyone. She grabbed her cell phone from the passenger's seat, checked her mirrors one more time, and opened her door. Without a moment's hesitation, she darted into the backyard.

As she bounded up to the top of the worn concrete steps, she prayed again. Surely, the back of the house would be unlocked. She yanked open the old screen door. It flipped outward, smacking the wrought-iron railing of the stoop like an oversized child's toy. Dory realized that her shaking hands would have to fumble with the key if the deadbolt had been set. Precious time would be lost trying to get in, get hidden, to find Susan.

Her hand reached for the knob. She knew that it would be open. This was Mount Robert, after all. Who locked their doors in the middle of the day?

Grabbing the round weathered handle, she turned furiously. It was locked, and refused to budge. Dory swallowed hard. She looked quickly over her shoulders into the overgrown backyard. The only sound she heard came from the creaking bird feeders swaying in the midday March breeze. The eerie squeaking reminded her of a horror movie.

She quickly dug into her back pocket to find her keys. Her hands trembled, and she instinctively kicked the door out of frustration. She banged one arm onto the wood, and worked the metal into the lock with her other hand.

The door suddenly pulled open, and Dory almost fell into the kitchen.

"Whoa," said Susan, almost a soft warning, as Dory grabbed her keyring from the door and tumbled towards her arms.

When Dory lunged forward, both women stumbled in the doorway. Dory grabbed the bell sleeves of Susan's white blouse to steady herself while she quickly lifted her foot behind her and kicked the back door closed. She dropped Susan's arms and spun around to turn the deadbolt.

"What's going on?" Susan began with a hint of scolding. "You're making enough noise to wake the dead."

Dory looked up at Susan, raw fear contorting her face.

"What is it?" Susan asked, concern rising in her voice.

Dory went to speak. Everything was going to tumble out of her mouth. Her eyes glistened with tears again. She stood there waiting for her brain to find the right words.

At that moment, Dory's arms went around Susan. She hugged her with a fierce strength, as a sob came from her throat.

Susan put her arms around Dory and held her. "Okay," Susan said. "It's okay," she repeated softly as she stood there embracing the young woman.

"What is it?" Susan asked gently.

Dory sobbed.

"It's okay," Susan reassured her.

Suddenly, Dory let go of Susan. She looked around the kitchen frantically. In one movement, she pulled Susan towards her while spinning around to push them both behind the door. It was the one spot in the room that remained hidden from any windows.

"Ouch!" Susan cried out, as Dory pinned her into the corner. "What are you doing?"

"We're in trouble. Not just us . . . everyone. It's Peter Elliott . . . he's . . . he's . . ." Dory's voice trailed off into silence. Her eyes were huge.

"Hang on," Susan said calmly.

"No," began Dory fiercely. "No, you don't understand." Her head was spinning, but she knew she had to tell Susan. "It's Peter Elliott. He's behind everything. He's behind the college closing."

"What are you taking about?" Susan asked, now seeming totally confused.

"I overheard him talking. I was at his house, but I didn't know it was his house. Way out on Lake Manning Road." Dory's eyes looked large, and her fingers were beginning to dig into Susan's forearm.

"Why were you at Peter Elliott's house?" Susan questioned.

"I was out looking for a lost dog on Lake Manning Road, and I found Peter Elliott's house," Dory explained. The words were starting to find their way out of her mouth. "But I didn't know it was Peter's house. He was there. He was having some sort of party."

"Did he hurt you?"

"No, no," Dory answered rapidly. "I was hidden. He didn't know I was there. At least, I think he didn't know I was on his property. But maybe he did." Dory's eyes darted around the kitchen again. She felt ready to jump out of her skin. She looked back to Susan and held her eyes as she continued. "I heard Peter talking to someone. I don't know who, some other man. This other guy has some company—pharmaceuticals, I think he said. They have a plan . . ."

Dory was ready to sob.

"Okay, I'm not following. What kind of plan?" Susan asked steadily.

"They want the college. Both of them—Peter and these guys. They want to shut Mount Robert College so it can be a drug-testing place, like a lab. And they want to use kids." Dory started to cry.

"What do you mean a drug-testing place? And what about kids?"

Dory grabbed Susan's upper arms. Her grip was relentless.

"Peter Elliott and this guy—I don't know his name—want the college. They want to turn it into some kind of a lab. It's going to be for the testing of new drugs. They said they're going to let the Children's Home use the campus, and they're going to test the drugs on the kids."

The words had finally escaped from Dory and they hung in the air. Susan frowned as if she was in shock.

"You heard all this? At Peter's house? And he saw you?"

"Yes, I heard it. I was hiding, underneath his deck. He thought he was alone with this guy, but I heard it all."

"And they said they want the college for a lab?" Susan asked again, seeming to need the facts. Dory knew she had to slow down and tell her cousin everything she'd heard.

"Don't you get it?" Dory almost shouted between clenched teeth. "They want the college—all of it—for some sort of testing place. They haven't told anyone in Mount Robert yet. And anyone who does know was paid off to keep their mouth shut. And they want to use little kids, the orphans from the Children's Home, to test their stuff. They want to try all their medicines on little kids."

Now Dory's eyes were on fire as Susan stared in silence. Dory held Susan's upper arms, ready to shake her if Susan failed to comprehend.

"We have to call someone," decided Susan quickly, her eyes darting to the wall phone in the kitchen.

"No," Dory commanded. Her voice dropped at least two octaves as she said, "We can't. The cops already know. They're in on it. I'm pretty sure they've been paid to keep quiet."

Dory yanked Susan's arms again, causing Susan to stare back at her.

"All that Peter needs to finish the deal is my house and land. He told the guy that when he gets my property, the deal is complete. He'll move kids onto the campus, and then they'll start testing drugs on them."

"I'm sure you misunderstood," began Susan. "Let me call Craig Cartwright. We hired him so—"

"No," Dory hissed at her. "He's in on it. Don't you get it? That son of a bitch works for Peter Elliott. I heard them talk about Craig. Peter hired him to get us to sell the land."

"No," responded Susan. "I hired Craig. He's our attorney. He worked on our behalf."

As Susan had said the words, her voice had grown weaker, softer, seemingly less sure. Dory could read her mind. Susan believed in Craig. Dory had watched the two, knowing instinctively there was an undercurrent between them. Their body language had been a dead giveaway of their feelings. There were the coffee dates and lunches Dory knew they'd shared. Suddenly, Dory found herself hating the whole thing even more, but she needed to make Susan see that they had been used.

"Craig made us a low offer, remember?" began Dory, staring intently at Susan. "He told us to take the deal. Some mysterious unnamed buyer, he said. But he never brought us a better offer. That's because he never really went to bat for us. And then he wanted us to sign the papers really fast, remember?"

Susan blinked. Dory could practically see her mind putting the facts together.

"We can't sign those papers. The ones that Craig brought to us," Dory said firmly, bringing Susan back to the crisis. "We're the final roadblock to the plan."

Susan opened her mouth to speak, but she seemed too stunned to think.

"Maybe we can go to an Asheville news station," continued Dory, as she started to look over Susan's shoulder to the old wall phone. "They can investigate and break the story. I think that's who we should tell."

"Papers?" murmured Susan.

"Yeah, the papers," Dory answered. "We can't sign them."

They stood for a long moment, staring at each other.

Slowly, Dory asked the question, "Susan, where's the contract?"

Susan swallowed hard. "Dad signed it. He took it to his office to be notarized by one of the secretaries who didn't go on spring break."

"Okay," continued Dory slowly. "So all we have to do is tell Uncle David and get the papers. Nobody but our family knows we accepted the offer. We can destroy them, and expose the truth."

Susan shook her head negatively. "Dad is in Raleigh today. He took the contract to work. He was having it notarized before he left this morning. I'm supposed to go by his office and get it. I'm going to meet Craig at the college this afternoon at three o'clock, after Mom's settled at home from the doctor," she said numbly, as if she were rehearsing a schedule from her day planner.

"No, no, no!" Dory said, her voice rising to a shout. "You can't do that. Call Craig and tell him that you can't meet him with the contract. Tell him something came up and you'll call him later."

They stood in silence and looked at each other.

"What time is it?" asked Susan, suddenly calm.

Dory pulled her eyes away and glanced at the old wall clock that ticked a steady rhythm.

"It's a quarter to two," Dory answered as she met Susan's eyes.

Suddenly Susan straightened up, squared her shoulders, and ran a quick hand over her eyes. She knew what she had to do.

"I have to go to Dad's office to get that contract. He left the papers in his desk. He told me where to find them. I'm going to get everything, and bring all the documents home to destroy them."

"I'm going with you," said Dory, determination filling her face.

"No," replied Susan. "No. I need you to stay here with Mom. She had lunch when we got home, and she's resting in her room."

"But I need to go with you," pleaded Dory.

Susan looked at her.

"No," Susan said, firmer now. "If Craig or anybody comes by, I want you to be with Mom. We can't leave her alone. If these people are as secretive and determined as you say, then she can't be by herself. She's sick and frail. What if someone comes to the house?"

Susan broke away from Dory and grabbed her handbag from the kitchen table. She fumbled for her keys as she pulled open the back door. The outer screen panel pushed against her hand as she turned to Dory.

"I'll get the contract. You stay with Mom," Susan said, as Dory stood in the middle of the kitchen. "Don't let anyone into the house."

Quickly, Dory moved to the back door and turned the deadbolt behind Susan. Her legs moved away from the door until the kitchen sink rested against her back. Turning around, she gripped the metal edges of the basin and stayed in front of the old faded yellow-and-white counter for a full minute, until the sound of the car motor faded into the March wind. She was all alone now, except for her sleeping aunt.

With the lightness of a cat walking across the floor, Dory began to move down the hall. She went from room to room in hushed movements.

First, she locked every door of the old house, and then she checked and fastened every window. Finally, she stood outside her aunt's bedroom. A raspy sound, a rhythmic throaty gurgle, came from the door that had been left ajar. Dory peeked inside. Her aunt was asleep on her back, a knitted rainbow afghan covering her lower body. Harvey slept curled in a ball next to her, and Toby had his eyes shut as he stretched on the floor. Dory desperately wanted to check the windows in her aunt's bedroom. Could she do it quietly?

Dory shook her head at the idea. She feared waking her aunt. Besides, Dory felt sure that she looked like a mess, with her tears and emotions of the day written all over her face. It was best to just let her aunt sleep. Without a sound, Dory pulled the door shut. She craved something else more than she needed to lock the windows.

With the same unheard footsteps Dory had mastered during the past two years of living with her aunt and uncle, she backed away from the bedroom door. Her feet took twelve steps. She knew the exact number, even though she hadn't thought about this sort of thing in months.

But today was different. She really needed the help. The last time she'd felt this way was before Dan had come into her life. He really hated all of it, she knew. And Dory didn't want Dan to find out about any of this, but she couldn't stop herself, not this time. There was only one thing that would give her any relief from her fear.

The location of the hall bathroom created the abundant space she wanted. Now that she shared the sink and shower with Susan, everything stayed neat and orderly. Soft white towels hung on the rack like textile soldiers standing at attention. Dory silently closed and locked the door.

She had not looked in the bathroom for months, but that didn't matter. After all, whoever searched in her hiding places? If her aunt or uncle, or even Susan, had found her stash, they would have already created a big fucking deal, Dory thought. She knew they would certainly have freaked out, lecturing her and threatening her with some kind of punishment.

Quietly, she opened the second drawer of the white painted vanity. The makeup bag was right there in the back. If anyone had opened the zipper, they would have only seen the little contact cases from the optometrist. Most likely, they would have ignored the small Velcro pouch on the bottom of the bag. Dory opened the tiny hidden pocket and silently rejoiced at the contents.

She took one out and held it in her fingers. The paper felt so good, so neat and wrinkly all at once. It had been a long time since she had felt the reassurance that came from holding a joint.

The purple Yankee candle on the tiled vanity still had the matches beside the jar. With a quick strike, Dory lit the wick and let the vanilla and lavender scent spread into the room.

With two steps, she reached for the light switch. Dory never needed illumination, only the aid of the bathroom fan.

She picked up the same match she had used with the candle, relit it, and held the wooden stick up to her joint. Her hands continued to tremble from fear. That would stop pretty quickly, she thought. It had been months; the pot would probably really kick her butt.

Dory strolled over to the toilet and opened the lid. When she straddled the seat, the water swayed underneath her denim-clad thighs. Getting high like this sucked, but disposing of the evidence was so easy if anyone started knocking on the door. She took a few hits and listened to the whirl of the fan. As she leaned her back against the upright toilet seat cover, her eyes shut.

"I really need to go to Susan," she muttered to herself. "I know she really needs me." Dory always talked to herself when she got stoned. The sound of her voice made the words more real.

As she sat there, she could feel herself relax. Her thoughts were getting bigger; her feelings were also coming closer. It was the best part of weed for her. The connection and letting go both happened at once.

Dory opened, and then closed her eyes again. She would go find Susan, just as soon as she'd finished getting high.

CHAPTER 36

S usan gripped the steering wheel. Her hands shook with a tremble that she couldn't control. Her knuckles were white. This was some sort of misunderstanding, she told herself as she pulled out of the driveway and drove down the street. Whatever had happened—however Dory may have misconstrued the facts—she would get all the details straightened out and understood.

Right now, Susan just knew she needed that contract. Hard breathing came from her throat as the town slipped unnoticed past her vision. Speeding toward the college, she started to tell herself that maybe everything wasn't so bad, that this was some sort of mistake. But as she chewed her lower lip, Susan felt the beginnings of fear. The story made a weird kind of sense.

"I just have to get that paperwork," she muttered out loud as the March afternoon sunshine streamed warmly into her front seat.

Susan tried to push her shoulders down as she drove along the nearly deserted roads. She forced herself to relax. After all, real estate deals fell through at the last minute all the time. She knew all about broken deals. But now her stomach began to churn.

She'd just called Craig, her cell phone now tossed onto the console. Susan wasn't surprised that he'd failed to pick up the call. For four days, there had not been a word from him. Several messages she'd left on his phone had gone unanswered. For the first time, Susan silently felt grateful for his lack of response.

When she'd called a minute ago, Susan had done her best to steady herself, to try to sound nonchalant while speaking to his voicemail. "Something came up today. I can't meet you in my father's office with the contract. I'll do so tomorrow. I'll call you later."

Her words were forced. She was sure that her staccato tone made her voice sound strange. Maybe Craig would just assume there had been a problem with her mother's appointment. Or maybe he could really care less about the change in plans concerning the contract, only relieved to not have to see her. Susan glanced down at her phone. Hopefully, she wouldn't hear from him until she gathered the contract and figured out what was going on with the offer.

Driving along, she sensed a warmth spreading across her face. The whole situation felt so embarrassing. How could she had been so foolish about Craig? She had wanted to believe in him. Her thought, really more of a hope, was that maybe he had started to feel about her the way she'd begun to care for him. If he really worked with Peter Elliott, like Dory said, then he had only used her loneliness to gain an advantage in the deal. Susan grimaced. *Well,* she thought, *the old saying rings true. There's no fool like an old fool.*

But a second wave of discomfort danced through her mind as she pushed her foot on the gas petal and shifted in her seat. What did this really say about her as a real estate agent? She was supposed to be a professional, to ask thorough questions, to understand the deal. More than once, she'd tried to press Craig for more details, especially in the beginning. But every time she approached him with a question, his words were reassuring, almost smooth.

"It's a cash deal," he had told her. "The buyer wants to remain anonymous. The money will be in your father's account within twenty-four hours of closing, but you should remember that there's an expiration to this offer."

Little nagging questions had always stayed in the back of her mind. Who in Mount Robert would ever want to remain anonymous, especially when it came to property that once had belonged to the one famous citizen the town had ever produced? And why did Craig seem to be in such a hurry a few days ago to have her father sign the deal, telling them all that the offer might be withdrawn if they hesitated? Something had felt off, even then. Now as she drove along, the answer to each dismissed question always seemed to somehow end with Peter Elliott.

Maybe, Susan thought, she had been so busy with her mother that she just hadn't really paid attention to what was right in front of her. She knew that illnesses had a way of squeezing everything else to the side in life. And the last few weeks had been such a struggle for their family that perhaps Susan was more overwhelmed than she wanted to admit. Perhaps, she had never really been able to get a handle on her mother's cancer, and all the treatments with the new experimental drugs.

As Susan pulled her crossover through the brick-columned entrance of the college, she noticed immediately how different the school appeared. Everything looked incredibly desolate. The guard house sat empty. Even through it was spring break, and classes were on recess, the campus had an air of bleakness about the grounds, as if even the landscaping could sense the pending closure.

Susan scanned the abandoned buildings as she drove along the main road. For most of her life, she'd come to the college campus and felt comfortable, almost like an extension of her own living room. After all, she had grown up here, in every hallway and courtyard. Now the school seemed to have a foreign air, like a place from her distant past. It was the end of an era, she reminded herself. The college she knew was disappearing before her eyes.

The science building, on the far end of the quad, loomed up ahead. Its windows were dark, giving the building a forlorn air. The sun slipped behind springtime clouds, making everything appear washed out and gray. Susan almost shivered at the sight of the emptiness.

She pulled into a spot in front of the main entrance to the biology hall. Such a coveted space would never have been found so easily in the past. Well, thought Susan, convenient parking was the one and only advantage of the day.

Grabbing her phone, she noted the time. It was ten past two. Craig planned to meet her at three o'clock. If the papers were locked in her father's desk, as he had told her, she would only need a few minutes to get them and leave.

Susan hopped out of her car, her bundle of keys plopping with a soft metallic thud in her palm. She decided against the need to lock her cross-over. After all, her visit would be a quick one.

As she walked to the large glass entrance, she pulled the handle of the main door. It was locked. The blackened hall inside acted as a dead give-away to the shuttered school.

She fumbled only momentarily. Even now, she still had a key ring with passkeys to most of the buildings on campus. Growing up in the days before security had become a serious business at the college, Susan's easy access had allowed her to help her father as a teaching assistant of sorts. Most of the professors' children could do the same thing as well. The learning environment was one of the few perks of being the offspring of tenured faculty at a small college.

The lock clicked as Susan turned her key. She pushed the heavy door open and went into the chilly, darkened hallway. Forgoing the light switch on the wall, she pulled the glass door closed behind her. There was no need to relock the door for such a quick errand, she decided. She started walking.

Her father's lecture classroom and office stood at the end of the hall. Growing up, the building had seemed enormous and busy to Susan. Now only dim, hazy recessed lights flickered in the ceiling tiles as she made her way down the hall. The soft, steady sound of her own footsteps echoed in the quiet.

Susan turned the knob to her father's classroom and the old worn door opened easily. As always, the room was flooded with light. The floor-to-ceiling windows on the far side of the lecture hall gave a stunning view of the mountains.

As a child, these windows had been her favorite ones, far better even than the simple colored glass panes in the old church she attended with her family. Susan glanced at the vast Blue Ridge Mountains and the adjoining veranda.

She hurried towards the front lecture area. Her father had clearly been in the classroom before he'd left for Raleigh. On the center table, the skeleton of a large raptor rested in elegant display. The bones were disconnected but carefully placed on the black-topped examination surface for discussion. Susan instantly knew the purpose of the eagle that had been left prominently in view.

Every year, after spring break, her father's students would study the mechanics of flight. It was one of her father's famous lectures. He would most likely take his students out onto the veranda that functioned as an outdoor classroom, with the skeleton as his teaching tool. Susan had heard the lecture many times in her life.

She looked at the corner of the room and saw that the door to her father's office was ajar.

Quickly, she moved to unlock her father's desk with the tiny access key he had left for her. The real estate contract would hopefully be right on top.

All the paper rested in the drawer. Susan grabbed the paperwork, checking hurriedly through the sheets in her hand. Her father had signed the deal, with Dory's signature added at the bottom of the last page. Susan ran her fingers over the lumpy notary stamp and the indentations that made the deal official.

With swift determination, Susan relocked her father's desk. She grabbed the contract and slung her purse onto her shoulder.

It was only after she pulled the door to her father's office closed behind her that she felt the shift. Something was just slightly different in the room.

Susan looked at the doorway. She was not alone.

CHAPTER 37

Susan gave a startled jump. Her breath caught in her throat.

"Hello, Susan." The words were carefully said, casual but pointed. It was Peter Elliott.

"Peter!" exclaimed Susan, her eyes wide. "You frightened me. I didn't hear you. I . . . I thought I was alone."

"It's delightful to see you, as always. You do look well." Peter had not moved from his position in the doorway. Only his dark eyes seemed to grow more intent as stared at her.

"Um, um, yes," Susan stammered. She gulped, but her mouth felt dry. Her heart thudded in her chest. She needed to get out of there.

"I do believe that you have something for me." Peter nodded in the direction of Susan's hand.

She could feel the papers in her now damp fingers. So this was what he wanted.

"How did you know I was here?" Susan gave a forced smile and a quick laugh. It sounded uncomfortable in her ears, and fake in the empty classroom.

Peter let a slow smile spread across his face. The upturned lips reminded Susan of a Cheshire cat.

"Your father was kind enough to call me this morning. He was on his way to Raleigh, I believe. As the executor, he wanted me to know that you were meeting Craig Cartwright this afternoon at three o'clock. I thought I would stop by and save everyone an extra trip to my office."

Susan swallowed hard. She could see the dimly lit hallway over Peter's shoulder. Her desire to get out of the building made her want to bolt for the door.

"Well," Susan began. "We've been talking as a family, you know, and um . . . we, um . . . think we need more time to think over the deal. Um . . . we really aren't ready to sign the papers, or anything."

The smile now slipping from Peter's face, his gaze hardened by the second.

"Susan," he said slowly. "I know that those papers have been signed. They're in your hand as we speak."

Susan could feel the panic rising in her throat. This was all wrong. She would have to stall.

"This isn't the best deal for us," Susan said suddenly, her voice rising forcefully. There was silence in the room. She stared back at Peter, and she knew she had to continue. "My Dad just called me on my cell phone. He wants us to wait." Her words were getting shaky, almost echoing in the empty lecture hall.

"Give them to me." Peter slowly walked towards her.

"No." The word had escaped Susan's lips with a force that surprised her.

Peter stood several feet in front of her now. He was taller than Susan remembered, his arms broader. His eyes were locked on hers hypnotically.

"Give them to me. There's no better deal out there. You know it, and I know it. I want that contract."

"No," Susan repeated, fury starting to rise within her. "We're not ready."

In a sweeping motion that surprised even her, she brought the paper in front of her. With two hands, Susan ripped the contract into pieces. She faced Peter with defiant eyes, her hands now trembling.

"That was a stupid thing to do," growled Peter.

"We have the right to decline the offer," said Susan louder, more emphatically.

Peter put his right hand in his pocket, and suddenly Susan saw the cool gray metal of a small handgun. Peter pointed it at her.

"Actually, you don't," he said.

CHAPTER 38

S usan stared at the gun. Her heart beat in her ears, and the room gave a nauseating sway around her.

"What, what . . ." stammered Susan.

"The 'what' is the contract," replied Peter coolly. "And now you've made it much harder for both of us."

So this really was it. Dory had been right all along. The sale of her Aunt Julia's home was just a part of a bigger plan. Susan stared up to Peter's face. She could see his anger, smoldering just beneath the surface.

"I know why you want this so much," Susan heard herself say. She had to say something. Taking a gamble might not pay off, but she had nothing else. "I know all about your deal, the one with the pharmaceutical company. I also know about your plans for the college. And most of all, I know about your plans for those children, the ones you want to use for drug testing."

There. Susan had said the words out loud. Maybe if Peter knew she had discovered the truth, then he would back off and leave her alone.

Peter looked Susan up and down now, his mouth now upturned. The gun had not moved from his hand. Susan felt terrified, vulnerable, like she was naked before him.

"Very good, Susan," he said in a complimentary tone. "You figured it out. But then, you always were a smart cookie." He continued. "Few people in this town even know what's really happening. They're much too consumed with their own lives to really think through things. They get easily overwhelmed by chaos."

Susan stood frozen in place. This couldn't be happening.

"For the record," Peter added, "I always saw that you were intelligent. It really was a shame that you didn't go on to law school. Choosing marriage and motherhood always seemed like such a waste of your natural talents."

Susan stared at Peter. Time felt like it was moving in slow motion.

"But why?" asked Susan suddenly. Her emotions were swirling. If this was really happening, then at least she wanted the truth. "The college is breaking even, maybe a bit in the black," Susan continued, a hint of pleading in her tone. "But you know all that; you sit on the board of regents. And the Children's Home, you sit on that board, too. You're the one person who was supposed to protect those children. They have no one else. You know that, too."

"The why," Peter began, "is because the world has changed, Susan." He spoke now, an almost weary logic in his voice, "The days of the beloved small liberal arts school are coming to a close. Most progressive people can see that. America is moving to value technical skills above anything else."

"But what about the children?" Susan had to know, to hear it all.

"As far as the children are concerned, we live in a different time now. Wards of the state, welfare recipients, even immigrants, are going to have to pull their own weight. Handouts are quickly becoming a thing of the past. Our entire country is moving in another direction. From Washington on down, people now realize that we can't take care of everyone."

Susan stared at him, a chill running down her spine. His words almost sounded like a propaganda argument from history.

"Besides, the children who'll come to this campus will have a rare opportunity, if you think about it. They can get an education at this school, and they can be agents of change, if you will. By becoming the subjects of drug trials, they cease being a burden to society. They'll be a bloodline for the future good for mankind."

Susan stared at him. He was mad.

"By the time I get through with my PR campaign, the residents of the fine city of Mount Robert will think I did everyone a favor," he continued with a smile. "With the relocation and expansion of the orphanage, they'll celebrate the fact that I created more jobs for the common man. They'll also realize that I found a way for the children—wards of the state, really—to be useful. Most of the youths who are going to fill these buildings have parents strung out on meth and heroin, costing the state and society an incredible financial burden. All I've done is facilitate a solution, to think 'outside of the box,' so to speak." He paused, seemingly to let the ideas sink in to the woman in front of him. "The only thing I don't need is you or your family trying to stir up objections to an excellent master plan."

"So what are you going to do now?" Susan asked with a calmness that surprised even her. "Do you really want to add murder to everything else?"

"I don't want to, but then you've left me little choice," responded Peter smoothly. He motioned with the gun. "Out the glass door now. We're going onto the veranda."

Susan dropped her purse and backed up toward the glass-windowed wall. She felt like she might trip over her slow-moving feet.

"Go on," Peter said coldly. "Unlock the door."

Susan wondered if this was a trick. Did he plan to shoot her in the back as soon as she turned to unlock the outside door? She realized that she didn't have any choice. Slowly, Susan turned away from him, clicked the metal lock downward and slid the heavy glass door open to one side.

"Walk," Peter said.

The stone veranda, her father's own outdoor learning laboratory, stood deserted, overlooking the fresh spring mountains. Only the sound of the sharp March wind blowing across the stone floor could be heard.

"Up against the far railing," Peter commanded.

Susan stood, now facing Peter, her back pressed upon the round metal tubing that enclosed the deck. It was the only barrier between her and the steep sixty-foot drop that ended on the wooded ground.

Peter pulled out a white cotton handkerchief and a leather glove from his back pocket. He moved with incredible speed. Quickly, the gun was wiped clean. Peter stuffed the square linen into the front pocket of his pants and swiftly put the black glove over his right fingers. In a smooth movement, he pulled the leather up to his wrist. The gun barely moved.

"Give me your hand," commanded Peter. He squinted for a moment in thought. "Your left hand. If I remember correctly, you're left handed."

The request startled Susan. Was he going to shoot her in her hand? She imagined the white-hot bullet piercing her palm. Thinking of the agony made her light-headed.

"For God's sake." Peter sounded almost annoyed now. He grabbed her left hand and pressed her palm around the gun. He closed his fingers over hers, all around the barrel and down the back of the gun.

"You're left handed, are you not? Of course you are," he answered his own question, as if he were explaining a simple solution. He gazed at Susan. "Your untimely death will be ruled a suicide," explained Peter calmly. "I plan to tell everyone that you told me you weren't yourself, and you tore up the contract. I'll also tell them you were depressed, primarily because Craig Cartwright spurned your affections." Peter dropped his voice now, as if he were speaking to an old friend. "Yes, I saw you and Craig having coffee one day. I could tell immediately how you felt about him."

Even now, Susan sensed her face getting hot at the mention of Craig's name.

Peter continued. "With your dysfunctional family, and their many challenges, the authorities will be quick to conclude that your issues were all too much for you. It will appear to everyone that you shot yourself in the head with this stolen gun, and then your body merely flipped back over the railing."

Susan was stunned. It was a perfect plan.

"Oh," added Peter, "and before I pull the trigger, you're going to place your left hand by your ear. That way the gun powder residue will land on your dominate hand."

Susan could hardly breath. How could this be happening?

Peter added a final thought. "Don't worry. Your poor family will be so distraught over your departure that they'll quickly sign another contract. So you see, it all works out for me." Peter stood there gazing at Susan with satisfaction.

For a brief moment, Susan saw her life flash before her eyes. She had a vision of holding her son as an infant, of watching birds with her father as the sun rose, of her mother on the day of Susan's graduation. She blinked, the sunlight now in Susan's eyes. *So this is how it feels to die,* she thought.

"Put your left hand on your cheek," he barked.

Susan jumped, startled, and raised her fingers to her ear. Peter moved the gun towards her left temple.

As she raised her eyes to meet his gaze, she suddenly saw a dark figure behind Peter. It was Dory. Susan had told her not to follow, to say home. Susan gulped. She started to pray that Dory wouldn't come any closer.

"Please get away. You can save yourself," Susan murmured, her lips barely moving. *This is it,* she thought now. Her mind focused on her one final hope for Dory. She cried, facing Peter and the gun. In her last moment, Susan finally knew what it felt like to have a sister. Her family had been a precious gift. She had just learned it all too late.

CHAPTER 39

Susan looked into Peter's eyes for the last time. The gun would explode next. She had always heard people say that a bullet fired from a gun sounded like a firecracker, a loud pop, fast and booming. Susan wondered how loud the metal would be next to her temple, if she would feel the heat hit her flesh.

Suddenly, Peter's eyes went wide. Susan could see his eyebrows arch and his mouth open in surprise. In an instant, he arched his back. His gun stayed pointed at her as he turned at his waist. Craig Cartwright stood behind him.

The talons attached to the end of the bird skeleton stuck in Peter's back. Craig had driven them into his spine and pulled them down into Peter's flesh with all his strength. As Peter twisted around, Susan could see the blood spurting out from his white shirt. Little bits of skin and muscle were laid open in long streaks down his back.

With a sickening shriek, Peter reeled and lunged. A left arm hit Craig squarely on the jaw. In retaliation, a right punch sent Peter up against the silver railing. Susan sidestepped and screamed.

Craig had both hands at Peter's neck.

"It's got to stop," Craig said between clenched teeth.

Peter looked him straight in the eyes. He still held the raised gun. Craig pushed him back farther so that Peter's head and shoulders dangled beyond the railing.

The handgun was almost in front of Susan now, its barrel desperately trying to find Craig. With one great push, Peter flipped over the edge. From where she stood, Susan saw that Craig was starting to lose his footing. He was going to plunge over the railing, too.

Instinctively, Susan grabbed Craig's belt, another hand around his waist. For a moment, everything moved in slow motion. It was suddenly silent. Susan gasped for air and forced herself to look below.

Craig had Peter's left arm in both of his hands, gripping with all his strength. Peter's body was completely suspended in the air. A look of utter disbelief rested on his face. His eyes widened with fear.

"Don't be a fool!" shouted Craig. "It's over."

The finality of the words hung in the air.

Susan began to brace herself. She and Craig would both pull Peter back up over the railing. If she reached over the edge and grabbed him too, they could lift him to safety together.

Now Peter's eyes hardened. Gone was the terror of the previous moment. He looked at them both with hatred. With his right hand, Peter raised his gun; he was going to get one of them.

Then Craig simply opened his hands and let go. A shot rang out, and he grabbed Susan and pulled her down to the floor.

CHAPTER 40

Susan would always remember the blue lights. It seemed that every police car in Mount Robert had arrived at the college. The revolving cobalt beams that seemed to bounce in an endless tempo off the mountains were all that could be seen as the dusky sky began to fade to black. Police cruisers and trained dogs combed every inch below the veranda. Peter's body, his neck broken by the fall, along with the stolen gun, had been retrieved. A shell casing was also found, and marked with a small red flag in the wooded ground. Susan stared out into the night. She wondered if it would ever feel safe again.

Wrapped in blankets now against the night chill, Susan and Craig continued to talk to the detectives. They had been questioned all evening, first together, then separately. Susan was too tired and shocked to do anything but tell the truth. Somehow, she knew that Craig would do the same.

"It is a fantastic story," remarked the lead detective, a middle-aged man with piercing brown eyes that reminded Susan of the Cherokee natives of the town. She noticed his blue jeans and flannel shirt, as well as his attention to every detail. She guessed that he probably had been at home, and then called back to investigate.

"Yes," Susan said wearily. "It is fantastic. I also wish it weren't true."

"You realize we'll have to run a full investigation. That being said, you need to remain in town. No leaving and going back to Tennessee until we complete our work."

Susan looked over at Craig. He caught her eyes, a steadiness passing between them.

"Don't worry," answered Susan. She thought about her parents, about Dory. "I'm not going anywhere; I have family here that needs me."

Shortly after ten o'clock that evening, Susan and Craig were cleared by the police to leave the building. As the detective escorted them to the front door, Susan marveled at the sheer number of television news stations that were lined up on the front lawn of the college. It would be quite a story, quite a bit of notoriety, for the school and the town.

Craig offered to take Susan home.

"This is a mad house," Craig said as he peered through the glass door of the science building and surveyed the situation on the quad. "I need to speak with your parents and Dory," he said as he turned to Susan. "Why don't you call them quickly to let them know you're okay, and just ride with me?"

They dashed to Craig's car before the reporters could reach them. Once inside, the doors were locked. The motor started and Craig quickly drove the car down a service driveway that led to a side street away from the college. They rode in grateful silence. Exhaustion had stolen the need for small talk.

"Are you hungry?" Craig asked once they had turned onto the main road in front of the college. "I mean, before I take you home, are you hungry?"

For a moment, Susan had to think about how she felt.

"Actually, I'm famished," she answered. Food had been the last thing on her mind for hours, but now the thought of something hot sounded irresistible.

They headed to a little café on the edge of town that had earned the reputation of being a local greasy spoon. With its dim lights and truck-driver clientele, both of them thought it might be the one place they could eat in peace.

As they walked in, Susan felt relief to see only two other customers, each eating alone. The tiny restaurant was quiet except for a beat-up orange radio that broke the silence, tuned to the golden oldies.

Craig and Susan slid into a corner booth. The vinyl matched the color of red wine.

"Can we have coffee?" Craig asked the line cook who caught his eye through the pickup window.

"Thanks," Susan said to the cook, who came out of the kitchen with a glass coffee pot in his hand. His apron and shirt were outlined with ancient stains.

"Also, can we also have two sandwiches? Turkey," Craig asked the older man. He looked at Susan and she nodded her approval. The cook set the coffee pot on the table and pulled his green order pad from his front pocket.

"Fries with that?" he asked them with a country twang.

"Sure," they said in unison.

The middle-aged man picked up the glass pot with his toughened hands and returned to the kitchen.

Susan and Craig sat in silence. The remaining tension of the day seemed to weigh on both of them. It would be a long night. And they both knew they wouldn't sleep.

"Susan," Craig began. "I owe you an apology. In fact, I owe your family an apology. The truth is that I got momentarily blindsided by Peter. Or maybe I really got blindsided by my own desires. I hope you can forgive me," Craig said to Susan. "I'm truly sorry, and I want to make things right."

"You're asking for grace," Susan said quietly with a tired smile. She thought back to her conversation with her father around their kitchen table. The one simple word—*grace*—that could build bridges between two people.

"Yes," Craig admitted as he met her eyes. "I need grace."

They sat in the quiet of their thoughts for a moment.

"So, what happens to us now?" Susan asked as she lifted the dull white mug to sip her slightly stale coffee.

"Well," answered Craig, with a weary tone to his voice, "the whole story will come out, and Peter Elliott will be exposed for the plan to close the college. My best hope is that possibly, with the right leadership from the board of regents, and maybe from your father, the college can remain open."

Susan stared into her cup. Swirls of oil danced on the surface from the cream she'd added. Her hands finally felt steady as she wrapped them around the warm cup.

"So, what happens to us now?" she asked again, looking up at Craig.

Craig turned his face to look at the almost empty diner, and ran his hand through his slightly curly hair. He turned back to her, and held Susan's green eyes in his own.

"Unfortunately, it won't all be a quick fix," he replied in truthfulness. "Dory's home and contents will still have to be sold. And the artifacts that are in the house still have to be placed correctly. Dory may have to live with your parents until we get the details finalized. The whole process could take a while, but it can be done." He looked at Susan as he spoke.

Susan's face softened as she smiled at him. So much had passed between them.

"I can help you with all of it," offered Craig, folding his hand over hers as she cradled the mug on the table. "That is, if you want me to."

Her eyes looked down at his hand on hers. For so long, Susan had hoped that Craig would stay in her life. She wanted him to feel the same way about her that she knew she felt about him. When she raised her eyes to his, Susan saw that what they had was undeniable.

We are right where we should be, thought Susan. *Maybe this good can last.*

She turned her hands over and laced his fingers into her own. Maybe, she wondered, they were both finding a way—their own way—to each other. Maybe they were both coming home.

"But what happens to us now?" Susan asked.

"Everything," he smiled.

EPILOGUE

Susan glanced into the tall mirror in the church parlor. She couldn't help but smile at her own reflection. Everything looked so right.

As she smoothed her blue satin dress with her fingers, her hand moved up to gently tug at the matching short jacket. It was already perfectly in place. The dress looked beautiful, she thought. Her mother, feeling better with each day now, had gone to Asheville to help her shop. Sylvia had even shed a tear when Susan walked out of the dressing room modeling it.

The sunlight caught the gold locket that glittered around Susan's neck. She touched the smooth metal, adjusting the chain slightly. With a beautiful link to her past, they would have a lovely wedding.

The outside door opened, and Susan turned as she felt the cool rush of air. Autumn in the mountains had always been her favorite time of the year. The weather for the weekend was perfect.

Susan's father came in, holding the door for Dory. As Susan turned away from the mirror, she could see that Dory was glowing. Susan immediately caught her breath.

Dory had managed to have her mother's white satin gown redone into an A-line dress that just swept the floor. With her dark hair pulled up and loosely pinned at her neck, fall flowers haloed her veil. A locket, identical to the one Susan wore, gleamed around Dory's neck. Susan marveled at what a radiant bride Dory had become.

Susan moved towards her.

"You look beautiful," Susan said admiringly.

"Do you have any advice for me? Any words of wisdom?" she asked Susan excitedly.

Susan leaned forward, and could smell the flowers in Dory's hair.

"Be happy," she whispered in Dory's ear. She kissed her on the cheek. "And best wishes to both of you."

Susan pulled back and saw that Dory's face reflected her own happiness. She was composed, yet her eyes danced with joy.

Her father smiled proudly at both of them. He put out his arm, and Dory rested her hand on the sleeve of his dark suit. He smiled, and Susan noticed how relaxed he appeared. He stood proudly with Susan and Dory, seemingly at peace.

Susan pulled out her cell phone. She took a quick picture of Dory and her father. She had been tasked by the family to write up the wedding for the *Mount Robert Gazette*.

Her article was already planned in her head. She would write that the beautiful bride had been escorted down the aisle by Dr. David Upton, the interim president of Mount Robert College. She would describe the simple ceremony and the lovely reception. Susan smiled as she tucked her phone in her matching handbag. She had already decided the event details were all that needed to be shared with the town. After all, not every secret had to be revealed.

"I think that everyone is seated now," said Susan to both of them. "I'll go in, and then you can both enter when you're ready."

"Do you have the rings?" Dory asked.

"Right here," Susan answered as she opened her palm to reveal the two simple gold bands.

Susan handed Dory her bouquet, and picked up her own flowers as she slipped passed them to open the parlor door. The fall air felt wonderfully cool as she stepped onto the old brick pavers that lined the side of the small country chapel.

As Susan mounted the front steps, she heard an overhead sound. It was the honking of geese. They were just above the church, flying south for the winter, their pointed pattern etched against the sea-blue sky. She watched them as they followed each other with beating wings. The birds were a family, Susan realized, as she stood watching them. They stayed together for a long journey. She looked back at the chapel doors. The birds echoed all that her own family had endured.

Inside the old sanctuary, Susan saw that the pews were filled with family and friends. A hammer dulcimer began to play. Dan, flanked by the minister, walked out from the side doorway in the front the church. With blue and yellow flowers in his lapel, he stood smiling. He waited for Dory. Susan slipped her purse onto an extra seat at the back of the church. With the rings in her hand, she walked towards Dan. She would stand up for both of them.

As Susan watched, she couldn't help but marvel as Dory came down the aisle. When had Dory grown up? So many things had changed. Susan suddenly realized that maybe she had never really known Dory, or even her own parents. Maybe it was impossible to always understand each other. And yet somewhere along the way, they had all become a family.

Susan felt Craig's eyes on her and she returned his gaze. He sat with his own son next to Susan's mother and Ryan. They all looked so happy, she thought.

A lifetime of things had happened, Susan remembered as she stood at the front of the church. In the past few months, she'd finally come home, back to Mount Robert. Her house in Germantown had been sold. A "perfect" family, new to the area, had offered to buy it during the summer, and Susan was happy to sell.

In September, she'd opened her own real estate office on the Mount Robert town square. Having her own business felt like an amazing beginning. New visitors to the mountains increased both home and rental sales.

As the sound of applause rose in the chapel, Dory and Dan moved down the hardwood aisle and out the chapel doors. Family and friends followed them into the late afternoon sunshine.

The bride and groom now walked together, and went to the side of the old weathered building. Falling burnt-orange leaves littered the side cemetery that nestled up against the church. A granite marker with the name of Julia Upton stood on the edge of the grass. Susan watched as Dory placed her bouquet of asters and mums on the headstone. Dan put his arm around her.

Watching them, Susan thought about the other grave she had visited with her father. Peter Elliott rested on an isolated piece of land on the edge of town. A windswept and forgotten place, the grave stood unadorned. Susan had needed to see it. She had needed the closure.

Seeing Dory, Susan felt a lump in her throat for the first time that day. The wedding had been beautiful, but there were things she should have said. Things she should have told her sister. As Dory rested her head on Dan's shoulder, Susan knew there was so much more she should have put into words. Why hadn't she said the most important things to Dory?

She should have told her that it wasn't in the living and dying, the breathing and the burying, that we truly find ourselves. Dory needed to know that life itself was a gift. Through the years, there are things we all lose, and things we all find along the way, but living is precious. Susan should have told Dory all of it, and so much more.

Blinking back tears, Susan felt Craig's hand on the small of her back. The boys, two different sons, were heading towards the parked car, laughing together as people headed to the reception.

As they drove across town to the inn at Mount Robert, with family cars in a steady procession, Ryan asked about the toast.

"So are you ready with great words of wisdom, Mom?"

"I'm working on it," Susan joked to her son.

Susan had been thinking about the toast, about what to say. Everything had changed so much. The problem was that she wasn't sure how to put their life stories into words. What was the best way to wish for hope and love?

The inn had closed the dining room for the evening meal service. Dan, the beloved chef, was being honored by his staff with a reception supper.

As drinks were passed, Susan looked at everyone. Faces glowed in laughter and smiles. Ryan was talking with his grandparents. Craig had his arm loosely on the back of Susan's chair. As she rose to make her remarks, Craig nodded at her. They would make their own announcement after the holidays. Now a hush fell over the group.

Susan held up her glass, and champagne flutes and copper mugs rose in the air. The firelight from the stone hearth reflected on the raised drinks.

"To us," Susan said.

"To us," they repeated.

She paused for a moment. *We realize,* she thought, *sometimes before it's too late, what is really important.*

"To us, and to the journey," she finally said.

Susan smiled at all of them. Hope and love filled the room. Somehow, they were all right where they were supposed to be.

CONVERSATION GUIDE

---

1. Who is the nest keeper? Does it change as the novel unfolds?

2. Animals are present throughout the story. What roles do the various animals play for each human character in the book?

3. The desire for grace and forgiveness is requested by more than one person in the novel. David Upton tells Susan that "maybe you can never really know grace until you're in need of it yourself." Do you agree?

4. Dory is a rebel. Is she understood by her family? Is she likeable?

5. Peter Elliott and Craig Cartwright have fairly similar backgrounds and professions in their small town. Why do they choose such different paths?

6. Peter Elliott is seduced by powerful people. Do you think that evil is often enticing and attractive? How does evil play to our weaknesses?

7. Both Susan and Dory ultimately dismiss their concerns and unanswered questions about the events in their lives. Do we often fail to listen to our own inner voices?

8. How does Susan go from merely fulfilling obligations with her family to a desire to have deeper relationships?

9. Susan Abbot is at a crossroads in her life in much of the novel. Do most women fear that their past will dictate their future? How does she find hope for her life ahead?

10. Susan wishes that she had told Dory about the important things in life. She regrets not saying, "that it wasn't in the living and dying, the breathing and the burying that we truly find ourselves. Dory needed to know that life was a gift. Through the years, there are things we all lose and things we all find along the way, but living is precious." Do you agree?

ACKNOWLEDGEMENTS

A first novel is conceived in the writer's mind but only comes into the world with the help of many people. I am incredibly grateful to the following individuals and groups that enabled me to start my journey of storytelling.

I would like to thank Laura Grabowski-Cotton for her excellent instruction in the fine art of writing.

This book would not exist without The Palmetto Publishing Group. My thanks to Jack Joseph for his introductions to the company. Kevin Sass and his team deserve my deepest gratitude for their tremendous project and editorial support. I also want to thank Abbey Suchoski for her excellent cover design and creative coordination.

I would not have my story in the hands of so many people if it were not for the expert guidance of Rick Miles and Red Coat PR. My thanks to him for the wonderful publicity so the novel could be discovered and read by a truly large audience.

Having my friendship with Peggy Thomson is a treasure. I am grateful for her writing encouragement and peer support.

There were endless contributions that I received from Laura Carter Jowers. I thank her for the most thorough editing process during the story formation and reading countless drafts, often after long days of teaching. Her daily support and hours of cheerleading were more important that she will ever know.

Richard and Jordan Carter spent a great deal of time reading early manuscripts. They provided much needed excitement and encouragement for my pilgrimage into the world of writing and I am grateful.

I wish to also thank William Carter for his belief in the story and the ultimate challenge from him. "Okay, I am going to go get my undergraduate and graduate degrees so now it's time for you to write your book."

And finally to Gray Carter, I want to offer my heart for being my first and last editor and reading chapters by the hour with the red pen. How do I ever say enough words of thanks for the time and space to write and the help given to create a novel? I am blessed by his understanding, patience and love-and for everything.